MW01593213

KRISTINA TRACER
BEAUTIFUL WORLD

KRISTINA TRACER
BEAUTIFUL WORLD

PUBLISHED BY FURPLANET

Editing by Nickolas Brienza.

Cover art by Kevin Pease. (*www.absurdnotions.org*)

Book design by Jessie Tracer / Electric Keet. (*electrickeet.com*)

ISBN 978-1-935599-72-2.

to the Mess and its denizens;
practice makes perfect.

01 | ADAM WATSON
INTERVENTION

JOHNATHAN ANSWERED HIS DOORBELL ON THE THIRD RING, GLARING across the threshold. His normally unkempt mane of hair had been swept back into a semi-coherent tail, but the tie around his neck was still untied, the collar of his light blue dress shirt unbuttoned. His cheeks were clear of stubble, but a dark patch under his neck suggested that I had caught him in the middle of shaving.

"Adam, hi," he said, forcing civility into his tone. His gaze was tight, unflinching. "I'm sorry; did I or did I not tell you that I had a date tonight?"

I sighed. *This is it,* I thought. *Make or break time.* "That's why I'm here, actually."

A scowl crossed Johnathan's face as he turned away from the door. "You don't like Mitsuko," he said half-accusingly as he stepped back into the apartment. It wasn't an invitation, but he didn't slam the door in my face either. Maybe he wanted to have this out as much as I did. "You never did."

"It's not that I don't like her, Johnathan, it's—" My voice cut out as I stepped into the front room, which served as both living and dining space in Johnathan's cramped studio. Outer space seemed to be the theme of the week. Last Saturday, the wallscreen opposite the entrance that had been a bay window letting in the last rays of sunset across a distant beach was now a porthole to a starry sky, an orange sun rising over an alien planet filling the bottom-left corner of the viewport. The other holoframes dotting the walls echoed the theme, the images flickering from vintage spacesuit cheesecake to drifting starfields to futuristic shots of silver cigar-shaped ships docked at spindly stations.

The only static image in the room dominated the wall to the right, opposite the entrance to the tiny kitchenette. In it, an anthropomorphic raccoon in a jade-green teddy stretched luxuriously against a sea of darker forest velvet. Her tail curled over her legs and she gazed upwards towards the frame with a warm smile. Yellow and white camellia petals dotted the image, clinging to both background and subject. It looked as though someone had tossed a handful of flowers into the scene, and then captured her just in the moment before she began to laugh.

I turned towards the short hallway that led towards the bathroom. "It's that.... How can I even say this?" Frustration mounted in my voice, and I blurted out, "She's not *real*."

The snap of an electric razor coming to life punctuated my statement, followed by the drone of it doing its work, the only sound in the apartment. An eon of uncomfortable moments later, it snapped off again, leaving the whole room silent. Finally, into the empty air, Johnathan said levelly, "You've met her."

"You know... you know that's not what I meant," I called down the hallway towards him. "She's not... I mean... she's...." I was at a loss for words. Nothing seemed like the right thing to say; I'd blown my entire argument in the opening statement.

Johnathan stepped out of the bathroom, buttoning his shirt. "She's a digital sentience inside one of Tadashiissei's systems." From his inflection, he might have been talking about the weather forecast. He grunted, lifting his head to fasten the top button on his collar. "Your point?"

"I.... My point is...." I fumbled for words, backing up towards the entrance as he continued his advance back towards the living room, trying to make eye-contact with him. "Johnathan, what kind of relationship do you really think you can have with her?"

He grinned, a genuine smile just shy of laughing, eerily reminiscent of the raccoon's in the picture. "I'm about to go on a date with her, aren't I?"

"No, that's not...." I shook my head. "I mean, what kind of life can you have?" I was trying to be nice, trying to bite my tongue, to be reasonable. There had to be words to express what I was thinking, and I fumbled for them desperately, trying to say something that would make sense to him. "You can't go every week plugging yourself into their network. You can't afford it. It was fun once in a while, but you can't keep this up forever, can you?"

His grin spread. "I don't have to."

As he spoke, his eyes opened wider, and I saw within them a glimmer that made me pull away as he brushed past me into the living room as he tied his tie. "What do you mean?" I asked his back. "I mean...." I froze as realization dawned. "You can't be serious."

He turned around, smoothing out his Windsor knot, his expression thick with false innocence. "Serious about what?"

"You... you're...." I didn't want to say it; that might have made it real. "You're going in there. Permanently."

"The industry term is 'upload'," Johnathan replied. "And yes, I am."

I stared, incredulous. For a moment, my eyes slid past Johnathan to the viewport, and I felt like I would simply fall past him and out into empty space beyond. "How're you going to afford it?"

Johnathan's expression toned down to a serene smile, and he picked up a remote off of the short table in front of his sofa. Turning towards the picture over the mantel, he thumbed a button and Mitsuko's portrait flickered out to be replaced with a pair of raccoons in the same setting, their arms and tails entwined. Mitsuko still wore the same teddy as before, while the other, a male, bore only a pair of pajama pants made of the same near-translucent fabric. My eyes widened in recognition; it was the avatar Johnathan had worn the last time I had gone with him into Tadashiissei's servers.

The frame beeped again, and the scene changed, this time to a shuttle landing bay, where Johnathan-the-raccoon and Mitsuko wore immaculate orange mechanic's uniforms, tool belts at their waists and hats in their paws. Another beep, and Johnathan stood at the doorway leading to a shuttle; he wore a silvery steward's uniform with a translucent green bubble helmet tucked under one arm, while Mitsuko stood opposite him in a classic chunky spacesuit, reading flight plans from a palmtop computer. Another beep, and Johnathan was motioning out the window of the shuttle towards a space platform.

"Tadashiissei's offered me a job in their design department," he said as a flood of similar images flickered past. "Their first space expansion is due in three years, and I'm going to be part of the lead team. I'll even have a job in-world as chief steward, and Mitsuko's thinking about applying with the station hospitality staff." With a final beep, the screen snapped back to the original image of Mitsuko gazing up at the camera, dotted in chrysanthemum petals, just about to giggle.

"You're serious," I said, turning away from Mitsuko's picture, back towards the person I thought I had known as my best friend. "You're really serious," I couldn't look him in the eye. My gaze slipped up to the picture of his girlfriend, to the alien world behind him, to the remote that he'd been wielding moments before. "You're really going to stick yourself inside the computer for good."

Johnathan chuckled. "Yes, I am." He stopped, and his face became a mask of earnestness. "Adam, I know I can't explain this to you, but I'm happy. It doesn't matter to me that it's all inside a computer. It doesn't matter to me that she's made of ones and zeroes instead of flesh and bone. What matters is that I love her, and that she loves me, and that we have a chance to be together, that I have I chance to be doing what I want to do, with someone I care about. I'm happy, damn it, and I don't understand why you and the guys can't just be happy for me."

"But... but it's not *real*," I protested. "None of it is! It's all just a game!"

"What is real?" Johnathan asked as he shook his head. "We could all be brains in jars, for all you can really prove about the world. You don't know for sure that you're not a simulation already. Science can only answer so far up the chain of metaphysics before it has to throw up its hands in disgust. You can't conclusively prove that we didn't all come into existence five minutes ago, that this isn't some grand simulacrum being run by a cosmic computer preloaded with this configuration, our argument included. So what's wrong with going down a level, instead of up one? Why should Tadashiissei's worlds be considered any less real just because we know where they came from?"

His words gnawed at my heart. I wanted to answer him, to deny him, but I knew that even if I could prove my point, it wouldn't matter. "She doesn't love you, Johnathan," I snapped. "She can't. She's programmed to respond to stimulus, not to feel. She's an AI, not a person." I was lashing out now, but I didn't care.

Johnathan's expression darkened. "The polite term is 'digital sentience', Adam, and now you're just being rude. You and I, we're just programmed to respond to stimulus, too, only our programs run on organic lubricants and glands, instead of silicone wafers. What's the difference? Her code's as complex as mine, and she's as blind to her underpinnings as I am to mine. She has thoughts and emotions and hopes and dreams as much as I do. The only difference is that in her world, age is a myth, scarcity is only limited by processing power, and literally anything is possible, if you're willing to work for it. Damn it, Adam, who *wouldn't* jump at a chance to live forever in a world like that?"

I turned away, back towards the door. "I can't explain it any more than I already have," I mumbled, eager now to make my escape. "You just don't get it. I'm about to lose my best friend, and all you can do is play messiah."

"No, Adam," he replied sadly as I retreated out the door, "it's you who doesn't get it. I'll be in paradise in six months, and you'll still be here, wondering where your world went. Good-bye, Adam. I can't spare you any more time, or I'll be late, and reservations at Junsei-en aren't easy to replace."

I turned around to answer, but the door was closing, Johnathan already gone behind it. The last thing I saw before it snapped closed was a rocketship blasting off from the surface of the alien world in his holoscreen, heading for the station.

02 | JOHNATHAN DART
REGRET

THE FRONT OF TADASHI ISSEI'S BEAUTIFUL WORLD FACILITY WAS BELOW ground level, flowering hedges shrouding the entryway. A ramp of multicolored tiles ran between them, leading from the sidewalk down into the earth, giving the illusion of descending inside one of their digital realms even before I had gotten inside. It always felt a little disorienting, the outer world disappearing behind me as I prepared to dive into the inner one, but I always got the impression that the effect was intentional. If so, it worked; before I had even gotten in the door, I felt a little bit like I was leaving the old world behind.

The rainbow of interlocking tiles continued on the far side of the glass double doors, spreading across the floor in ripples of color. On the white stucco wall above the row of counters sat a number of digital clocks showing local time in major cities. At the far end of the line-up hung a single analog disk, a wedge of color-wheel running from hour to minute indicating the time in Irokai. Beneath the timepieces, signs printed in English and Japanese directed travelers towards their destinations: New Arrivals, Returning Travelers, Special Assistance, Gift Shop.

The line in front of the first-timer's window was filled with teen-agers laughing and gabbing with each other, while adults stationed at regular intervals kept the cluster moving in an orderly fashion towards the window. *Some kind of class trip,* I guessed as I eased past them, over into the Returning Travelers line, eying the arc of color overhead and doing some quick calculation: eighteen-twenty, give or take a minute.

If I spent the money for a teleport directly to the restaurant after transition, we could still make our time slot. Given the option, I'd have much rather taken a tram from Mitsuko's block, but even with the frequency of their runs, the chance of catching one in time was slim, and the last thing I wanted was to miss the reservation. We'd been looking forward to dinner at Junsei-en for a month, and I wasn't going to be the one to disappoint my girlfriend.

While the counter clerk helped the couple in front of me, I dug my palmtop out of my pocket and snapped it open, revealing a tiny screen on one face and a thumbboard and trackball on the other. It took only a few taps to bring up the quick-messenger, a few more to select Mitsuko's name out of the contact list. «In line at the transit desk,» I pecked out in a hurry. «Almost home.»

A few seconds after I hit 'send', the screen lit up in a response. «I can't wait,» said the message. «Is everything okay?»

My thumbs hesitated over the board, then pecked out a reply. «Sugoi.» I glanced up as the couple in front of me accepted their passcards back. «See you soon.» With a click, I snapped the palmtop closed and approached the counter.

The woman behind the counter wore a white shirt and dark green slacks, with a multicolored ribbon pinned to her shirt just above her nametag. She smiled as I stepped up to the window, her hands folded in front of her. "Welcome back, Mr Dart. Here for the night, or just the evening?"

I took the holographic passcard from my wallet and handed it to her. "The night. I'll need an extended-stay booth."

She nodded in response and swiped the card. "We already have your reservation in the system," she confirmed with a smile. "You can proceed back to room seventeen. Enjoy your evening!" With that, she handed me back the small rectangle of plastic, which I swiped through the reader on the wall before I stuffed it into my pocket. With a wave, I pushed open the security door and headed down the corridor towards the transfer chambers.

THE PATH FROM JUNSEI-EN'S FRONT DOOR BACK TO THE TRAM PASSED over a wooden bridge crossing a small pond topped with floating lotus blossoms. To one side, a few meters away, a low waterfall flowed down over a rock wall, churning the clear blue water into a white froth. On the other, the pool deepened and widened, with brightly colored *koi* dancing and darting in and among the flowers that drifted across the surface. The whole was surrounded with rocks beyond which grew a bamboo forest that obscured vision and completed the illusion of peaceful isolation.

The first time I had come here, it had all been a game. The water in the waterfall didn't come from a river or a recycling pump. It came from an algorithm, a clever piece of code that gave the appearance of running water. If I put my paw in it, it felt wet and it made the individual strands of fur wave, but those, too, were just tricks of the mind, more data pumped into my head from Tadashiissei's servers. I knew, but didn't bother to test, that if I spent the money and flew up to the top of the rock wall, I would be able to see that the water didn't come from anywhere. It just poured out of the side of the cliff, without origin or destination. It was all just ones and zeroes, just like Adam said.

The second time I came here – the first time with Mitsuko – none of that mattered. It was beautiful, and that was enough. Gone was the wonder in how they had rendered it all, the questions about bit rates and throughput and storage. All that remained was the quiet joy at listening to the breeze blow through the bamboo while gazing up at the sunset. I bought a votive candle in a paper boat from Junsei-en's gift shop and watched Mitsuko kneel down on the bridge to float it out onto the water. I folded her paws in mine and watched the boat bob on the surface as colorful fish nudged it from beneath, trying to make it tip. It had been a perfect moment, the nature of the sensations lost in the sensations themselves, the wind and the sky and the water all coming together to a single unforgettable impression, like an Ezra Pound haiku.

This time, I stood on the bridge, short claws digging into the wooden railing. Tonight, the breeze was stronger, and the bamboo hummed and chattered softly as the wind tapped stiff stalks together. The fur of my arms and tail fluttered, sending a shiver up my spine. I lifted my eyes to the full moon rising over the horizon, trying at once to remember and to forget.

Soft, warm paws touched my back, then slid around my waist as Mitsuko pressed herself to my back, holding herself close to me. I let go of the bridge and enfolded my arms over hers, curling my tail back around her waist. The rise and fall of her chest added its gentle percussion to the symphony of sensation, and for a moment all I wanted was to stay forever in this position, lost to the rest of the world.

After several moments of silence, Mitsuko spoke. "Something is wrong." Her voice was gentle, the hints of her Japanese accent giving a distinct sing-song to her words. It had been one of the first things to draw me to her, back when I first came to Irokai and she had been assigned to our group as a tour guide. There had been no illusions then; she was cheerfully honest about herself, and it had entranced me. I had spent as much of the trip as I could just listening to her talk.

I looked down from the moon to the dance of its reflection against the rippling surface of the pond. "It's nothing, really," I replied quietly, wishing I were as convinced as I tried to sound.

Mitsuko squeezed me once around the stomach in a soft hug, then stepped back. She coaxed with her motions for me to turn away from the waterscape to face her, and I took her gloved paws in my own. Her eyes were a deep emerald green, almost black in the twilight, set in a sea of short ebony fur. Beyond the mask, the white fur looked greyish-blue. "What happened?" she asked gently, her head tilting to the side in a gentle expression of concern. "You were so quiet over dinner."

My gaze drifted down from her face to take in all of her. The green silk dress she'd chosen for the occasion shimmered softly in the moonlight. The stripes on her tail bobbed slightly as the wind ruffled the fur at their borders. Her feet, like mine, were bare, a concession to the difficulty of making sandals that looked good with toeclaws. Her forearms were sheathed in the same silk as her dress, giving her entire ensemble a touch of antique elegance.

My eyes came back to hers, and I smiled, my ears arching as I squeezed her paws gently. "You're beautiful, Mits."

Her ears reddened in response, but she smiled, her eyes sparkling from the compliment. "You are changing the subject," she chastised gently.

Looking into that warm radiance, I knew I was making the right decision, no matter how hard it was going to be. I shrugged with one shoulder, making a moue of my muzzle. "It's Adam," I said, as if that explained everything. In a way, it did, but I kept talking anyway. "He's not making this easy on anyone."

Mitsuko sighed, nodding as she leaned forward, resting her head against my shoulder. "He is afraid, and he is angry," she replied. "He thinks he is losing a friend."

"He will if he keeps this up," I rejoindered testily. I regretted saying it almost as soon as the words were out of my muzzle, but it was true. I hugged Mitsuko's shoulders and leaned back against the wooden railing, my tail entwining with hers. "I shouldn't be like that. It's not *us,* or even *you.* It's...." I tried to find the words for it, but none came. I didn't want to use his epithet. If it had been rude before, it would've been insulting now.

Mitsuko didn't spare me the indignity. "He thinks it is all a game, that none of it is real." She sounded more disappointed than hurt.

I winced and nodded. "Yeah, that's how he put it. He's why we were almost late; he came over while I was getting ready and tried to pick a fight."

She lifted her head from my shoulder, looking into my eyes, one hand on my chest. "Should I talk with him? I could call or send a message."

I shook my head. "Somehow, I think that would just make things worse." I quietly urged her to rest her head against my shoulder. "If he doesn't think of you as real, he'd just write it off as company propaganda or something."

Mitsuko giggled, her ears flicking against the underside of my muzzle. "Oh, *hai,* that would be it," she said, stressing her Japanese accent into a bad parody of broken English. "Ikanobari Mitsuko, Irokai propaganda minister. I will convince you to move forever to my country through pretty word-pictures of chromatic landscapes and impossible acts of beauty." Then she made a face and stuck out her tongue. "Hnngh."

In spite of my best efforts, I laughed, a full-throated bark that took the wind out of my lungs. Mitsuko joined in with her own giggling, and together we just held each other and shared a moment of humor. By the time I'd caught control of myself, the spectre of Adam had been banished; it was just Mitsuko and I again.

When the laughter subsided, I leaned down and tenderly nosed one of her ears. "I love you."

She lifted her head and smiled, pressing her muzzle softly to mine. "I love you too, John," she said when she broke for air.

Then she leaned back against my shoulder, and I held her in my arms. Together, we leaned back against the wooden railing and let our gazes wander upwards, watching a million pinpoint votives float slowly across the midnight sea.

03 | ADAM WATSON
CONFRONTATION

I WAS WELL INTO MY THIRD BEER WHEN JULIA SLID INTO THE BOOTH across from me, jacket-sheathed arms folding on the scuffed laminate tabletop. She locked her fingers together and rested her chin on them, leaning on the table. "So, this is about John." Her tone made it a statement.

I scraped a line of frost from my mug and looked up at her. This month, her back-length hair, tied back into a tight braid, was a dark forest green that could have passed for natural on the first take. She hadn't bothered to remove her wraparound dark glasses, creating the illusion of a "censored" bar obscuring her identity. Beneath it, her mouth was twisted into her usual smirk. She'd turned up the collar of her black windbreaker, and the tee-shirt beneath it had a text-picture of pi comprised of its digits.

I smirked and lifted my beer in a mock-toast. "You know, you haven't changed since college, Julia."

The quirk of her mouth bent into a frown. "Neither have you, Adam; you're still the only one in the group who doesn't call me Jules. This isn't about me, though. It's about you. Rather, you think it's about John, which is why you called me."

I shrugged and set down my mug again, flagging down a waiter.

"Call it a point of pride; I hate diminutives. And yes, it's about Johnathan. What're you having? I invited; my treat."

Julia shook her head, holding out a hand, palm extended. "Nothing for me; I'm ankle-deep-head-first in a project. You sounded desperate, though, so I got things to a breakpoint."

The waiter made his way to the table, pulling a notepad out of his apron. "Can I get you two something?"

"Just a burger for me, no tomato, no mayonnaise," I asked, emphasizing the removals. "Seasoned fries. Oh, and a refill. Julia, anything? I'm paying."

She leaned back against the bench, grunting her acquiescence. "Yeah, okay, I'll have the turkey club and an iced tea. No salt on the fries, and bring it in a to-go box?"

The waiter nodded. "I'll get these started and be back with your drinks." Then he was gone, leaving me alone with Julia's frown.

"Okay, Adam," Julia snapped as soon as the waiter was out of ear-shot. "I'll stick around for half a sandwich because we're friends, and because we've been friends, and I hope because we're going to keep being friends, but I'm not interested in solving your problems with John."

I frowned, but before I spoke, I took the time to drain my mug, setting it back down against the scratched plastic. "I just... don't get it," I said, looking down at my empty glass. "I mean, how can he turn his back on all of us for this?"

Julia's smirk reasserted itself as she rummaged in the pocket of her windbreaker and pulled out a heavy refillable lighter. "Long as you're phrasing it like that, Adam, you're not going to get it. There's a difference between turning away from one thing and turning towards something else."

My frown deepened as I fidgeted with my mug. "Maybe," I conceded, but I came back quickly with the real point of my ire. "But... Mitsuko?"

Julia groaned quietly, covering her glasses with one hand, rolling the lighter around in the other. "I don't even want to try to discuss Mitsuko with you."

"Oh, c'mon," I said, leaning forward in my seat and pushing the empty mug to the edge of the table for the waiter to remove. "You're in software design. Of anybody in his circle of friends, you'd be the one most likely to be able to tell him."

"Tell him what, Adam?" she asked, her voice low and tight. "That he's dating a pocket calculator?"

"Now who's not respecting whose opinion?" I huffed in response. "I'm sure she's a very well-coded expert system, but at the end of the day, she's still just that: software. She's a program. C'mon, Julia, you do this stuff for a living."

Julia shook her head again. "I work on expert systems, not digital sentience. One's programmable; the other's not." She nodded a thanks as the waiter set a glass of tea in front of her, then a fresh beer next to me, before whisking away the empty mug.

"See, that's my very point!" I hissed as soon as the waiter was gone again, stabbing the table for emphasis. "He's not in love with a real thinking being. Not a person. If he were falling for somebody from Japan and said he wanted to move out there, I'd be fine with that, but that's not what he's doing. He's talking about turning his brain into so many sample-slides and rendering himself as some kind of expert system inside one of Tadashiissei's networks, all so he can spend the rest of his life... or whatever... with a programmable sex toy!"

Julia's frown reasserted itself on her face, and she leaned forward, elbows on the table, ticking points on her fingers. "One, just because I said digital sentiences weren't programmable doesn't mean they don't exist; it means they can't be written." Her tone of voice had picked up a hard edge that suggested it would brook no interruption. "They can be evolved from expert systems with a sufficiently high degree of interconnectivity and a matching firmware base on which to grow. You're not into electronics, Adam; you're a biology professor. Stick to what you know.

"Two, the process of uploading doesn't to anybody's knowledge destroy anything other than the physical shell; every case of it that's been studied to date has shown no ill effect, no trauma, no disorders, and no loss of creativity or mental capacity. How many books has Imogen Franklin written since her conversion? Seven? Eight? And her literary critics say they're better now that she's no longer worrying about getting the whole thing done before the cancer kills her. Hell, imagine where cosmology might be today if this had been around during Stephen Hawking's time. John's an artist; if he really thought loss of creativity were a concern, he wouldn't do it, and Tadashiissei wouldn't let him if they were going to hire him. I know the idea of willingly giving up organics in favor of silicon squicks you, but that's a personal preference, not a fact, and no amount of wishing otherwise will change that.

"Three, Mitsuko is not a programmable sex toy; she's one of Tadashiissei's tour guides, and you're lucky that you said that to me and not to John, because he would punch you for that kind of crack. He may be just an art type, but I doubt he's forgotten his Jeet Kune Do, and he still hits the gym pretty regularly."

I slumped back against the padded bench seat. Her blunt point-by-point had sucked a lot of the thrust out of my argument, but I wasn't prepared to grant that to her in public. "I don't see why he bothers hitting the gym if he's just going to go throw his body away in six months," I sulked.

"Procedural memory," Julia replied, grinning smugly. "Different part of the brain from regular memory. I'd have thought a biologist of your caliber would have realized that much."

"Oh, very funny," I snapped, then sighed. "I'm sorry, Julia, I'm just – wait." Something she said during her rant came back to me. "How did you know about his new job?"

For the first time that night, Julia chuckled. "Oh, he told me the day he got it. I've known for a week. We *did* date for a few years."

I slumped back in my seat, defeated. "Am I the last person to know about everything that happens?"

"Not always," she said, leaning back and tucking her lighter into her pocket as the waiter slid a plastic box in front of her. "I was the last one to figure out John and I weren't going to work out."

I sighed in response, looking with mild distaste at the burger I'd ordered and began picking at my fries. The conversation had killed my appetite. "I'm sorry; could I get a to-go box as well?" I asked the waiter, who nodded and left.

Julia took that as her cue to rise out of the bench. "If you're not eating, then I need to go. Tonight's a deadline I really can't miss." She stopped beside the table, one hand on her hip, the other holding her sandwich. "Look, I'm sorry this is hard on you. You and he have been best friends for years, and he's going through some changes that you're just not ready to face. I have it on good authority that he wants to remain friends with you, but this is something he's not prepared to give up, and you're going to have to decide either to accept it and stay friends, or give it up and him with it. I can't tell you which is the right answer, but I can tell you which answer he and I would both prefer."

I didn't look up at her. I couldn't look up at her. "Don't tell me you're on his side in this."

"I didn't break up with him because I quit caring about him, Adam." She sounded as tired as I felt. "I— Never mind. Point is, I don't want to see the group split up over this. I want to see Mitsuko become part of the group, as much as possible. She's not the roadblock in this, and neither is John, for all his hard-assery. He just wants to be happy, and

Mitsuko makes him happy. Being in Irokai makes him happy, happier than he can be out here."

Our waiter breezed by the table, dropping off a plastic box and a small tub of mustard. "So when are you going in there after him?" I quipped as I scraped fries off of my plate. I was burning every bridge at this point, but I was past the point of caring. I just wanted someone to understand, and here was Julia lecturing me like I was her student.

She turned away from me. "I'm not, Adam, not for a long time. I'll be glad to visit, but no way am I moving there right now."

"Why not?" I asked, trying to come across as genuinely curious, but probably sounding accusatory. "I would've thought a software designer of your caliber would've been the first in the group to jump at the chance to live a completely digital existence."

She chuckled darkly. "Touché. Let's just say I have my reasons and leave it at that. Look, I really have to go, or I'm going to miss my deadline, and then things will really suck. G'night, Adam. Next weekend, I'm free and I should have the cash from this project in hand. Give me a call, we'll get with John and maybe Mitsuko can join remotely and we can play Bartok or Barbuda or something."

I shrugged, closing up my box. "Maybe."

Julia paused a moment, weighing the tone of my response, then shrugged. "Whatever, man. Take care." Then she was out the door, leaving me alone with my beer and my frustration.

04 | JULES PENNROSE
DISTURBANCE

BY THE TIME I MADE IT BACK TO THE APARTMENT, THE LAST SUN-
LIGHT had fled the sky, leaving only grey and silver streaks of moonlight across the carpet from the open window blinds. I shoved the
door closed behind me with one foot, waiting for the soft chirp of
the electronic lock and the thunk of the deadbolt before stepping
out of the entryway, past the kitchenette and into the dining area.
"Bedroom, light dim," I called out ahead, pausing next to the card
table – still scattered with unopened envelopes and a plate from this
afternoon – to drop my windbreaker, keycard, and pocketbook, waiting for the fluorescent panels in my room to light the hallway ahead.

I paused at the bedroom doorway to kick off my shoes and socks,
not bothering to untie the laces. As I shifted my weight, my eyes
jumped around the room, my home and office since graduation.
Multicolor printouts of data and code diagrams bearing inscrutable
handwritten notes from projects long past covered the walls, interspersed with the occasional fantasy or futuristic art print. Directly in
front of the entryway, a massive computer desk – too big for the room,
or even the door to it – dominated the floor, turned to obscure all
view of the monitors from the hall. Behind it was the captain's chair I
acquired years ago, reupholstered and restuffed multiple times since

its purchase. Beside that sat an unfolded futon, the mattress wrapped in an oversized sheet and topped with a jumble of blankets. Opposite my nesting space, my bureau sat with one drawer perpetually stuck half-open, accompanied by a half-full laundry basket. A well-abused entertainment center filled the remaining wall space, loaded with an old television, various antique gaming consoles, and the occasional forgotten computer component, covered in dust.

Thinking of Adam's first words at dinner brought a rueful grin to my lips. *I really haven't changed much since college, have I?* I stepped into the half-lit room and shucked off my jeans, then tossed them half-heartedly towards the laundry basket, muttering as they fell short of their target. It wasn't that I hadn't grown since then, to be sure; I'd learned a lot about myself since those days, and I'd gotten better at knowing what I wanted to do with my time, good enough for self-employment, charging small companies inordinate fees to design self-teaching information management systems. Telecommuting had mostly spared me from having to absorb part of office culture, which meant that I'd really just become more of what I was, back in school.

Maybe that was part of what was splitting Adam away from the group, I mused as I dropped the dinner box on the desk and then slumped into the captain's chair. Of the three of us at the center of our circle of friends, he'd been the only one who had gotten a "real job." John had gone into professional design before he'd even graduated, and his models and landscapes commanded more than enough money to make rent. I'd stepped into the working world, doing the business-casual thing, but as soon as I had a decent portfolio I slid right back out and went freelance. Only Adam, with his research projects and his never-ending stream of students, really had to worry about inter-facing with the outside world on a regular basis; that forced him into a mindset that, while not bad by any measure, just wasn't like ours once we'd found our respective niches away from the prying eyes of others.

I took a big bite of turkey club, but a thought struck me that made me almost choke on it. Maybe Adam wasn't the outsider after all. He was the one dealing with regular people day in and day out, while John and I had been free to insulate ourselves against others' opin-ions. Freed from the responsibility of actually interfacing with nor-mal people except under laboratory conditions like the shops or the next contract review, maybe we'd allowed ourselves to grow inward. Adam, meanwhile, was the only one who'd managed to keep evolving with the rest of the so-called real world. Maybe he really was the nor-mal one of the bunch, and John and I were the freaks.

I set down the sandwich and grabbed for my headset, trying to grin and swallow at the same time. On one of the computer screens, an arctic wolfmorph swayed in time with a silent song. His fur was shock-white, so stark that it seemed to glow against the near-black of the digital display. Hints of gold glinted from the tips of his ears and the fur on his chest, as well as from one of his fingers. Around his neck was a gold chain whose links jostled against each other in response to his motions. His only other attire was a pair of oversized black bondage pants littered with zippers. An assortment of glow-sticks that hung from his waist left rainbow trails as he danced.

Freaks indeed, I thought as I cleared my throat into the microphone, making the idlescreen freeze. "Computer, unlock," I said once I had the headset in place. A prompt-box asked for my password, and my fingers rapped against the keyboard. Moments later, the wolfmorph vanished, replaced a myriad of windows. Some held code segments, some contained flowcharts or data diagrams, and still others were blank, waiting for input. The one that dominated the display held a program debugger, a small yellow arrow pointing to the line of code at which I'd paused for Adam's call.

"Debugger, resume," I said, fingers already at work, bringing up other windows as the program stepped forward. I flipped over to a database monitor, watching values set and reset themselves as lines of code crunched in the background. "Debugger, stop, restore to breakpoint. Editor, open weather, open terrain. Switch to weather." I made changes on the fly as the computer rewound the simulation, changing values, adjusting commands. "Debugger, resume." Again I swapped to the data tracker, then back to the code, muting the microphone to grab another bite of my now-warm sandwich.

The hours cranked past as I continued my editing, until well past the time when any sane person would have crawled into bed and collapsed. Finally, as the sun made itself known outside the window, I saw the codes I needed to see show up in the database. "Debugger, pause," I grumbled, then switched to a fresh screen and called up an expanse of artificial meadow. With a few keystrokes, a few dandelions grew among the grasses, and an impossibly yellow sun hung in the unnaturally clear blue sky.

"Debugger, resume." With a spreading grin, I watched as black storm clouds rolled in from nowhere, blotting out the sun. Lighting flashed between the cloudbanks, followed moments later by thunder rumbling in my headset. Seconds passed, stretching ominously to nearly a minute before a searing blast of white burst from the center of the storm front, arcing towards the ground and setting fire where it touched. Another bolt followed the first, then another and another, until the space between earth and sky was filled with a virtual sheet of electricity spattering the ground. The memory of the scent of ozone filled my nostrils as I watched.

Then, a minute later, the lightning was gone. The clouds broke apart, then dissipated, leaving behind only the sun and the pristine sky. However, where there had been only flowers and grass, there was now a patchwork of embers and soot, clearly spelling out "Jules was here" in bold, black letters against the sea of green.

Looking at the results of my handiwork, my stomach briefly clenched, threatening to give me the chance to revisit my turkey club in all its glory, but the moment passed, and with a few deep breaths I was feeling level again. I'd made it no secret on the Irokai fan-forums that I wasn't happy with Tadashiissei's brand management or trademark prosecutions, and I definitely hadn't been quiet about my dissatisfaction with their autocratic approach in-world, but that was all civil disobedience. This... this was vandalism at best. I didn't want to think about what it could be at worst.

"E-mail, title, quote offer of business proposition unquote, decrypt, open," I said, and the scorched earth disappeared behind a text window. The text had obviously been passed through some kind of low-quality translator, but the meaning was unmistakable:

> *Jules:*
>
> *I desire that your service is hired in order to write the program which writes message on landscape in Irokai. The method of this I leave for you, but behavior should as lively as possible for pulling much interest. I need this which is ended next month. Protocol everything which we decipher until present, and Irokai data dictionary, is in this e-mail; is this sufficient? If you accept, to this you should answer; at the bottom of this message the key is to encode your response one time. Attach your program to the e-mail of the reply. The payment will be by the method of your suggestion.*
>
> *We wanted none of this, and you too, coming to this especially. However, Tadashiissei will not to us listen until we prove it is serious. All of us love Irokai, and you too, but with us, you agree that we cannot love Irokai without its freedom.*
>
> *You are welcome to Democracy Revolution.*
> *Fuki*

The document held several compressed files, each encrypted with the same key, the one Fuki had sent in the last message. Inside, they held the connection protocols that Tadashiissei used to transmit data between servers, as well as core object models for the environment. It wasn't enough to hack directly into anyone's head, but with this and enough time and effort, I could probably rewrite most of Irokai by hand.

Whoever Fuki and the Democracy Revolution were, they were skilled enough to crack Irokai's database and dedicated enough to take on the company that owned it. Ever since I'd gotten the message, I'd wondered why they'd contacted me, given what they obviously already had going for them. Were they looking for a fall guy? Would any of this work on the real systems? I'd heard of pranks like this being pulled before, but I'd always assumed that they were people inside the system setting off jokescripts on each other; this was the first time I'd ever seen a suggestion that outside forces could be at work. Did I really want to be associated with this sort of thing?

Did I really believe in freedom for Irokai?

While I was lost in my thoughts, the computer snapped up the screensaver. Within a few moments of the monitor going dark, the wolfmorph was once more gyrating hypnotically to unheard music, lightsticks flashing. I watched him move for several seconds, then spoke into the headset. "Computer, unlock." The image froze once more, covered by the dialog box, and I entered my password again.

"E-mail, reply." My fingers jumped across the keyboard, hooking up source code, data dumps, configuration scripts, build instructions and a quick intro file to the response. "Encrypt." A quick cut-and-paste dumped the previous key into the input box, and a progress bar flashed up on the screen for a few seconds while the computer locked the files. "Send." The screen flashed once, and then the message disappeared.

With a groan, I peeled the headset off of my ears and dropped it onto the keyboard with a clatter, then stumbled to the futon mattress with a heavy sigh, not bothering to finish undressing. With a bit of thrashing, I arranged pillow and blankets to cover my head from the encroaching sun, then pressed the palms of my hands into my eyes, rubbing away the headache I knew was settling in my brain.

Sorry, John, but I'm not letting you jump into this naked and alone. You may be blinded by love... but maybe so am I. "Bedroom, light off," I said, then rolled over, waiting for sleep to drag me into the darkness.

05 | JOHNATHAN DART
ASCENSION

FROM THE OUTSIDE, MITSUKO'S HOME LOOKED LIKE ANY OTHER IN Midori Prefecture: a traditional post-and-beam structure made of aged bamboo that had weathered to lustrous grey, topped with clay roofing tiles stained in a range of greens from creamy jade to deep forest. It sat atop a low hill overlooking a garden, on a slightly uneven platform that provided both front and rear deck. However, as we approached the building, Mitsuko raised an arm and waved, and the thin paper walls came to life, a steady light from within illuminating the entire house.

As we approached the front door, Mitsuko's fingers brushed against the frame, and a soft chime announced that the lock had been disengaged. One silk-sheathed paw resting on the seam of the front door, she turned to me and smiled, her tail curling around her waist to brush against my hip. In the filtered light from within the house, her mask was half-bathed in shadow, the rest cast in shades of green, her emerald eyes almost black. She brought her other paw to my cheek and cupped it gently as I slid my arms around her, urging me to bend down into a deep and tender kiss. Moments stretched into minutes as we stood embracing, until finally she pulled away just enough to speak. "I had a wonderful time tonight," she murmured, her cheek resting against my chest.

"So did I, Mits," I breathed gently into her ear, the underside of my muzzle brushing against the top of her head. "I always do when I come here."

She was still for several moments, as if storing up memories of the contact for the time we'd be apart. Then, quietly, she asked, "When do you go back?"

I smiled at that and pulled just far enough away to look down into her eyes. "After lunch tomorrow," I said quietly. "There's something I want to show you tonight."

At that, her eyes widened and the smile on her muzzle spread, her tail stroking slowly down my side and leg, teasing my own. I cupped her with mine against the door frame, then helped her slide open the front door, letting soft unfiltered light from the high ceiling spill out onto the bamboo deck and back down the hillside. I stopped just within the entryway, wiped my feet on the stiff-bristle scrub since I had no shoes to remove, then stepped lightly across the woven *tatami* into the main living area, drawing Mitsuko inside and sliding the door closed behind her.

Once inside, I touched a finger to her muzzle for silence, then leaned in for a quick kiss. "One moment, love," I said as I withdrew, grinning from ear to ear. "I'll need a little bit to set this up."

Mitsuko blinked, her head canting to the side curiously, tail weaving slowly behind her, almost cat-like. For a moment, I stood, just admiring the pose. Her traditional Western dress clashed so beautifully with the Japanese neotraditional surroundings, a perfect juxtaposition of past and future, without suggesting which was which. For a moment, I considered abandoning the rest of the show to call up a terminal and capture that image, but then the reason for the trip came back into focus, and my smile broadened.

I knew that some people found calling up the hardline optical interface with their eyes open to be incredibly disorienting, but by now I'd done it so often that I hardly noticed it at all. It took only a moment's thought, and then ghostly red text floated around the periphery of my vision. My subscriber ID – the unique digital signature that Tadashiissei knew as "me" – hovered in the bottom left corner of my view. My current financial balance sat in the bottom right. Earlier, I'd paid for the trip to Junsei-en with a few quick glances, summoning up the bill, checking the amount, agreeing to the transaction and signing the receipt with nothing but a turn of the eye. It was lower than I'd have liked, thanks to dinner and the teleport I'd had to buy to make the reservation, but I was still riding high from the advance I'd received. I could afford a bit of extravagance, and I could think of no one better on whom to spend it.

A spiraling color-disk – the stylized clock common across Irokai – hovered in the top right corner. Currently set to Irokai time, the wedge of the color wheel visible showed the time as twenty-one-and-three-quarters or so, but my real focus was in the top left, where the primary menu interface waited. If I needed an emergency exit or staff assistance, I could access it through that system, but I passed all the standard options for a selection not present for most of the people who came to Irokai: the small section near the bottom of the list marked Development Access.

When I activated the interface, a voice began speaking from nowhere, female and very polite, but with a hint of firmness, her English tinted with a faint Japanese accent. "Attention, please. Traveler Johnathan Dart has requested developmental access." The words lacked the inflection of sentience; I'd heard the same statement in the same intonation dozens, maybe hundreds of times. "Ownership of this area is registered to Resident Ikanobari Mitsuko. Before developmental access can be granted, owner permission is required. Ikanobari Mitsuko, do you agree to allow developmental control to Traveler Johnathan Dart? A backup of this region will be made as a precaution."

Mitsuko's eyes widened as she tried to catch my gaze, then turned towards the ceiling quickly. "Oh, *hai,* I agree."

"Your agreement has been recorded, and the backup has been made," the Voice of Irokai replied. "Please be aware that you may revoke your permission and request a restoration from backup at any time. In the event that an incompatibility occurs, we will automatically restore from backup. If at any point we must restore from backup, developmental access will be temporarily suspended until any incompatibilities are resolved. No permanent changes can be made while developmental access is active. Traveler Johnathan Dart, you have been granted developmental access. Please enjoy." Then the voice went silent, and the number in the bottom-right corner of my vision suddenly dropped by a significant amount.

Still, for what I had in mind, I knew it would be worthwhile. I dismissed the hardline interface and turned to Mitsuko, who was now staring at me intently. Her warm smile had shifted into an expression of bemused interest, as if she had already guessed what I had to show her, but was waiting for me to say it myself. She held her arms behind her, paws clasped, her tail waving behind her. "So what is all of this?" she asked.

"Ah-ah, that would be telling. I'd rather show, but first...." I waved my arm expansively, and a cedar chest materialized beside me with a twinkling of light. "We'll need to change."

"Change?" Mitsuko asked as she stepped over to the small chest and knelt in front of it. She glanced up to me, then looked back down and lifted the lid, gasping as she inspected the contents. Inside were a pair of two-piece bubble helmets, each held together with a magnetic seam. Beneath those lay two *uchūfuku* – slim-cut vacuum-safe softsuits – adapted to meet the needs of tailed beings. Beneath those were two small pressure tanks, each set for an hour of breathing time.

"I got my simulation running," I said; it was all the explanation needed. "Care to see it?"

She gathered the smaller suit into her arms, then rose again and nuzzled my cheek as she walked past without saying a word, then pulled one of the thin paper dividers behind her to form a makeshift screen. With the light behind her, I watched her silhouette slowly slip free of the silk dress that she wore to dinner. I could have – would have – eagerly stood there admiring her lithe raccoon figure, but I had my own change to make.

Quickly, I peeled off the jacket and slacks, leaving them in a small heap beside the chest. The tie and shirt followed quickly, and finally my briefs, leaving me free to start drawing on the softsuit. The silvery fabric felt slick and slightly cool to the touch, just like I remembered it. I pulled apart the two halves of the neck collar, stretching out the opening until I could step inside and slide the fabric up my legs, aligning the magnetic panels with the pads of my hinds. Working my own banded tail into the pouch in back made me wince as I tugged the fur against the grain, and I made a mental note to revisit the design again, through I'd yet to find a solution that satisfied me. This wasn't the time to get lost in design work, though, and I pulled the sleeves down my arms and tucked my fingers into the gloves. Finally, I reconnected the halves of the magnetic collar, then broke the seal on the helmet, affixing front and back pieces to the suit around my head. Once the tank was in place, I would be completely enclosed within the softsuit, the magnets forming a perfect seal against the vacuum.

Mitsuko slid back the panel and stepped back into the main room. The shimmering softsuit clung to her body, emphasizing every curve and line of her figure. She smiled at me from within her helmet and turned a slow pirouette, the flat magnetic plates in her feet shuffling oddly against the straw tatami mat. "Am I wearing it correctly?" she asked with a mischievous smile, her voice echoing slightly from the radio system built into the helmet.

All I could think to do in response was nod; some areas of my own suit suddenly seemed more snug than I'd remembered from the design tests. I pulled the tanks out of the cedar chest, then passed one to her with one paw, motioning for her to turn around with the other. She did so, and I slid the tank into the restraining straps on her back, hooking up its lead to the airhose. I turned a valve, and her airflow started with a soft hiss. Once hers was secure, I turned around and showed how to attach mine. Soon, I heard the same release of pressure and smelled the familiar tang of ozone. We were ready.

I turned to face Mitsuko and flashed her a quick grin and a thumbs-up, then focused back on the front door. I waved my arm with a flourish, then stepped up to the entrance and slid aside the thin paper barrier. Beyond, a gray ribbon of metal stretched out into the distance, surrounded by emptiness. The wooden deck had vanished, along with the rest of Midori Prefecture, replaced with a limitless expanse of space, speckled with a myriad of stars.

I took a deep breath, then stepped across the threshold, the magnetic pads beneath my feet clacking softly as they made contact with the metal hull, holding me in place as gravity shifted across the threshold. I paused just beyond the doorway, waiting for the lightheadedness to pass as I transitioned from Mitsuko's world to my own. Once I was clear of the doorway, I turned and reached back, extending a paw in invitation to the woman I loved.

Wide-eyed, Mitsuko took my suited paw in her own, then took a few cautious steps across the gap, swaying briefly as the same vertigo overtook and then left her. I reached past her, then closed the doorway leading back to her home; once it was shut, all that remained in its place was the solid bulkhead of the station. I motioned upwards, and Mitsuko tilted her head back, then leaned back and gawked at the column that rose overhead. Thin metal spindles reached out into space from the central trunk like branches of a silvery-grey tree. Spaceships of all shapes and sizes hung from those metal limbs, docked at all different points. Directly above, past the very tip of the tree, hung a giant blue-white-green sphere, shining like an alien sun.

"That's—" Mitsuko's voice cut off sharply in a giggle of delight.

I squeezed Mitsuko's paw in my own, taking a moment to follow her own gaze, up towards the Earth. I wanted to say something, to say anything in that moment, but there were no words I could offer that would match the feeling I had inside. The faint whiff of ozone from the pressure tanks, the slightly clingy pressure of the softsuit, the tension of Mitsuko's fingers against mine, and the sight of my homeworld overhead all fused into a single indefinable sensation, one that I wanted to never end.

I knew that feeling couldn't last, though, and I had one thing I wanted to share before relinquishing the development flag. I knew Tadashiissei would never approve it; I'd never even planned on submitting it to them. This was still my development environment, though, and I was going to enjoy it to the fullest extent that I could. I glanced at the clock in the corner of my view, then again through layers of development menus, before dismissing the hardline once more. I turned, walking backwards as I urged Mitsuko away from the central tower, out to the edge of the communications array, until we were surrounded on all sides by empty space, only a few magnets holding us in place against a narrow metal platform, keeping us from drifting away into the void.

I smiled at Mitsuko through the tinted grey bubble helmet, then said just loudly enough for the radio to catch, "Don't be afraid, Mitsuko."

Her eyes widened, her tail twitching behind her, the words catching her by surprise. "John?"

I gave her paws a final squeeze, then let them go, stepping back away from her, balanced at the very edge of the walkway. "Trust me, Mits," I said, fingers feeling for the seam on the helmet holding the hemispheres of reinforced glass together. "I love you."

Mitsuko stepped forward, her paws clacking against the metal walkway. "John?" she called out, her voice trembling. "What are you doing?"

Her fingers met my wrists, to try to pull my paws away from the helmet. I smiled at her, then gave a final pull at the seam. With a rush of wind against my face and a flare of light from within the suit, the halves of the helmet split, then tumbled apart, freed from each other and the ring around my neck. Mitsuko's muzzle twisted into a silent cry at the sudden decompression, jerking away, covering her helmet with her paws to avoid seeing my body burst or freeze. She stood trembling, just shy of the edge of the array, frozen in shock.

When my still-suited paws gently brushed her shoulders, she stiffened, but then slowly uncovered her helmet, staring in shock, traces of tears wetting the fur beneath her cheeks. Slowly, the corners of her muzzle turned up into a smile, and she began to laugh, silently shaking inside her suit as she wrapped her arms around me, clinging to me tightly. I encircled her with my arms, squeezing her tightly.

I told you not to be afraid, love, I transmitted to her, not in speech, but in a direct broadcast of thought, words sent directly from my mind to hers. Then I pulled away, carefully, coaxing her back from the edge, and began to strip away the now-unneeded softsuit. As the material fell from my shoulders, a pair of broad wings covered in iridescent bands of feathers that matched my shimmering fur spread from my back, unfurling to their full width to help catch the solar winds. I turned to look at them with glowing yellow eyes, then flexed them and flapped, propelling my legs and tail out of their useless encumbrances, leaving me naked against the vacuum.

Once the transformation was complete, I turned back to Mitsuko with a smile and held out one paw to her; balanced on my pads sat a gently pulsing sphere, a copy of the transcendus module, the modifications that made the softsuit and airtanks unnecessary. She smiled up at me through her helmet, then took my paw in hers, wrapping her suited fingers around my gift. It sank into her paws as she reviewed and integrated the new code, and then moments later she pulled open her own helmet with a burst of air and light. Then she opened her eyes, a brilliant emerald light shining out of their depths as she spread her shimmering wings, her softsuit falling away from her, trailing out away from the deck as the station slowly spun in place.

Despite the vacuum surrounding me, Mitsuko's paws were warm against my shoulders, as I knew mine would be against her waist. Freed from gravity and our artificial modesty, we floated away from the station, wings flapping in near-unison as we learned the rhythms of each other's new forms. Once we were out of the station's shadow and bathed in the full light of the sun, I turned back to Mitsuko, drifting away from her briefly to admire the results of my work against her already-sublime figure. She smiled and silently laughed, then turned a lazy somersault, her wings and tail provocatively splayed to show off my handiwork, and I felt my body respond.

I want you, I sent to her, flapping my wings and catching up to her, taking her paws in mine.

Mitsuko urged me closer, then wrapped her wings about us. *I want you, John,* she replied soundlessly. She guided my paws to her small, firm breasts, then rested her own on my shoulders. Her skin beneath the fur was as warm as the rest of her, her nipples already firm beneath my thumbpads as I caressed them gently. She shivered beneath my touch, her head tilted back, her muzzle half-open as I stimulated her. Watching her respond to my stimulations made my cock pulse in its sheath.

Moving carefully, I ducked my head down, kissing along her neckline and down her chest, nipping playfully with my teeth against her fur until my muzzle was at one of her breasts. Placing a soft kiss against the nubbin of stiffened flesh, I slowly slid my lips down around her nipple, tugging at it carefully as I began suckling. It was as if electricity had arced through her, her body stiffening beneath my tender touch before curling up against me, as if to try to wrap herself around me, holding me against her. The taste of her was sweet and faintly musky, and my tongue tingled from the brush of her fur as I swirled it around her nipple.

After a quiet eternity, I kissed my way across to her other breast, repeating my performance there. She shivered and shuddered in my arms, pressing herself eagerly against me. Despite the lack of air in simulated space, her chest rose and fell in heavy breaths as I teased her. Her wings tickled mine as she wrapped herself around me, urging me onwards with her touch and motion. Then, finally, with a silent gasp she pulled away. *Too much!* she sent, trembling from the overload of sensation. I stopped, then, and a moment later, she drew closer again. *Please, John... more.*

I floated over to her, this time wrapping my wings about her as I took Mitsuko in my arms. She rested her paws on my shoulders as I placed mine on her hips, my cock fully engorged as I pulled her against me. She spread her legs, wrapping them around mine, and then it took only a moment to position myself before smoothly pressing myself into her. Her sex was hot, her flesh tingling against mine, sending sparks from my groin up to my brain as I filled her, one gentle thrust carrying me fully within her. Once inside of her, I paused, hugging her tightly to my chest, then began slowly pistoning myself back, pulling away and then pressing forward again, making love with Mitsuko in deep space.

In the absence of gravity, sex truly was a two-person endeavor. Where before one could lie still and let the other do everything, now it took the effort of us both to consummate our passion. As I pushed myself forward, pulling her towards me, she thrust back, using her legs to encourage me deeper. Our wings fluttered and flapped, by turns encircling or just brushing against each other, the new sensations compounding the rest. I closed my eyes, filling myself with her taste and feel, then opened them again and smiled into those orbs of luminescent emerald. *Yes,* one of us sent, or perhaps both, minds moving as our bodies, urging each other closer to climax. I trembled against her, my body shuddering. With every stroke, my cock throbbed within her sex, the heat of her body suffusing mine. Her claws glided down my back along the sensitive join between wing and spine as I held her hips against me to help me find purchase. She twitched, moaning silently in the void, nodding as I thrust faster, deeper, the urge to orgasm overwhelming. I bit my lip, stars dancing at the edges of my vision, my nerves singing soundlessly as with one last push, I came, a burst of heat and seed filling her sex. She threw back her head, claws digging into my back as her entire form tensed, climaxing in response.

In the afterglow, we hung there, twinned stars against a black backdrop, shuddering and quietly nuzzling against each other and riding out the aftershocks of our shared passion. Then, finally, we separated, smiling at each other, and turned back to the station, our wings flapping as we dove back towards the communications array. At the panel in the side of the station, I turned back to the suits, still clinging to the far edge of the platform, then winked back to Mitsuko and shook my head. If the code ever got approved, it would prove an interesting artifact for the first maintenance crew to find.

I waved my paw at the smooth metal wall, and the same section as before slid aside, revealing Mitsuko's main room beyond, just as we had left it. I touched down just outside the door, then stepped lightly through, Mitsuko following closely behind. Once within, I turned and shut the front door, then brought up the hardline one last time for the night. It took only a few seconds to dismiss the development flag, and the wings and glow disappeared as soon as I did so. A few seconds later, Mitsuko's vanished as well, leaving her with only her natural radiance and a smile.

"Thank you, John," she said, stepping closer to draw me into an embrace. "That was beautiful."

My ears flushed in response, and suddenly I felt very awkward. I knew that she loved me for me, but there was always that moment, right after I had shown off some new bit of in-world wizardry, in which any praise I received was colored with doubt. I knew she loved me, as I loved her, but did she love me for me, or for the things I could do?

Was there a difference?

I wrapped my arms around her and hugged her tightly. "I'm glad you enjoyed it," I whispered back, resting my cheek against hers, my tail slowly swaying behind me. "I'm sorry if I scared you back there, but—"

She shushed me softly, then rested a finger across my muzzle. "I understand," she replied. "You are an artist. It is one of the things I love about you."

The words struck home, perhaps more deeply than I wanted to admit, but I was still riding high on the afterglow. "Thanks, Mits," I murmured in response, kissing her ear softly. "Let's go lie down; that took a lot out of me."

She nodded in response, then turned her muzzle to kiss me tenderly, before taking a paw in mine to lead me back to her bedroom. Once sprawled out on her low futon, she curled up next to me, pulling a thin cotton sheet up and over us as we snuggled up together. She turned towards the ceiling and dismissed the lights, plunging the house into near-total darkness. I curled up against Mitsuko's back, one arm beneath her head, the other around her waist, her tail draped over my leg. My mind drifted as sleep came for me, imagining myself floating with Mitsuko through that perfect void.

06 | IKANOBARI MITSUKO
PREMONITION

THE SKYBRIDGE CONNECTING THE THIRTIETH FLOORS OF THE Nanakōsei and Everest Research buildings was glass below as well as above, cool beneath my bare pads as I stepped out into open space. Overhead, the sky hung low from the broadcast towers that topped Murasaki Prefecture's spires. From here, the moon seemed to stare down at the city beneath it, its lurid gaze just as taken by the flashing lights and flickering signs as those surrounded by them, far below.

My gaze briefly followed the moon's, down through the floor to the sea of lights that ebbed and flowed below me. A moment of vertigo ran over me, making me shiver, but as soon as I felt it, it was gone, quashed by the same part of my mind that had let me interpose countless times before when one visitor or another had inadvertently risked self-integrity while part of my group. The sense was the same every time, an instant of sick giddiness just before my training took hold of me and suppressed it. Staring down at the glittering expanse, I wondered what it would be like to live outside, where that sensation could be had at any time, for more than a few brief seconds.

Once the vertigo passed, I walked out onto the bridge, cinching my kimono around me as proof against the chill in the air. The service request that had woken me gave me only a location and a sense of urgency, but nothing else. I'd taken only enough time to make sure Johnathan was still asleep and then to meet the basic needs of decency before leaving. I had actually considered referring it to my shift-replacement; I had little enough time to spend with Johnathan as it was, at least until he moved to Irokai. However, the request had been by name. I might have been on vacation, but a priority call of this nature simply could not be ignored.

Halfway across the skybridge stood a fox, tall and thin, his red-furred ears standing straight above his head. The split hem of his black longcoat shifted slightly with every move of his white-tipped tail, but aside from that he stood still as a statue; even his bare hinds remained fixed in place against the transparent floor in defiance of the cold. His gaze remained level, his narrow muzzle as blank as the wall in front of him. In the reflection of the glass, his large violet eyes met mine. He nodded once, and the sense of urgency dissipated.

As the request faded to a background impulse, I queried the local dataspace about my host. It took only a few glances through my menus, and then I had as many questions as answers. The first name that came to me was Giri, but the family name gave me pause, a string of characters that could have been static. Quietly, I wondered why he had changed it, but it would have been rude to ask before a proper introduction. Attached to the name was a link to his public employee record. I followed the reference, and Giri's title and station were mine: security lead, Ōseito Ward, Murasaki Prefecture. I ignored the web of contacts and reports that followed; what mattered was the mindset of the person that had summoned me, and knowing his role in Irokai would help me understand that. It was little enough with which to work, but it was more than I had before the summons.

Giri remained still through my investigations, but as I studied his personnel records, a stream of fresh static, much like his family name, begin to flow out of him. A request for key exchange followed a few moments later, a few meaningful droplets masked in an empty sea. Even as he waited for acknowledgement, the steady pace of nonsense continued, though his violet eyes remained fixed on the view, acting as though he were silent.

I smiled as graciously as any hostess would to a sullen guest and stood next to him on the bridge, paws resting on a railing near the wall. I did my best to catch his gaze in the reflection off of the glass, but all I could do was study his eyes as they stared into the distance. "It is a beautiful night, is it not?" I spoke the words lightly, hoping that some geniality might set my summoner at ease. The privacy request hung unanswered, a subliminal nagging just out of normal sight.

36

His silence stretched out into seconds, but then the digital babbling faded out and the security request disappeared with it. The fox didn't turn to look at me, but instead raised one paw, waving it to encompass the view of the stars. "Check the local edit history," he said quietly, ignoring the question I had asked. His tail twitched as he spoke, expressing irritation that he kept from his voice.

The frown that I felt never reached my muzzle, though my own banded tail flicked once in response to his own. "Perhaps introductions are in order," I replied with a smile, turning away from Giri's reflection to face the fox directly. "My name is Ikanobari Mitsuko." I half-bowed at the waist, extending the most courteous greeting I could without dipping into unnecessary formality.

Again, the fox paused, waiting for several seconds before responding with a bow of his own. "Giri," he said in the same soft tone as before. He held the position for a moment, then rose.

I followed his motions, smiling again as I looked into his eyes. "You have no family name?"

At that, one corner of his muzzle rose into a smirk. He parted his jaws, and a burst of static and dissonant beeps and trills escaped it, making my fur bristle. "You asked," he said after the noise abated.

I rubbed at one ear with a paw. "Oh, *hai,*" I admitted with a rueful smile. "Why did you change it?"

Giri shrugged. "It is a hash of my codebase at incept. I thought it was more fitting than what they named me."

"Oh?" I tilted my head to the side, filing away that bit of information. "What was it before?"

The fox shook his head. "Unimportant; it was not me."

The exchange, eccentric at the mildest, made me hesitate. I could find little in the brief exchange that invited further conversation, and in a few sentences, Giri had managed to put me on guard. Rather than push that line of discussion any further, I fell back to my training. I clasped my paws together at my waist and inclined forward slightly. "How may I help you this evening?"

Giri scowled at the question, then turned back to the window, motioning again towards the window. "Please review the local edit history." He transmitted a set of coordinates along with his words, indicating a section of the sky out beyond the buildings.

Now I frowned. "My administrative access is limited," I said as politely as I could, keeping my eyes on the side of the fox's muzzle, ignoring the direction of his gaze.

The fox's own expression soured at my words. "You work in Tadashiissei's Hospitality Division; I know what access you have." He sighed, hints of petulance in his voice. "I am asking you to review the local edit history, not randomly delete a building."

I held back a sigh of frustration, and turned from Giri back towards the window. Obviously he had no interest in letting this go. As glad as I was for the system interface and as easily as I relied on some of what it allowed me to do, I disliked having to tap into my administrative access; it always felt like cheating. It took only a few moments of silence, and then I began paging back through logs of the indicated region.

It wasn't hard to find what Giri wanted me to see. Just over two hours ago, someone had replaced a section of the heavens visible to almost the entirety of the Prefecture. I called up the display engine and passed the captured edits through it, and the constellations became letters. I spoke aloud the English words written in twinkling motes of light: "Why do you pay to live?" A series of Japanese kanji floated in comet trails beneath: *Irokai no Minshukakumei.*

I turned from the window back to the fox that stood beside me, cocking my head to the side. "Democratic Revolution of Irokai? What is—"

Giri held out one paw, forestalling the question. "I do not know. If I did, this would be resolved by now." His other paw went to his waist, and a traditional katana shimmered into place within an ornate sheath beneath his fingers. "What I do know is that this is not the first breach of this sort. To date, I have backup logs of seventeen such incidents in the last calendar year, and their frequency has been increasing." A fresh stream of encrypted data began to pour out from him, followed a few moments later by a new request for key exchange. "Please review these revision logs," he said quietly.

This time, I accepted his offer with a nod, and the nonsense resolved into sets of log files and database entries showing both original and altered content. None of them contained a source or owner. I compared the records before and after; in most, innocuous text had been replaced with more slogans. In some, Tadashiissei's logo had been replaced by one that looked like the symbol of Irokai, but its colors were inverted. The only constant across them all was the same kanji that I had seen emblazoned across the sky.

I frowned and released my specialty access, then adjusted my kimono and folded my arms across my chest. "Any incident such as this surely would have attracted some sort of attention by now, by the media if not Tadashiissei."

The fox's expression remained implacable, but pride and anger flickered in Giri's eyes. "Irokai Security is both efficient and proactive. I have also brought every such assault I have encountered to the attention of my superiors, and every time I have been told that appropriate actions will be taken and that anyone violating Irokai's codebase or harming its residents will meet with stiff punishment."

I waited a few moments, then prompted Giri gently. "They have not caught the perpetrators?"

One of Giri's ears twitched. "The security logs have been rotated and sent to external storage."

I let his words – both what he did and did not say – sink slowly into my thoughts. The implication of his statement was clear: no-one working for Tadashiissei had responded to his reports. I tugged my kimono more tightly around me, shifting from one hind to another against the cold glass. "Does anyone else know about this?"

Giri shrugged. "I have made efforts to make Security aware of the situation, and many have expressed concern. As to whether anyone outside of Security knows or cares...." He left the rest of that thought unspoken.

I tugged my kimono more tightly around me. "Why did you ask for me, then? I work in Hospitality, not Security."

The security agent smiled tightly in response, holding up two fingers. "Two reasons. The first is that Hospitality specialists have access to any level of emergency administrative authority deemed necessary in order to protect the well-being and happiness of residents and visitors to Irokai. My access is much broader, but requires specific permission from my management."

I nodded once. "And the other reason?"

He hesitated, then turned to face the sky once more. "Your lover, Johnathan Dart. He has development-level access, does he not?"

I tilted my head, tail twitching in response. "He does, yes, but why—"

Giri again stopped me with an outstretched paw. "I have made every attempt to notify my superiors, both within and outside of my management, of the seriousness of this situation. These changes have either no name attached or else obviously fraudulent ones. I have been unable to identify a source for any of the attacks. Every last one of these should have started a full-scale audit both of internal and external security. So far, it has led to nothing. I can only assume, therefore, that upper management within Tadashiissei is aware of events and does not care. I therefore cannot continue to trust internal responses as adequate."

His eyes narrowed as he spoke, his voice becoming hard. "Your lover is not yet a part of Tadashiissei. If it becomes necessary to take action without their approval, we may need his assistance."

My eyes widened. "You are suggesting rebellion."

Giri shook his head, his paw once more at his waist, fingers curling about the hilt of his sword. "I am protecting my home. My primary role, both as an employee of Tadashiissei and as a resident of Irokai, is to safeguard both this place and the people who live here. If Tadashiissei will not take action, then I must act on their behalf. To do less would be dereliction of my duties." He turned back to face me. "If these attacks continue as they have, we may soon find ourselves fighting to protect everything we value. What I need to know from you, Ikanobari Mitsuko, is whether you will help defend Irokai or not."

I looked down to the blade at Giri's waist, then back into the fox's eyes; they glinted like polished amethyst, cold and hard. I wanted to doubt his analysis. I wanted to question his conclusions. I even briefly considered a flat denial, but everything was too well-considered, too well-argued. Given what he had seen and heard, his explanation seemed consistent with all of the facts at his disposal. As I had no alternatives to offer, it made his position a difficult one to deny.

"*Hai,*" I said quietly, nodding once in response. "I will help."

07 | SASAKI REI
COMMITMENT

ENTERING THE OBSERVATORY, I ALWAYS FELT THE URGE TO PAUSE AND bow my head. Air came and went from the room through evenly-spaced ceiling grates, with white noise to muffle the circulators' steady hum. Soft white LED panels glowed dimly near the floor, casting the room in a faintly blue artificial twilight. Every section of the window-less walls had been fitted with matte black baffling panels, further dampening both light and sound. No matter the noise level outside, the silence was sepulchral once the door closed behind me.

A round pedestal the size of a boardroom table dominated the center of the room like an altar, its obsidian surface glossy and reflective. At intervals around its edge were a number of simple, black, cloth-covered chairs, neatly camouflaged against the matching carpet and walls. In front of one chair, a small section of the desk glowed with a keyboard and trackpad projected upwards from within onto touch-sensitive glass. The remainder of the surface remained blank, as close to true black as light could produce.

I settled into the chair in front of the control station and began tapping out commands, occasionally sweeping a fingertip across the motion-capture pad. In response, the remainder of the glass surface of the boardroom table blossomed with light. In the center of the table, the symbol of Irokai beamed, slowly cross-fading into an over-head relief view of the digital world itself. Five large islands, each slightly tinted a different color, sat in an boundless sea. Tram lines connected them together, crisscrossing the deep blue gulf in a silvery spiderweb.

For several minutes, my fingers hovered over the keyboard as I watched the world rotate beneath the surface of the desk. The ambient light was a near-perfect imitation of night-time, but Irokai – like the world beyond its borders – had escaped the tyranny of the sun as a timekeeper. Kigiku Island's nature preserves and broad forests teemed with simulated animals, while Murasaki and Beni Prefectures throbbed with more urban nightlife. The Bazaar at Hana was far less busy than during the day, but even it never truly closed. Only Midori Prefecture seemed quiet, but scattered lights across the residential districts showed signs of life as well. Irokai continued to pulse quietly beneath my gaze, ignorant of its observer.

I lowered my fingers to the keys beneath them and resumed my typing. In a few moments, the world dimmed into the background, and a series of red and yellow dots flared across the map. For each marker, a window filled with text opened, attached to its location with a thin, angular line. One of the yellow dots pulsed regularly, asking for immediate attention. I cycled through each of the other spots first, skimming their contents for issues requiring actual urgency. Most of the texts contained "Irokai Security" somewhere, flagging visitors for improper behavior or asking for supervisor approval. I closed each after a few sentences, moving from one to the next rapidly until I came to the flashing light. As I opened it, a familiar name leapt out from the screen.

In its essence, the report was another documented hacking attempt, caught and reversed by attentive Irokai Security staff. However, in the depths of its presentation, it was a cry of despair. Intricate details suffused every paragraph, meticulously analyzing which of Irokai's data structures and network protocols had been violated to cause the attack. Attached images showed in graphic detail how the constellations had been rearranged into English letters, with comets altered and added to write kanji across the nighttime sky with their trails. The author had dedicated two full screens to a list of previous attacks, complete with dates, locations, and Tadashiissei responses. The report finished with a single question: "Do the responsible authorities intend to allocate resources to manage this escalating situation?" Each word had been selected for maximum precision and dispassion, but the plea in the subtext was equally clear: *Do you even care what happens to us?*

After a few more keystrokes, Giri's job history and personnel entries scrolled over Irokai's projection. Commendations decorated his service record. A few incidents blemished his career, but each of them could be explained away as a clash of personality with his chain of command. In a frame to the side rotated a three-dimensional model of a lanky *kitsune* in a black leather longcoat over a sweater and slacks. A *katana* in a traditional sheath hung at his waist, and one paw rested upon its hilt. Within his window, the model of the fox turned his head, gestured with his free arm, and shifted his weight, as if studying me from the other side of the display.

One of the red dots hovering over the Bazaar faded from view. Another one turned yellow and began to pulse. I let my focus drift from the security agent's impassive gaze to the latest report and skimmed it. Someone had attempted to make an unauthorized copy of a vendor's program, and a local member of the security staff had been scanning the market and noticed the attempt. He used his administrator access stop her, which caused one of the lights on the map to turn red. The agent had then escorted the offender out of the Bazaar with instructions not to return without a security officer as escort.

At the bottom of the report, the security agent said it was her fourth unsuccessful theft, which suggested more that had gone unreported. He'd even taken the time to comb through past incident reports to corroborate his claims. His had recommended in his personal notes that the offender be exiled and had flagged his report with a request for review, prompting the golden highlight on the map.

I opened the offender's transit file and reviewed her history. She had, in fact, been the perpetrator of multiple thefts inside Irokai, both from the Bazaar and from shops in Murasaki. However, she'd also been to Irokai at least once a month ever since its inception and spent a great deal of money within its borders. Her purchase record showed a wealth of teleports, short flights, custom model modifications, and other special features she'd bought. She'd accumulated a number of complaints from vendors on her security record, all for suspicious behavior and suspected theft. Her social reputation, however, was excellent, with a number of people explicitly praising her for gifts she had given them for no apparent reason.

I smiled and drew my chair closer to the table while my fingers worked quickly over the illuminated glass. Coaxing administrative access into Irokai's traveler database without leaving a record in the security logs took longer than I'd have liked. Resetting her criminal history and then imperceptibly corrupting the incident report took longer still. Afterwards, though, I had every reason to believe that her unexpectedly clean slate would give her plenty of room to continue.

That resolved, I closed all of the report windows and turned my attention back to the image of the kitsune. The smile that had come to my face as I worked faded again as I studied his features. At times, the image's ears rose, and the corners of his muzzle lifted in agreement, but never did his smile reach his eyes. One of his paws rested lightly on the hilt of his sword, but his fingers never strayed far from a ready position, and his posture suggested both a knowledge and willingness to use it.

Giri's report might have been asking for assistance, but even if he never received it, he wouldn't stop fighting for his beloved Irokai.

«The safety of Irokai and its inhabitants is of utmost concern,» I wrote at the bottom of the incident report. «We are currently reviewing your request and will keep you apprised of any change in status.» I attached my digital signature to the bottom of the file, then flagged it as needing no further action and committed the update. The window closed and the flashing marker faded to a solid yellow, then disappeared.

The bulk of my work finished, I logged out of the security system, then opened my contact archive. Sifting through the list, I found the number that I needed and set up an encrypted communication channel. A speaker hidden within the ceiling buzzed twice, then twice again, followed by a beep and a woman's voice speaking Japanese. 「Yes?」

I leaned back in my chair, elbows on its armrests, fingers steepled before my face. 「Fuki-*san,* I must apologize for calling you so late,」 I said quietly, taking the most respectful form I could.

A brief pause followed, and then the woman replied in kind, her voice tired. 「Sasaki-*sama.* As always, it is good to hear from you.」

I smiled again, watching the world turn. 「Did I wake you?」

「No,」 Fuki replied. 「I am curious, though, why you are calling me instead of messaging. Did we not agree this was a security risk? I could be heard, or this call could be monitored.」

I nodded at that. 「It is, but it's late in Midori and a text can't wake you if you're sleeping. I think someone is starting to become suspicious. Giri's latest offering is as much a diatribe as it is a report. How goes your project?」

「Not as well as we may have hoped,」 Fuki confessed. 「I have

acquired an additional resource. He is dedicated and skilled, but he is still new to the team and is not yet integrated with the group. I must commend you, by the way, on your training methods. Irokai Security is very efficient.」

I allowed myself a smile at the backhanded compliment. 「I'm taking what steps I can from within, but there's only so much I can do myself. I don't like saying it, but I believe that it's time to advance to phase two.」

The voice on the other end of the call paused again, then spoke more hesitantly. 「So soon?」

「I'm afraid so,」 I replied, sitting up in my chair. 「As long as Giri's able to undo our best efforts single-handedly, this isn't going to go anywhere. We need something big enough that even he won't be able to fix it alone.」

「Understood,」 Fuki said wearily. 「I will ensure that we are ready. Is there anything else that you wanted?」

I paused a moment, then nodded again, even though Fuki couldn't see me. 「There is, yes. Giri's going to continue to be a problem unless we deal with him. I can do that, but I need a justification.」

「That will be difficult,」 she said after an extended pause. 「I am hardly in a position to set up such a situation, and Giri has a spotless reputation.」

「Not spotless,」 I said with a slight smirk. 「Merely very good. He has a history of personality conflicts in his personnel file. It seems he's a little too willing to follow the spirit of the law, but not the letter.」 I called up his file once more, reviewing specifics. 「Questioning orders and refusing to implement lockdowns on vendor request, among other things. As you know, disobeying management can be grounds for termination.」

Fuki was silent for a time afterwards. 「Are you not disobeying management as well?」 she finally asked. 「Inciting revolt against Tadashiissei can hardly be said to be in the best interest of the company.」

I chuckled at that. 「I'm doing what is best for Irokai in the long term, which is my primary job responsibility. I have faith in your abilities, Fuki-*san,* and in our vision. Democracy for Irokai.」

「Democracy for Irokai,」 Fuki replied, and then came the terminating beep.

I stood and turned back to the table, letting myself be hypnotized by the lights glimmering across the different districts for a time. Then, with a few keystrokes, I shut down the overhead view and the world of Irokai disappeared, leaving me in silent twilight.

08 | JULES PENNROSE
WARNING

AS SOON AS I OPENED THE DOOR TO MY APARTMENT, I HEARD THE chime indicating a new message in my personal inbox. I groaned and shuffled over to the card table in the living room. *Ten hours on-site consulting, and work awaits me when I get home,* I thought with a weary chuckle. *I had more free time when I worked full-time.* Leather flats, dress slacks, and knee-high stockings melted off of me as I walked, spilling in haphazard puddles of cloth across the carpet as I headed for my bedroom. I flung my professional-looking sweater towards the laundry basket, not bothering to see where it actually landed, and I quickly replaced it with an oversized black tee-shirt decorated in neotribal patterns. My stomach grumbled at me, reminding me of exactly how long it'd been since lunch, but I ignored it and dropped heavily into the overstuffed captain's chair behind my desk, grabbing my headset and fitting it in place.

"Computer, unlock," I said into the microphone, fingers reaching out and jumping across the keyboard. "E-mail, open, display new messages." The computer blew a raspberry at me and the screen flashed to match. A dialog box opened: «Message encrypted; please provide pass phrase.» At the bottom, a cursor blinked inside a text entry box, patiently awaiting my input.

I leaned back in my chair. The header of the new message indicated it was from Fuki, with a blank destination address, meaning I was one of several people receiving it, but we weren't supposed to know who else did. I spent a few moments wondering if it was worth the effort to try to figure it out, then turned my attention back to the interposed window. She'd put no new passwords in her previous letter, or even any hint she was still interested in doing business. The deposit she'd made for the last job had cleared without any hint of fraud, and nobody had flagged my bank account for illegal activity, but she'd still gone silent as soon as she'd gotten the code drop from me. We'd exchanged public keys to allow for secure communication, but that obviously wasn't enough to open this new document. Whatever this was, it was important enough to go to a list of anonymous people, and unwholesome enough to be worth keeping away from the uninitiated.

That still didn't tell me what the key was. Fuki, whoever she really was, seemed too cautious to make a mistake such as sending out an encrypted message to the wrong person. So, it almost certainly wasn't an accident that I'd received this. That meant that I had to know what the pass phrase was, but not know that I knew it. That meant it had to be something she'd said to me before, something universal enough that everybody on that hidden distribution would've gotten it already. My stomach gurgled again and I scowled at the computer, as if it were the source of my hunger. *Cloak-and-dagger games are fine, until they interrupt my dinner.*

I wanted to shut things down and go get food, but now I was curious. "E-mail, cancel. Disable new message alarm. Inbox, search." As soon as the new screen opened, I typed "Fuki" into the search bar and hit enter, eyes scanning the results as they displayed in the match window. "Stop. Select message two. Open." The requested entry in the list blinked twice, then expanded to full-screen. Quickly I scanned the document, looking for... I didn't know what.

I paused on the last line of the message, right above her name. My eyes narrowed and I shifted in the captain's chair. "Display new messages," I repeated into the microphone, and again my inbox asked for a pass phrase. Into the text field, I typed *Democracy Revolution.* I bounced my finger twice on the Enter key, then snapped it down, committing my guess. Immediately, a progress bar opened, its color shifting from white to green as it unscrambled the message.

As soon as the bar filled, it vanished, and in its place opened the message that Fuki had sent:

Jules,

Thank you to help the future of Irokai, safe from dictatorial Tadashiissei. Our common goal is shared, and we did great everythings expanding our messages with just the tools of ours. Unfortunately, the response of Tadashiissei has not been to open Irokai, instead covering up in regard to our efforts. They do not accept the attack, therefore the time for increasing is now.

We must attack Irokai itself. Not destructively or permanently, but clearly. Noisy. Very brightly. As for the citizen of Irokai, they must see. As for Tadashiissei, it must not hide us now forever.

You, I know you may be who hesitates, but now is time for action. If the self-proclaimed owner of Irokai does not transfer control, those who believe freedom and democracy must take them for any power. John Adams who says "Liberty must at all dangerous be supported; we have a right to possess it." Under Tadashiissei, all the "citizen" of Irokai are servants who must pay for the fact that their life is maintained. Tadashiissei is not a government.

We tried that our messages come to the people of Irokai and Tadashiissei knows that we are buried. We must forever not be silent. If you are not, say nothing. If this message is deleted, I do not send again ever. If you want to help, the key which is attached can encode your sent response. You will receive everything the equipment which is necessary to succeed this effort.

Democracy for Irokai.

Fuki

I scanned the screen several times, the veins in my head throbbing a little harder each time. Finally I snarled, "E-mail, close!" I yanked the headset off of my ears and flung it irritably at my monitor. I shoved myself backwards from the desk and grabbed the lighter from its surface. The captain's chair tipped backwards when I stood, then thumped back down onto its coasters behind me as I struggled into a pair of discarded jeans, then stalked out of the bedroom in search of an open pack of cigarettes. I never lit up inside; this was as much to make myself take regular breaks as to protect my health or my deposit on the apartment. Right then, I really needed a smoke. I paused only long enough to shove my feet into a pair of sneakers, then stepped out onto my balcony.

A thin metal railing enclosed the concrete slab that jutted out from the side of the building. On it precariously balanced a small glass ashtray, already half-full with remnants of previous visits. Beyond the narrow ledge, the city spread in a jumble of narrow streets and crowded tenement buildings, a mishmash of uninspired tans and stained greys. The sodium glow from the streetlights and windows obscured the stars with a beige haze of light pollution, washing out the sluggish clouds overhead in burnt sienna and umber. A petulant wind fluttered the hem of my shirt as it blew down the street, stirring up the ash in the ashtray and carrying it off into the distance.

Once the door to the apartment was closed behind me, I robotically went about getting the cigarette out of its package, put it between my lips and lit it. I was doing my best to focus on the process, but I couldn't push past the knot of anger that Fuki's little "suggestion" had instilled. I drew in a meditative breath, glanced down at the orange embers, then tilted my head back and exhaled noisily, gazing upwards into space. For several minutes, I concentrated on bringing hand to mouth, on inhaling and exhaling, on tapping grey ash into eddies that landed on the matching concrete, and on trying to stare beyond the sky. The sting of a hot coal against my fingertips snapped my attention back down to earth, making me wince. I steadied the ashtray with one hand and ground the butt into it with the other, then fished a replacement out of the pack.

Only after I had the second cigarette lit and stuck between my lips did I turn my thoughts away from the washed-out skyscape to the message that the enigmatic Fuki had sent me. As soon as I did so, my mouth curled into a grimace. I leaned against one of the metal support poles holding my balcony to the one above and let out a stream of smoke, then sighed as it dissipated in the breeze. Even just her name made my stomach clench and my hands want to do the same. This was getting out of control, fast. I understood what she wanted, and even why she thought it was a good idea, but it wasn't going to work, and she had to know that. This wasn't a game any more. This wasn't a silent protest, or even a noisy one. This was no longer vandalism; this was destroying something beautiful to try to protect it, and the idea put bile in my throat.

The sad truth was that, at some level, I agreed with her. Tadashiissei possessed the money, the servers, and the ability to keep Irokai running. As long as they had all of those, they dictated the terms, and everyone else either played by their rules, or they didn't play. I'd played along for a while, until I realized just what they were asking, with their special charges and their access fees. Want to teleport from one place to another? That'll cost you. Want to fly? That's another fee. Want to create something out of thin air? The more complex it'd be in the real world, the higher the price tag. Never mind that everything in Irokai was digital, that gravity only existed because they'd coded a physics engine. The only real cost to having – or being – anything you wanted was the time to design it. Tadashiissei made it all possible, and then they made anyone with vision and desire pay for it, step by costly step. It was hard enough having an impossible dream; endlessly paying someone to live it, knowing that one day the money could run out, was infinitely worse.

I looked down at the remainder of the cigarette between my fingers, then brought it to my lips and finished it in a single deep breath, going slightly cross-eyed as I watched the coal burn red-hot. I held the hot, acrid smoke in my lungs, letting it burn along with my indignation, then let it all out in a grey-brown stream, my shoulders sagging. Then the stub joined the others in the ashtray, and I went back inside, kicking off my shoes next to the sliding door and shucking my jeans beside them. *I'm not going to do this,* I told myself firmly as I set down the cigarettes on the kitchen counter. *Whoever she is, she can play all the games she likes, but I don't have to play along.*

Once back in front of my computer, I dropped back into my chair, sinking into the excessive cushions, and fumbled for the headset. Instead of fitting it back over my ears, though, I just held it, eyes fixed on the dancing anthropomorphic wolf on my screen. In each hand, he had a glowstick hanging from a black thread, the lights dancing around him in a hypnotic pattern, splashing blobs of color across his fur and glinting off of the piercings in his nipples. More hung from the belt-loops on his baggy cargo pants, reflecting off of a patchwork of zippers. His eyes were closed, his head tilted back and his muzzle open in a look of quiet ecstasy, listening to music that only he could hear. He looked happy, capable of snapping out of his self-imposed trance at a moment's notice, but otherwise completely blissed out in a world of his own creation.

I remembered that look; I'd worn it myself, when I'd been him.

My stomach still tight, I leaned back in my chair, eyes glued to the screen, as absorbed in my avatar's dancing as he was. I knew that using it as a screensaver was a mistake, but I'd told myself for years that it would've been rude not to do so; John had made it for me, after all. He'd given it to me after I'd broken up with him, telling me not to give up so easily on Irokai or on the company that made it. It was an easy thing for him to say; he wasn't the one that had gotten kicked out for arguing with Tadashiissei's lawyers. He wasn't the one getting banned for daring to ask for help. No, he was the one about to move permanently to the digital world, to have the body and the life he'd always dreamed of having – the life that I'd wanted for years.

I dropped the headset into my lap and squeezed the arms of the chairs in a vice-grip, doing my best to ignore the uninvited tears that trickled down my cheeks. I'd been within a hair's breath of accepting Tadashiissei's insane costs, of signing my life away to them, and only Adam's pleas and demands for sanity had shaken me. He'd been wrong about so much, but on that one point he'd been utterly right, more than he could understand. If I'd agreed to the terms of the upload, I'd have put myself at the company's mercy, wholly dependent on their survival. What if they went under? It seemed unlikely, given the size of Irokai's economy and how much they made off of the people who visited, but unlikely wasn't the same as impossible, and it just wasn't worth the risk. It wasn't even worth the price I'd have had to pay every month just to keep my account in good standing and my mind out of backup storage. It didn't matter how desperately I craved it; I just couldn't afford it.

I'd written letters – handwritten notes on real paper – asking for a change in the terms. I'd called for clarifications, I'd posted on the forums, and I'd organized petitions, begging for a change to the upload account maintenance terms. The harder I'd tried, the stricter Tadashiissei's lawyers had gotten. They'd made no concessions, offered no apologies, and in the end they decided that the path of least resistance ran directly through my account. One day, John and I had gone to spend a weekend together in Irokai, and they refused my entry at the door, saying my account had been suspended. When I tried for an explanation, the clerk at the counter said only that I'd been flagged as a troublemaker, and there was nothing he could do. I'd tried to protest, but corporate security escorted us out of the building and asked me politely not to return. They'd won. I couldn't fight them any more.

I wiped ineffectually at my eyes and tried to snort my sinuses clear, then settled the headset back over my ears. *Maybe I can't beat them on their terms,* I thought, *but this isn't their game any more.* "Computer, unlock. E-mail, open, open latest message, reply." As soon as the window was on the screen, I began typing, fingers trembling only slightly.

> *Fuki,*
>> *I'm in. Tell me what to do.*
>> *Jules*

"E-mail, encrypt," I said, pasting the key from Fuki's last message into the text field the computer gave me in response. "Send." Then I slumped backwards in my chair, arms folded across my chest, hands balled into fists to keep them from shivering. I felt sick to my stomach, but my head felt light, almost giddy, as though I had dived off of the balcony and was now falling head-first towards the pavement.

In under a minute, my mail client started chiming. With turn-around speeds like that, she had to be watching her e-mail like a paranoid. I smirked and pulled my chair up against the desk until the edge pressed uncomfortably into my stomach. "E-mail, go to latest, open."

The screen obliged, popping up what little text there was: «Jules, I desire to speak to you in time current. Please send ‹Hello from Jules› to niji_fuki.» Other than the timestamp, that was it.

That sick, giddy feeling spread down from my head out into my arms, and my stomach twisted. I fought the craving for another cigarette and leaned back in my chair. "E-mail, close. Messenger, open. New message." I typed the handle and message that Fuki gave me, then hit the send button.

Seconds later, I received my reply: «Thank you for you saying yes, Jules. How soon time can you offer project completion?»

I shrugged, even though she couldn't see it. «That depends on how much information you can give me on Irokai's security structure. Something this invasive is going to have to look like it's native if it's going to survive.»

Fuki was silent for almost a minute, then replied. «In your inbox please find security protocol for all of Irokai access, encrypted with passphrase this name. It is not the administrator of all system but will work as local administrator on all everywhere for safety program.»

I didn't bother to open the message; everything else Fuki'd given me had been uncannily accurate. If this was entrapment, it was the most elaborate sting I'd ever seen. I leaned back in my chair, staring unblinking at the screen. Fuki must have taken my silence for hesitation; soon after her last message, she asked, «Is there elsewise that I can give in accord? How soon time?»

«Will those codes get through Tadashiissei's firewall as well, or will these have to run locally?» I asked, fingers drumming on the mahogany desk as I waited for a response.

Fuki's window blanked, followed by, «As to the outside I think yes but I cannot prove. Why?»

I bit my lip, then typed, «You can get me an induction rig and the adapters to run it.»

«You ask impossibly,» Fuki responded. «Where do you think I could get to you such an equipment?» I could see the sneer of indignation in her text.

I smirked, despite my trembling hands. «The same place you got the data dictionary and the security protocols.»

Both of us were quiet for a time after that, me because I was still shaking from my latest feint, and Fuki... I couldn't imagine what she had to be thinking. I forced myself to keep breathing, to count every breath as it left my lungs. At seventeen, her window flashed again. «I maybe can appear something, but you must make a guarantee. How soon time?»

I grinned, and my stomach knotted. «Three months, tops.»

«It is too soon, three months,» she replied. «You cannot so greatly affect Irokai in so small. Be true to real.»

«I am,» I shot back. «You've given me excellent motivation. What's the time frame for the protest?»

Fuki hesitated again, then replied, «Sadly, most are saying two times, so six. I will wait for all to be ready, and then at random. You accept?»

«I accept,» I returned. «In that time, I can get you two, or one big and a bunch of littles. A nice toolbox of tricks, to make your efforts worthwhile. Agreed?»

«Yes,» Fuki replied. Then the window's title bar announced, anticlimactically, that she had disconnected.

"Messenger, close." Six months meant that John would either have just moved to Irokai as a permanent resident by then, or would be just about to do so. Either way, he was in for a shock when he got there. I didn't like it, but with the right equipment and passwords, both supplied by the enigmatic Fuki, I might be able to help shield him and Mitsuko from the worst of it. I thought about trying to warn him, then shook my head against it. If he thought I was trying to talk him out of it, he'd treat me the way he treated Adam, and for good reason.

Mitsuko, though, was another matter. "E-mail, open. New letter to Ikanobari Mitsuko, title, 'Brace yourself.'" I took off the headset and set it down, typing with one hand.

Mitsuko,

John's welcome-home party is going to have unexpected visitors. I can't say much, but be ready for anything. If I can help, I will. I know this doesn't make any sense, but trust me when I say it will. Please take care of him, and please don't say anything to John. I'm

not trying to talk him out of this; anything but. I just know some
big things are afoot, and I don't want him caught in the middle.
I wish I could say more, but I've probably already said too much.
I know what you're capable of doing. Don't be afraid of using it,
when the time comes.

All my best for you both.

Jules.

As soon as I sent it, I pushed back from the desk and stumbled out
into the living room. At that moment, I'd had enough of the digital
world, and I really needed another cigarette. My phone sat where I'd
left it, on the card table in what passed for my living room, next to a
small pile of mail and my keys. I grabbed it and through the contacts
menu until the cursor was on Adam's name, then hit the dial button.

Adam answered on the second ring. "Hello, Julia."

I grimaced at the phone but decided it wasn't worth arguing over
the name. "Hey, Adam. Sorry about last time. Want to grab a bite to
eat? My treat."

Adam chuckled. "I'm shocked. I can't imagine you wanting to go
out with a neo-Luddite like me."

I laughed in response. "You help keep me grounded. Besides, I still
owe you one. Want to hit the diner again, or something fancy?"

"Now that you suggest fancy," Adam replied after a hesitant pause,
"we haven't been to Café Aquarius in a while."

I made a face. "You can't at least pick some place I can smoke?"

Adam rolled his eyes. "I don't see why you continue that filthy
habit; you know what it's doing to your lungs."

I sighed; this wasn't an argument I wanted to have either. "It kills
time and hurts less than cutting."

Adam *hmph*ed into the phone. "If you don't want to tell me, fine,
but you don't have to be grotesque. C'mon, it's been ages and I know
you like the place. Or don't you own anything other than jeans any
more?"

I blew a raspberry into the phone. "I do work for business clients.
I can dress like a professional. Seriously, now. I spent all day on-site
and I'm wound up; a couple of smokes would help me relax and take
my mind off of stuff. Plus, I just landed a pretty long-term project, so
before I hole up like a troglodyte I'd like some face-time, and John's
busy getting his act together for the move."

"One way trip to oblivion," Adam muttered.

It was soft enough that he probably thought I didn't hear it, and for once I didn't feel like arguing with him about it. Maybe it was because I knew what was coming. "Sorry, couldn't hear you," I said, saccharine-sweet. "Was that a yes or a no?"

Adam chuckled again. "I said that's fine. Meet you at Aquarius in an hour?"

"In an hour," I agreed. "See you there." I thumbed the off-button, then sighed as I set it down. *Back into the suit,* I silently groused. I picked up the pieces of my professional persona that I'd strewn around the room. Back in the bedroom, I retrieved my sweater from the pile near the laundry basket and squirmed into it. I retrieved the lighter from my desk, but my eyes went instinctively to the screen-saver that had activated in my absence, and I stood for a few moments, watching myself dance with a smile on my face.

"See you soon, I hope," I said to the wolf as I walked out of the room. "Lights, out," I said to the apartment, and everything went dark, leaving myself to dance in the darkness while I went to get a last meal.

09 | HASH(0x8BE0F03480CB) GIRI
DELINQUENCY

COLD AIR RUSHED INTO THE APARTMENT AS I OPENED THE SLIDING glass door leading to the balcony. The clock in the den said six-and-three-quarters local, a half-circle of color running from green to indigo; it was later than I liked to start my mornings, but after the late night, it had felt necessary. Those sections of the sky visible through the towers of Murasaki Prefecture were already a lighter blue, streaked with lines of gold and rose, hinting at the sunrise to come. Overhead, though, stars still filled my view, shimmering against a vast expanse of deepest black.

Nude aside from the sash tied around my waist, I stepped out onto the metal balcony, muzzle turned to face the sky. As I closed the glass door behind me, sharp winds cut through my fur, but I had long since become numb to the cold. One paw I kept at my waist, steadying the *katana* in its *saya* as it bobbed against my hip; the other I curled around the thin railing, bracing myself as I gazed upwards. Even with the morning fast approaching, I could still make out the constellations overhead. To the east, *Seiryū* had all but disappeared, only its eye still visible against the coming dawn. Opposite, *Byakko* shimmered against the darkness, her tail dipping lazily into a rising pond of brilliant blue. Elsewhere, the Tortoise and Phoenix chased each other across the heavens, and Rabbit and Fox danced. Beneath them all, I stood and faced them, entranced.

No matter how long I gazed upwards at the heavens, I never tired of watching the stars dance in the sky, watching them shine and scanning for the occasional comet. I knew, as a matter of fact, that the heavens were artificial. Far from being celestial bodies of burning gas, Irokai's stars were mere polygon clusters, spinning in place overhead and palette-shifting to give the illusion of twinkling in a sky unfettered by air pollution. They gave off no heat, only light. If I wanted, I could download a copy of the night sky and, in much-reduced scale, hang it from my living room ceiling.

Yet, for all that, I never tired of looking up to them. Stretched out against an endless blank slate, they gave Irokai a sense of infinity. The world was not boundless, but a night sky filled with stars fostered a sense that it could be. As far back as I could remember, the stars had transfixed me, and I could spend hours doing no more than lying on my back and watching them, imagining flying among them, reaching out and touching them. Knowing their truth had never diminished their impact. In many ways, it had heightened it; it put them within my reach.

For several minutes, I stood, watching the approaching day wash out the stars. The sky lightened, and streaks of rose and yellow streamed from the horizon. Then a flood of brilliant light broke through the skyline, outlining Murasaki Prefecture in gold, and I lowered my gaze from the sky. I had delayed starting the day as long as possible. It was time to begin.

Stepping back from the railing, I drew the scabbard from my sash. Kneeling, I rested it in front of me, then bent reverently over it, my muzzle not quite touching the ground, forehead just barely brushing against the intricately woven sheath. With arms outstretched, I held the pose of a supplicant, focusing on my breath as it entered my nostrils and then escaped between my lips. Prostrate before the sun, I emptied my mind, waiting to see what filled it.

As expected, the vision of the distorted sky was first to mind, and with it came a flash of anger. Stepping out of my apartment to be greeted by such a crude scrawl against the heavens was an offense both professional and personal. Until then, I had taken the graffiti in stride, the childish hacks of vandals who sought to destroy something they could never have built. Their acts against the stars themselves had been a blow too strong; it was proof that they, whoever they were, would stop at nothing until their aims had been achieved. It also served as the strongest proof yet that my superiors either did not understand the danger that hackers could pose, or did not care. It did not seem to matter how strident my demands, how imploring my requests. Every attempt I made to illustrate the threat to Irokai seemed to fall on deaf ears. My reports went unread. My support requests were closed, unanswered.

Eyes closed, vision turned inward, I studied my response, and my response to my response. It was no longer anger that motivated me, I realized; it was despair. I no longer believed that there would be an official response to my requests, any more than there would be a public revelation that anything had ever happened. In beautiful Irokai, hackers were an archaism, like paper currency. To admit that someone had, not once but multiple times, broken through the security measures in place and tampered with things publicly considered immutable would have revealed a world unready to be treated as just as real as any other. Even if someone were to answer my cries, it would be in a way that never admitted there had ever been a complaint. I would never know if someone were listening, until one day I found my prayers answered, with no sign that they had ever been made.

The weight of memory hung heavily on my shoulders, but I dragged myself consciously back into the now of meditation. *Your breath is real,* I reminded myself, ignoring the inherent absurdity of a digital sapience in a simulated world worrying about air. *In. Out. In. Out.* I focused on the sounds of my breath, on the feelings of the air moving, the rise and fall of my chest. *Feel, and accept the feeling, but do not succumb to it.* I felt anger and helplessness; this didn't mean I needed to be angry or helpless. The question was, what was there to do about my emotion? How could I resolve this tension?

I considered, briefly, quitting my job with security. In the past, I just manually reverted whatever changes that I found. Once, when an entire block of Murasaki became drenched in revolutionary graffiti, I went as far as to file a request for restoration from backup. For three days, even walking by those storefronts, knowing what had been done and being unable to resolve it, hurt in ways I still cannot fully describe. It felt as if someone had taken a razor to my arm and shaved an insult into the fur, just to prove he could. I knew something had been done about it, and that soon enough it would be as if nothing had happened, but that I had to ask for something like that to be fixed stuck in my throat.

I already felt an unpleasant nostalgia for that time. The problems were starting to arise faster than I could resolve them alone. Others within the department had helped me when I asked, and even my manager had thanked me for my efforts. It seemed, though, that outside of a limited few brave souls, most of Irokai's management had traded honesty and diligence for appearances. I could foresee a day, not too far into the future, when I simply could not keep pace with those trying to break Irokai from within. What would I do then? It would be better to leave a final warning and simply walk away from it all while I still had some dignity, to give up before burning out and coming to hate something that I enjoyed. The world would disintegrate around me, but I, at least, would not go with it.

And yet, were I to quit, what would I do instead? Where would I go? There was no "outside" for me, not in the way there was for the analogs who worked for Tadashiissei. Irokai was my only home, and I was as intimately tied to its existence as the world was to its hardware. The hackers were not just an artistic annoyance; they were a threat to my home. If the hackers were to get out of control, or worse, to gain control of Irokai, its creators might decide to simply end their grand experiment. What, then, would happen to those of us who lived within it? If Irokai were to disappear, I would surely go with it. The thought of death was alien to me, as it was to any resident of this world, but contemplating the end of Irokai itself was one that filled me with dread. There would be no waking up from that final shutdown.

I opened my eyes and leaned back, resting my paws on my hips, considering the sword that lay before me. If I was displeased with my decision, it was because the other options available to me were worse. No matter how pointless it seemed, the best option I could find was to keep my position with Irokai Security. At the very least, I could continue documenting every breach in hopes of forcing some form of response. I might never get a formal acknowledgment, but at least the problems would be fixed. Plus, as long as I held a security clearance within the company, I could continue to revert most of the changes myself. For those too invasive to manage alone, I could enlist others to help, people outside of Security, or even outside of Tadashiissei itself. I smiled tightly, remembering my conversation with the Hospitality specialist from the other night. Laid out in such bare terms, Mitsuko had been disturbed, to say the least, by the prospect of going behind her employers' backs, but even she had seen the necessity of action if Tadashiissei refused to do so. If she could convince her lover to help, so much the better.

I reclaimed the sword from the ground, bowed over it, then held it briefly upright, balanced on the tip of the scabbard, before sliding it back into the sash at my waist. My knees slightly spread, I waited until I felt still, then placed one paw on the hilt of the sword, drawing it and rising onto one hind as I slashed forward, the opening stroke of the *Mae kata*. In time with the blade, I launched the security interface and pulled up the administration panel. The tip of the sword wobbled slightly, my concentration split between the physical and practical. Turning to the blade to the side, I raised it overhead and gripped the hilt in both hands, sliding forward on one knee to draw the blade down in a vertical slice, accompanied by opening the local lockout menu. The blade wandered wide as I scanned through database references, then snapped down in a decisive stroke as I rose to both hinds and flagged an account. Then, finally, I closed the menu and completed the *noto,* returning the sword to its scabbard, sinking slowly back to the opposite knee.

Through each of the forms I progressed. Each draw matched an opening of the interface, each stroke a command, and each return of the katana to its home an exit from the terminal. I ran through the stances twice, once for thoroughness and once for speed. Then, practice done for the day, I bowed over the sword, then released it back into my personal archive. By the time I had finished, the sun had long since risen, and the clock in the den hovered at a few degrees shy of eight. I scowled at the time, tail and ears flat in irritation, then hastily dressed and left, making my way down to the lobby and the streets of Murasaki Prefecture.

THE GLOWING SIGN OVER THE FRONT DOOR SAID "SUNNY YOU," complete with stylized smiling yellow face. A sign hung on the door advertised expanded personal storage on sale, while a holograph turned beside the entrance, displaying a myriad of available bodies, all tastefully covered in a modicum of white clothing. The sense of need faded as I approached the shop, but I paused with one paw on the handle, watching the display. Someone had apparently decided that "bear" was this season's in-look; fully half of the figures that passed were ursine, in various colors and proportions. After a minute, I turned away from the shifting images towards the door, noting with an unsuppressed grimace the Tadashiissei "Sponsored Partner" image hovering next to the credit card logos.

Inside, the atmosphere was decidedly cool. The most incongruously unhappy element within the room was a female rabbit wearing a black shirt with an animated silver-and-blue logo advertising something called FutureShock and a skirt with some kind of pseudo-randomized texture running through the range of violets. The bright red security-rings around her ankles and wrists prevented her from leaving the store, but beside her stood a teenaged fox in a yellow employee's polo and black slacks, staring at her as though to lock her in place through the force of his gaze alone. He held his arms folded across his chest and was doing his best to loom over the rabbit, his tail curled tightly against his back. A few other patrons looked on with a mixture of interest and contempt, while an older female bear wearing similar corporate apparel, stood behind the counter, watching with a faint sneer.

As soon as they realized I was there, both the rabbit and fox started to speak, their voices canceling each other out in a blur of noise. Ignoring them and holding out a paw, pads facing them for silence, I walked up to the cashier's station and drew my security credentials out of the interior pocket of my coat. "My name is Giri. You called for security, *akibito-sama?*"

The bear nodded, clacking the claws of one paw against the yellow counter top. She pointed with the other towards the rabbit in the middle of the store. "She tried to make off with one of our specialty mods without paying—"

"I did *not!*" The outburst from the rabbit was automatic, her voice at once petulant and pleading. "I—"

The younger fox immediately snapped, "You did! I saw you! I caught you myself! I—"

"Oh, for æther's sake!" The rabbit put her paws on her hips, the silver rings in her ears jangling angrily as they shook. "I did nothing of the sort!"

The two fell instantly into bickering, their volume quickly rising as each tried to shout down the other. I sighed, shook my head, and opened up my security terminal. It took me a bit of time to remember where the options were located, but soon I put a local mute onto the two of them. Instantly, their voices stopped cold, but it took several seconds for them to realize what had happened. They both glared at each other, then at me, as though trying to convince me that the other was at fault.

Turning away from the bickering pair, I looked back to the manager, pulling up her name out of the user database. "So.... Eliott-*sama*, please explain."

The manager blinked and stood a bit straighter when I referred to her by name. She motioned towards a display on the wall near the cashier's station. Within a clear case, the figure of a bear-sow slowly spun, motes of light sparkling through her fur irregularly. Beneath the case, a sign in Japanese and English announced the Firefly package, available on sale now for forty-percent off with any other avatar upgrade. "I was up at the front of the store helping some other customers, but Aaron saw her standing there staring at the display. I heard him ask her if she needed any help, and she asked him how much the new Firefly mod cost by itself. When he told her, she started screaming about usury and monopolies. That's when I excused myself and approached. I tried to get her to calm down, but she refused to listen to me either, and then Aaron said she started to make an unauthorized copy! That's when I hit the security lockdown."

Throughout the manager's speech, the rabbit started gesturing more wildly, while the other store associate tried to grab her arms and pin them down. The confrontation appeared to be headed to blows, so I put a movement lockout on them both and then relocated the rabbit next to me. She jerked around in surprise, almost falling when her feet refused to leave the ground despite her vigorous response. I removed the vocal lock from her and frowned. "So, *usagi-san,* is this correct?"

The rabbit snorted, paws again on her hips. "Hardly." She turned first towards the fox, then the manager. "I was trying to figure out if they just used a pseudorandomizer or if they had a real analog random function on the lights, and he told me to stop trying to hack their code. I could've bought two custom bodies for what they wanted for one little mod, so I whipped out a decompiler – which, by the way, is neither illegal nor against the service agreement – to see for myself. The kid freaked out and screamed thief, and she hit the panic button."

The bear's silver-tipped brown fur bristled, her eyes narrowing. "You can't just go around trying to steal source code! That's illegal!"

"Terms of Service, Customized Avatars, section fourteen." The accused let out an exaggerated sigh. "I have the right to ensure before purchase that any mod I buy is compatible with other code I already have installed. I've got some heavy mods that I paid a lot of money for and I'm not going to plunk down that much credit for something that's going to clobber something else I already own. Legally."

The manger sniffed. "I don't see a single mod on you."

At that, the rabbit smiled tightly, and the logo on her shirt froze into the image of a single word emblazoned on her chest in metallic silver: *Possible.* "Yeah, well, I wouldn't wear most of them in a place like this."

At that, I held up my paws, forestalling them both from continuing. "I believe I understand what has happened here," I said quietly. "I will take custody of her, *akibito-sama.*"

As the manager smiled her approval, the rabbit's eyes went wide and jumped from me to her and back. "You gotta be kidding me! I've done nothing wrong!"

In the security menu, I switched the target of the rabbit's location lock from the interior of Sunny You to a five-meter radius centered on me. "Are you disobeying a direct order from Irokai Security?"

The rabbit's ears shook, her rings chiming angrily, but she looked down at the ground. "No."

I nodded, mostly to myself. "Good." To the manager, I bowed deeply. "Thank you for alerting Irokai Security to this matter, Eliott-*sama*. I will ensure this is handled appropriately." As soon as she bowed in return, I turned and walked out of the store, the rabbit dragging behind me on an invisible leash. I ignored the sales associate when he stuck his tongue out at my prisoner, but only as the door closed behind me did I relinquish his voice to him.

I made a point of ignoring the passers-by as I walked. I could see at the edges of my sight how they stopped to stare at the "criminal" in her awkwardly blocky red cuffs and anklets, but I did nothing to acknowledge them, other than to motion for the occasional pedestrian to step out of my way. To her credit, the rabbit did nothing to engage them, neither challenging nor pleading. She merely followed in silence as I led her to a nearby office building, up an awkward elevator ride and then three sullen flights of stairs, until we stood on the roof, alone in crowded Murasaki Prefecture.

When I did finally stop, the rabbit stumbled into me and then jerked backwards. "Sorry," she mumbled automatically, her eyes not meeting mine.

I didn't move from my spot for several seconds; I merely stood and looked over the edge of the building, down to the streets below.

"I said I'm sorry," the rabbit repeated, her voice louder but still nervous.

"What is your name, *usagi-san?*" I asked, not looking at her. Far below, people moved, little blobs of color against black asphalt.

The rabbit hesitated before blurting, "Briar." It was a challenge as much as a declaration.

I opened my terminal access and performed a quick scan. "Your account says otherwise, Summerfield-*san.*"

The rabbit snorted again. "Oh, yeah, clever," she sneered, reflexively. "You can look stuff up in a database. If you don't like my nickname, at least call me Caitlyn."

I turned away from the streets, back to face her, a frown on my muzzle and my ears flat. "I work in security; giving me an alias, even a common one, was not your wisest decision."

Briar rolled her eyes. "I told you what I wanted to be called. You gonna give me guff about it?"

I looked away, towards the skyline, watching the morning sunlight reflecting off of the buildings. "No."

Out of the corner of my eye, I saw her gesture at me with one paw, resting the other on her hip. "What's with the outfit, anyway? Coat, sweater, slacks. Samurai sword. Sure, you're Security, I understand, but do you have to *look* like a poorly-animated police officer?"

Without looking back at her, the corner of my muzzle rose in a wry smile. "Perhaps the fact that you knew what I was as soon as you saw me is proof of its effectiveness."

At that, she crossed her arms in front of her. "Yeah, insecure and trying to prove something." We both stood in silence at that, until finally she said, irritably, "Look, what's going on? Am I getting banned or not?"

I shook my head, still not facing her. "No," I said again.

The rabbit let out another heavy sigh and gestured to one wrist with the opposite paw. "Why all the theater, then? Why didn't you just tell them to buzz off?"

"I had my reasons, Briar-*san*." I looked back at her. "Sunny You has a partnership with Tadashiissei. I could not simply do nothing."

"Politics." Briar spat the word.

I merely nodded in response, taking a seat against the railing at the edge of the building. "Would you have stolen the upgrade, had they not caught you?"

Briar's face registered an instant of guilt before returning to her defiant glare from before. "You can't steal code. Code's just an idea given a form. I was trying to figure out how they did it so I could do it myself for cheap." She paused briefly, then continued. "Everything they sell is overpriced, anyway, and their code's always a mess. I know folks who could do the same thing in half the space."

"I see," I replied, more in response to her expression than her words.

"I didn't do anything wrong," she snapped. "You said as much." She drew away, then, looking down at the roof, as though suddenly remembering to whom she was speaking.

"I did," I agreed quietly. Before I could say anything else, though, a buzzer rang twice quickly in my ear, indicating a work call. I held out a paw to Briar, then tilted my head and checked my communication requests. It was from Mori Koneko, one of my analog coworkers. I accepted the contact. «*Moshimoshi?*»

«Giri? It's Koneko,» she transmitted unnecessarily. «I think we've had another incident like you described. This one's... it's big. You'd better come see for yourself.» Following her words was a relocation invitation.

I sighed. «One moment; I have another job to complete.» I closed the connection, then looked back at Briar. "I will let this one go as a misunderstanding. I suggest you stay away from Sunny You for some time." I dismissed the location lock, and the angry red circles around her limbs disappeared.

Briar blinked and rubbed at her bare wrists. "Wow. You had me worried for a while there. I thought I was busted again for sure."

At that, I raised one brow. "Again?" I performed a quick scan of her visitor history but found nothing in her record. "Your file appears clean."

The rabbit's eyes widened briefly, but then she shrugged. "It's... must've been a while. Maybe these things fade over time."

I frowned and filed away a copy of the last five minutes for later review; that was the sort of comment that deserved further analysis. However, if Koneko was correct, I had no time to research it presently. I waved off the excuse and stood up from the ledge. "I have more pressing concerns than someone trying to save a little money."

"You know, I like your attitude, I think." Briar sent me a contact information memo, which I filed automatically. "Next time I get in trouble, I'll call you."

I sighed and shook my head, then accepted Koneko's invitation to go survey the latest assault on my home, leaving Briar alone on the rooftop to contemplate the sun.

10 JULES PENNROSE
HOMECOMING

THE CLIENT-SIDE PROCESSING UNIT WAS AN AWKWARD BEIGE METAL box, crammed underneath the massive mahogany desk because it was too large to sit on top. Out of one side, a multitude of colored cables jutted like party streamers celebrating Expensive and Possibly Illegal Hardware Day. A thick optical lead, the induction rig's data line, fed into the back of my computer. A second massive cable plugged into the surge protector with an unwieldy power brick labeled in Japanese and in just enough English to make me worry about "flaming hazard." Finally, a collection of plastic rainbow-sheathed wires led up from the ugly tan cube to a flexible nylon helmet dotted with electromagnets along its inner wall and an integrated blindfold and earplugs to help block physical input. This last component hung nonchalantly across the back of my captain's chair, waiting for me to wear it.

It had taken me the better part of three hours to get the drivers for the induction rig installed and tested. I'd checked and double-checked the potential throughput of my system's network. I'd validated the integrity of the skullcap itself, reading and inducing a current through every magnet. I'd secured the power lines to ensure the total power drain wasn't going to brown out the building when I ran everything at once. I even ran a successful mock-connection to

Tadashiissei's network, aborting the connection right before logging into Irokai. Piecewise and collectively, I'd done everything but actually turn out the lights, put on the helmet, and activate the connection protocols.

During the fourth dry run, I consciously realized that I was stalling. I could only validate things in a vacuum so many times before I started second-guessing myself, but *something* kept me from actually sitting down in the chair and launching. I'd checked and double-checked everything system-related, so it couldn't be the software. The hardware itself was a black box to me, but all the tests I had done against it suggested that it was what Fuki had promised it to be: a hardware component for reading neural impulses and inducing state changes in the brain through electromagnetic resonance. I was as ready for this as I was ever going to get. Why was I still hesitating?

I bowed my head, letting out the breath I caught myself holding, forcing air in and out of my lungs. I didn't trust Fuki. That was at least part of it. She'd contacted me out of nowhere, citing some vague mutual acquaintances and suggesting that we had a lot in common, but really, I didn't know anything about her. I shook my head. *Scratch that,* I thought. I knew she either worked for Tadashiissei or knew someone who did; that was the only explanation for the amount of detailed information she'd been able to provide. No casual hacker, no matter how good, could have reverse-engineered so much about the company's codebase in such a short time. Even a team as good as the one she claimed to have couldn't have done this much research this quickly without internal access. That meant she had an angle, a reason for taking down the company from within... or a reason to go looking for people who did and get them to reveal themselves.

In light of that, I couldn't trust the rig either. Sure, it had the Tadashiissei logo on it, and it did look remarkably like what I saw on every visit to the transit facility, back when I could get through the front doors. That didn't mean that it actually was what I requested, or even that it did anything at all. It passed the initial checks, but any clever programmer could set up a dummy device to respond however he or she wanted, to look like a perfectly valid piece of hardware and then do absolutely nothing. Worse, what if she was a company agent, and this was a trap? If the thing could do proper induction, I had no way to control in advance what it would put into my brain, short of tearing the thing open and studying its guts.

Having admitted that, I had to know. With a groan, I crawled under my desk and jerked the cables out of the back of the box. With much grunting and thrashing, I dragged it back into the light of day, then rummaged in my desk for a multitool and set about to stripping screws and splitting security seals. When all the screws I could see were sitting in their rough locations two feet to the left, I grabbed my headset in one hand and spoke into the mic, not bothering to put it on. "Open search. Search for, quote, induction rig schematic, unquote. Go." That done, I braced myself for explosions or worse, and I carefully pulled off the ugly beige case.

Inside the box was exactly what I feared: a mass of colored wires, circuit boards, and the occasional corporate logo. I hauled myself up into my chair, scrolled through search results, and then started trying to compare notes. Nothing said "burnout circuit" or "possession virus", or even had a label written in English. I could see the firmware that handled the induction, the small solid-state drive for buffering. None of the diagrams I found matched perfectly, but all of them were at least six months old. Far from proving my theories, peering the inside the induction rig just made me more unsettled.

I ground my teeth in frustration. "You're still stalling," I said aloud, as though the words, given form, would somehow jar me into action. All it did was up my heart rate as I realized I was running out of excuses. Either I trusted it, or I didn't. If I trusted it, it either worked or it didn't. If it worked, I wound up in Irokai. If it didn't... my mind conjured a myriad of scenarios, from brainwashing to a silent alarm going off in Tadashiissei's offices to impossibly lethal feedback.

I shook my head again as I stood and walked out of the room, grabbing my cigarettes from the kitchen counter. The equation was even simpler than that, really. Either I trusted Fuki, or I didn't. If I trusted her, and that trust wasn't misplaced, then I got to go back to Irokai with administrative access. If I didn't trust her, or my trust was misguided, then I stayed outside, in the "real" world. Everything followed from that assumption, and that was the one line of the proof giving me the most trouble. Could I trust someone I only knew by pseudonym with something this risky?

The first draw of smoke hit my lungs in a burst of heat and nicotine, soothing my rattled nerves. I leaned against the balcony, cigarette tucked between two fingers as I stared at the sky, the sodium glare from the streetlights washing out the night sky. Nothing Fuki had said to me yet had turned out to be wrong, but that could all be an act, an attempt to lure me into her web. I had no reason to doubt her, beyond the fact that I couldn't make sense of her actions. Why would someone inside the company work to destroy its greatest asset, unless she were trying to get people to incriminate themselves? She had to have a motive, a reason for her betrayal, but I couldn't figure out what it was. I just had no idea.

I took a second drag, holding it inside until my chest burned, then let it out in a rush of grey smoke. *Did John understand why I left him?* I wondered, watching the wisps dissipate in the ever-present breeze. *For that matter, does Adam understand why John's leaving us both?* I shook my head, flicking the half-finished cigarette into the empty space. Some things, I realized, couldn't make sense from the outside. Even if I knew Fuki's reasons for what she was doing – assuming she was really a "she" and not a "they" or something else entirely – I couldn't guarantee that they'd make any kind of sense. Knowing something and understanding it were two very different things, and all this twisting around trying to decipher someone else's inscrutable motives was getting me nowhere.

The leather of the captain's chair was cool against my butt as I dropped, naked, into the seat. I took a few minutes to put the case back on the rig and shove it half-heartedly under the desk again. Whipping together a timer, a little watcher-script to cut my outside connection in an hour in case anything went wrong with the system, took a few more. The skullcap was tighter than I remembered, putting a faint pressure all around my head as I tugged it into place and tied the chin-fastener. "Lights, off," I said, my voice muffled by the earplugs. The light seeping around the edges of the blindfold disappeared, leaving only the faint glow of the monitor. "Timer, execute." I took a deep breath, closed my eyes, and leaned backwards, lifting my feet off the ground as the chair tilted me to near-horizontal.

"Inductor, execute."

An infrasonic thrum began pulsing through my head, and despite the absence of any light, my vision slowly filled with a field of grey. Faint rainbows rippled in the void, and then suddenly I was falling, but up and down refused to identify themselves. Bars of music resolved out of the background hum, chords coming together into a chorus of electronic pure tones, then diminishing into a digital hiss.

Swirls of color took shape and form, resolving like stereoscopic images into regular, asymmetric patterns. Gravity abruptly asserted itself, and I landed with a heavy thud onto my hinds, then staggered into the dart-tiled door. It gave way as my weight impacted it, and I tumbled out of the arrivals booth onto a concrete walkway. A collection of people stared as I struggled to my feet, and somebody in the crowd said, "Hey, buddy, you okay?"

Someone put a black-furred paw on my shoulder. I followed it back up the brown arm's length to the face of a raccoon, his brows furrowed in concern, an awkward mixture of sympathy and smugness at play in the set of his muzzle. Behind him, a group of his friends stood around twittering and watching their companion with admiration and annoyance. He extended his other paw to me and helped me awkwardly to my feet, offering a fraternal pat on the back. "First time through the transit system? That looked pretty rough."

I blinked, snapping my head from the raccoon's face back the wall behind me; it was concrete, like the rest of the tram station, but set with a series of multicolored tiles like the floor of Tadashiissei's transit station. The patterns extended briefly up onto the walls, and overhead a sign in Japanese and English said, «Beni Prefecture Transit Point. Welcome Visitors to Irokai!»

I grinned so wide my cheeks hurt, tail wagging madly behind me; even if I could have stopped it, I wouldn't have. I wiped at my face with one paw, relishing the feel of fur under my pads. "Yeah," I said, clearing my throat with a cough. "That last step's a long one."

The raccoon grinned, obviously glad of his chance to show off his superior gravity-management experience. "You gonna be okay? You need some help?"

I waved away the offer, shaking my head. "I'll manage; I'm meeting some friends at a club not far from here."

"Yeah?" The raccoon's eyes lit up and a knowing smirk crossed his face. "Which one?"

I looked back at my erstwhile-assistant and made a point of visually giving him the once-over. Out of curiosity, I went for a hardline and tried not to look too shocked when I got one, complete with administrator options I wasn't expecting. A quick scan using my newfound powers showed a bog-standard model, even down to the coloration. He didn't have a single mod or upgrade that I could spot. His clothes were custom-tailored, but a fast follow-up on the labels showed that they came from a corporate partner, probably part of a package deal. Even his tail moved in recognizable idle-loops; the overall effect was random, but the individual segments of movement were pure Tadashiissei baseline.

I smirked, giving my own tail an expressive wag. "I don't think you'll like it."

The raccoon frowned at that and pulled his paw away. "Suit yourself," he quipped with a shrug, then motioned back to the gaggle behind him. "We're gonna go have some fun now." Then he was gone, rejoining his group of little friends, which slipped back into the moving throng.

"Yeah, fun," I said to no-one. Then I was off at a dead run, sprinting past bodies as I exited the station.

THE SKIES OVER BENI PREFECTURE PERPETUALLY DRIZZLED, A LIGHT misting interrupted only by the occasional high wind or heavy storm. Even during the day the sun forever lurked behind the clouds, visible only by the stray streak of light that broke through the cover. Runoff gathered in haphazard puddles on the broad concrete sidewalks, reflecting rainbows from the street lamps. Away from the main strips lined with boutiques and cafés, the back roads and alleyways twisted and curved back on themselves. As a result, the whole district had a strangely organic feel, as though it had started from some grand plan and then quickly outgrown its design.

The front of the FutureShock looked like almost every other building in the district: low to the ground, with concrete walls and a corrugated roof, faintly tinted red with rust. Flyers advertising various bands, upgrade shops, and brothels blanketed the steel double-doors marking the entrance. The only sign for the club itself hung in the single window: a constantly-evolving logo filling the glass, beneath which were the words, "Anything is possible."

No bouncer stood at the doorway; instead, as I approached, the quick double-beep of an incoming message sounded in my ear. I opened the hardline and checked my queue; in it was a request for response from "The Association":

> *Dear Prospective Member,*
>
> *Please be aware that FutureShock and its participants do their utmost to live up to the organization's motto. Inside these sacred walls, anything is indeed possible. This venue is not for the faint of heart or the closed of mind. Anyone wishing to experience everything that Irokai not only can but should offer may enter the club after responding in the affirmative to this message, at which point The Association holds itself blameless for any loss of sanity, dignity, or innocence experienced within. In other words, don't say yes if you don't mean it, and don't try to hold us accountable later if you didn't really mean it.*
>
> *If you understand everything you've read above and you're still interested, respond in the affirmative and someone inside will acknowledge your acknowledgment as soon as possible. Thanks.*
>
> *The Association*

I'd forgotten about the application, and more importantly I'd forgotten that I wasn't using my old account. I considered searching through the administration console to find my old records, but good sense stopped me for a change. The last thing I wanted right now was to advertise to anyone else in charge that I might still be around, and checking for my old access information would probably trip somebody's flag somewhere. Still, it couldn't hurt to see if my old hangout had changed much in the time since I'd been gone, and this was part of why I wanted to be back in the first place.

It took a few minutes for someone to process my acceptance, while the light rain slowly soaked into my white fur, turning it a slick silvery grey. Then the double doors creaked open, inviting me inside. Synthesizer tones spilled into the streets, while softly strobing lights beckoned from the bottom of an unlit stairwell. I crossed the threshold into the concrete antechamber, and the steel doors closed behind me, shrouding me in shadows. Moments later, a red light came on behind me, illuminating the stairwell, throbbing gently like a mother's heartbeat, coaxing me further inside.

The stairs had no handrail, but each step was more than wide enough to find, even in the reduced light. Gradually, the glow filtering up from the basement replaced the red behind me, as the concrete steps gave way to solid black strips limned in yellow light. The edges of the stairs themselves lit the way further into the depths, their glow augmented gradually by a pattern of hexagonal panels on the wall that matched them, giving the appearance of a neon beehive. I paused and touched the wall, running my pads over the smooth surface; it wasn't glass, or plastic, or for that matter any material at all. It was an artifact of Irokai's nature, a wall defined solely as "wall," absent any property indicating substance. Light bordered each hexagonal segment, suffusing the hallway with golden radiance.

At the base, the staircase gave way to a broad tiled floor, each step sending up a soft reverberation that no analog material could naturally make. The middle of the room was sunken, dominated in the center by someone's artistic reinterpretation of a tree, circular clear trunk rising from arcs of roots embedded directly in the floor, while angular branches spread out overhead, decorated in fractal holofoil leaves. Translucent "fruit" in an array of Pythagorean solids and the occasional exotic surface hung at intervals, inviting those standing beneath to reach up and pluck them. Benches surrounded the "tree", free of any visible support yet easily carrying those who sat or sprawled across them. Instead of doors leading to other parts of the club, tinted pools of liquid mercury rippled at intervals around the edges of the room, and a long bar dominated one part of the wall. Inverted cones – primitive solids defined purely as functions in space, lacking texture or material – balanced impossibly on their points to serve as stools. Overhead, the walls rose in finer and finer tessellations, converging at the domed ceiling in a semi-spherical sundisk of luminous, impossibly pure yellow that filled the room with its light.

If the room itself defied conventional physics, then its inhabitants defied classification. On one of the benches beneath the tree, a glass statue of a domestic canine leaned against a liquid-metal rabbit, one transparent paw stroking along her silver thigh. At the bar, a holographic mouse drew lines of light through a cluster of violet rosettes floating in snow-leopard-shaped formation. Against one wall, a feline-shaped hazmat suit dripping with machine oil exchanged connector hoses with a blue-furred cat in a silver umbilisuit. As I watched, one of the portals began to ripple, then disgorged a butterfly-woman, her stained-glass wings coruscating rainbows behind her as they vibrated. Behind the counter, a topiary rabbit blooming with berries chatted amiably with a plush coyote, glowing wires stitched into its fur.

I smiled. It felt good to come home.

As soon as I stepped out of the tunnel leading down from the entrance, the rabbit-bush turned and waved. "Welcome to FutureShock!" she called, inviting some of the other inhabitants to turn in my direction.

My swagger died in midstep. *They don't – oh, yeah.* I waved sheepishly with one paw, ears flat against my head and tail trying to curl between my legs. *Of course they won't recognize me, even if they do,* I remembered. *New account, new identity.* In a place in which anyone could be anything, nobody took appearance for granted. I strode over to the bar, making a show of nonchalance. "Hey, Briar," I called out to the topiary, taking a seat on one of the conical stools. "What's blooming?"

The rabbit-bush's ears flicked upwards in surprise. "Sorry, have we met?" Suspicion tinged her voice.

"It's been a while," I admitted, scratching at the back of my head with one paw. "It's Jules."

The plush coyote huffed, its glass-bead eyes half-closed in a suspicious squint. "Nice try, officer."

I smiled wanly, ears back against my head. "You never change, Sparks." I motioned them forward and leaned over the bar, whispering, "I hacked my way back in." I put a finger across my muzzle and grinned.

That got their attention. Both coyote and rabbit leaned in close, ears arching forward to catch every sound. "If you are who you say you are," the rabbit challenged, her voice reedy and tight, "then prove it." Then she dumped a mass of encrypted text into my communication queue.

I dragged up my hardline and rummaged through my settings, then pulled up my bank of private keys and started decoding. As the algorithms cranked, I recited. "Why, the fact is, Miss, this here ought to have been a *red* rose-tree, and we put a *white* one in by mistake; and if the queen was to find it out, we should all have our heads cut off, you know. So you see, Miss, we're doing our best, afore she comes, to—"

The topiary rabbit held up a paw, ears arching forward and needles bristling in a smile. "Enough, Jules. Welcome back." Then she gestured towards the staircase. "So how'd you get here?" She waved the fingers of her other paw, and a cluster of bright red berries rose out of her palm, which she proffered. "Last I heard, you'd gotten banished."

"I was," I agreed as I took the bunch. They were sweet, mostly raspberry-flavored with a faint metallic aftertaste. "What is this?" I asked after I'd eaten about half of what Briar had given me.

"Something new," she replied with a shrug. "So how'd you get back in? And what's with the admin flag?"

Sparks nudged the rabbit with one paw and said to her, "I don't like this."

I finished the cluster of berries and handed back the stems, which vanished into Briar's thickets. "It's a long story, and I don't have a lot of time to explain it, but... yeah, I'm on a hacked account."

Briar grinned, her brambles rustling amusedly. "Tadashiissei's gonna be *choleric* if they catch you."

I smirked at that, but then the bottom fell out of my stomach, forestalling my clever retort. I put a paw over my gut and kneaded at it. The muscles beneath my fingers moved in very un-muscular ways, wiggling loosely, as though not quite attached. "What was in those, anyway?"

"Something new," Briar repeated with a giggle. "You'll see in a minute."

It didn't take that long. Despite the slow wave that my vision seemed to be doing despite remaining still against the bar, I could definitely tell that my fur was changing color, shading from white to a deep red. I brought a paw up in front of my face and squinted, watching with detached interest as the hexagonal wall-pattern began to shine through not just my fingers, but my pads as well. I looked down at myself, observing the changes as they spread, my fur losing definition, then vanishing entirely into my new rubbery skin. I couldn't see any bones or organs when I looked at myself, just an expanse of translucent red all the way through. I looked back at my tail and tried to wag it; it felt like I was dragging it through molasses.

Sparks snickered, then leaned forward and gave my arm a lick with a velvet tongue. "Raspberry," it pronounced with a smirk.

Carefully, I lowered one foot, then the other, letting them flop against the ground. Everything felt so *heavy* all of a sudden. I slid forward, but somehow my legs wouldn't support me, and I slipped bonelessly to the floor, ending up in a heap of tangled limbs. "Hey!" Even my voice was heavy, coming out slowly and ponderously, played back at half-speed. "Warn a guy next time." I stared up at the sundisk and brought my paws in front of my face, watching the way the colors before my eyes moved as I waggled my fingers.

Briar laughed. "That'd suck all the fun out of it." She came out from around the bar and sat down beside me, dragging one leafy paw over my chest and neck, making me squirm in slow motion. "Now, tell me, how'd you get back in here?"

"Induction rig," I responded immediately, though still on a heavy delay. "Hacked connection."

"Mm-hm," Briar agreed, "petting" me with her leaves. "So what's with the admin account?"

"Ask Fuki," I replied, slowly waving my paws in front of my face, then in front of her. The topiary rabbit swam in sticky red when I waved at her.

The rabbit-bush's ears flicked back against her head. "Who's Fuki?"

"Don't know," I admitted with a slow shrug. *Choleric.* The thought of the word made me laugh.

Briar's ears twitched, and I saw her look up at Sparks, who shrugged in response. "You sure?"

"Yeah, sure." I nodded, then tried to get a paw under me. I had legs, last I checked. Two of them, in fact, but they didn't really want to talk to each other. I contented myself with playing with the sun while they decided to be nice.

Again they looked at each other in silence, until Sparks said, "Is it *really* you, Jules?"

I nodded again. "Yeah." Yellow and red made orange. *Orange.* "Yeah, that's right."

The topiary frowned, and then berries were before my lips. "Here." They were blue, and I snapped at them eagerly with gelatin-teeth. They popped in my mouth, and strands of purple suffused me as the juice spread. "This'll help."

The weight slowly dissipated as the second batch of berries worked their magic, and I forced myself into sitting upright. "Whoa," I looked down at myself; the change was still fully in effect, even if the mind-bender wasn't. "Real nice, Briar, Sparks." I frowned at the two. "Nice way to say hello."

Sparks threw up its cloth paws in frustration. "How were we to know? Somebody comes in here with an admin flag claiming to be you, and we'd heard you'd gotten zeroed."

I held out a paw. "Okay, yeah, I understand. Do you believe me now, at least?"

Briar nodded. "Yeah, sorry." She stood, then helped me back onto my hinds and onto the stool. "So, how *are* you back? And why?"

I rolled my shoulders and grinned. "A guy gets lonely?"

Sparks chuckled, but Briar scowled in response. "I'm not taking it. There's something going on here."

I sighed and nodded. "Yeah, there is."

"So spill." The topiary folded her arms across her chest.

I looked at her, then at Sparks. "I can't say much. Mostly, I came to warn you. Some really heavy-duty disaster is on its way. Be ready to duck and cover."

Sparks' ears flattened. "Are they shutting this place down?" It huffed again, paws balled into fists. "We didn't do anything wrong! Well, I mean—"

I held out a paw to forestall the protests. "Not you, not here. Irokai. Does Minshukakumei ring a bell? Democracy Revolution?"

Briar and Sparks exchanged a glance, then looked back at me. "Rumors, mostly," Sparks admitted. "I've seen a few images of edits, but I thought they were faked."

I shook my head. "They're not. Not all of them, anyway."

The topiary rabbit frowned and leaned forward. "Jules, what's going on?"

I turned to the rabbit and smiled wanly again, showing translucent teeth. I leaned forward to rest my elbows on the bar—

—and pitched out of the captain's chair as the software timer expired, cutting my network connection. My knees hit the floor with a bang, my elbows following a moment later and only barely keeping my face from being next.

Unwelcome darkness and silence assaulted me, and for a moment I flailed in the void. Then sense reasserted itself and I clawed at the straps of the skullcap. I pried out the earplugs and then tore the whole thing off of my head. It fell in a heap of nylon and cables beside me as my eyes snapped around the room, the sudden change of sensory inputs making my head reel.

I put a hand to my stomach, trying to still a sudden burst of nausea and to get my breathing back under control. *So that explains the transit stations,* I thought, in between bouts of disorientation. The world slowly came together, and I poked at my skin, scowling at the pink flesh that had so recently been raspberry gelatin. It felt real enough, even if it wasn't mine.

Seconds ticked past as I stared at the discarded skullcap, paws – hands – clenched tightly on the arm of the chair. The urge to run back to FutureShock, to drop everything else for just a few more minutes of *self,* welled up, then broke out of me in a sob. *Get a hold of yourself, damn it!* I swore inside my head. *Every second you spend in there on that account is one more you risk getting caught!*

I choked back a second sob, wiping at my face with my hand, the sensation of fur against muzzle already gone from my mind. *You've already said too much. They're not stupid; they'll figure out what the need to know and what they need to do about it. There's nothing more you can do!*

Gingerly, I got my legs back under me, checked that the bones were intact within, and then pushed myself upright. "Successful test," I said to no-one in particular as I dropped back into the captain's chair and pulled it in front of the computer desk, shoving the skullcap out of the way with one foot. "Lights, on." I grabbed the normal headset next to my keyboard. "Timer, close. Inductor, close. Editor, open. Debugger, open, load file 'voice-over.' Synthesizer, open."

I had a lot of work to do to cover my advance payment.

11 | JOHNATHAN DART
TERMINATION

I ANSWERED THE DOORBELL ON THE THIRD RING, DOING MY BEST TO smile across the doorway. On the concrete porch, Adam slouched, his fists stuck into the pockets of his tan cardigan and his hazel eyes anywhere but my face. Despite his posture and the slight paunch around his middle, though, he still managed to look like he'd just left a photo shoot; his khaki slacks and brown loafers complimented his sweater well. His button-down shirt was dark green, a good contrast for his ruddy complexion. All past anger aside, I still thought he was as cute as I did when I first met him.

"Adam, hi," I said as warmly as I could manage, opening the door completely to him. "I'm sorry; I'm running late, as always."

Adam chuckled at that, but it was forced. "May I come in?" he asked, rising up on the balls of his feet to look over my shoulder.

I sighed. *This is it,* I thought. *Make or break time.* "There's really nothing to see, but if you want...." I stepped back, leaving the door open behind me as I made my way back down the hall, into the bathroom.

I heard footfalls behind me, then an uncomfortable stretch of silence, followed by a startled question. "Where's all your stuff?"

I eyed the razor, then myself in the mirror. I rubbed the scraggly growth on my cheeks and scratched at my neck irritably. I hated the scruffy look, but shaving seemed like a waste of time. *Fur or skin, but not these halfhearted weeds.* I wouldn't have to worry about it after tomorrow, anyway. Likewise, my hair bristled in an ungainly tangle behind me, but what was the point of brushing it? A quick scrounge through the drawers turned up an old hairband, which I used to pull my mop into a tolerable brush. "Sold, mostly," I said as I walked back into the front room, finishing the loose knot in my tie. The walls were bare, but dusty outlines revealed where all of my old frames once hung. Likewise, the room itself was mostly vacant, aside from the two of us standing in it. A single dejected chair remained in a corner, and only divots in the carpet suggested that there had been any other furniture. "What's left, I can manage through the company."

Adam's eyes fixated on the chair, but his voice was still addressed to me. "So, no last meal, then?" He was trying to put humor in his tone, but he just couldn't make it happen,

I chuckled quietly at that. "I thought we could go get something out?" I tried to make it a suggestion. "Less trash to clean up, that way."

"Yeah, okay." Adam's acceptance was grudging. "Where's Julia? I'd have thought she'd be here."

I tensed at the name, but then sighed and waved towards the front door. *Not my fight,* I reminded myself. Jules would say something when the time was right. Or maybe not. "Fighting a deadline, I think. I called a few times, left voice and text. No response."

Adam clucked his tongue disapprovingly. "She needs a new boyfriend," he quipped as he stepped back outside and unlocked his car. "She called me a few weeks ago, but not a word from her since."

I leaned against the roof, fingers drumming irritably on the roof. "You know, Adam, Jules really does prefer the nickname."

Adam wrinkled up his face into a frown. "I dislike diminutives," he grumbled. "Besides, 'Jules' is a man's name." Then he slid into the car, ending the conversation.

"Yes. Yes, it is," I whispered harshly once enough of the frustration had cleared to let me find my voice again. He couldn't hear me, though; he'd already started the engine. I jammed myself into the passenger seat, then slid it all the way back. I didn't look at Adam; I just stared out the front window as I put on my seat belt. "How about the Aquarius, for old time's sake?" I didn't want to be with him, but I knew I'd regret not trying one last time.

Adam nodded, and the car slid smoothly out of its parking space.

The trip was mercifully brief; Café Aquarius wasn't too far from what had been home. The building was ancient, weather-beaten wood that had been hand-painted in swirling spirals of blue and purple, with irregular splashes of gold. The driveway was mostly gravel, a few weeds and the occasional tuft of hardy grass poking through the rocks. The lot was almost devoid of other occupants, as was the interior, and it wasn't long before we were both seated with oversized glasses of iced tea, next to a window looking out at the street.

"So." I took a healthy swallow from my glass and set it down. "What's going on in your world, anyway? It's been weeks – no, longer – since we really had a chance to talk."

Adam demurred, waving away the question and turning to face the road. "C'mon, Johnathan, I know you wouldn't really be interested."

"No, seriously," I half-pleaded. "I'd really like to know."

"Well, I have one student in the Introductory Biochemistry class that I think I'm going to approach about an internship this summer," Adam began, leaning back in his chair. "He's had the kind of insight into some of the assignments that I've given out that I wouldn't expect out of a graduate. Most of my kids this semester have been fairly average, a good bell curve. We've just covered chirality, which is fun to watch. Everyone tries to solve the problems on-screen, and then someone figures out double-sided printing, and then the comprehension spreads."

I nodded encouragingly, and he continued. "I just wish my research were going so well, though." He thunked his glass down on the table, making the ice rattle. "We're tantalizingly close to a class of functions for predicting a few protein structures, but proof remains elusive." From there, his words dissolved into a sea of technical jargon. I knew his research involved some fairly esoteric subjects but I could never follow the specifics. His field of expertise was just too far removed from mine. I'd seen some of the models his software produced and they were incredibly beautiful, but I didn't understand what any of them actually meant beyond being organic molecules of some kind.

Adam continued to ramble, caught up in his own excitement, and I watched him speak with a grin. His emotions were infectious, and the joy with which he talked about his work made me smile. I remembered when he used to share that spirit about Irokai, back when he was so fascinated with the intricacies of how it all worked. He'd spent hours and days reading up on the induction rig, trying to decipher how it worked, and we'd spend days going into Irokai together, he and Jules and I, all taking in this fantastic world and exploring just what it could let us do. Then Jules broke things off, and then I met Mitsuko, and then....

I shook my head at the memory. Looking back at how it all happened, I shouldn't have been surprised at any of Adam's reactions. He didn't care about Irokai; he cared about the technology that could make us think we were in another world. He wasn't interested in exploring the limits of that world; he wanted to know what it could do to improve this one. Mitsuko, Irokai, everything inside those computers was all just a bunch of numbers to him. None of it meant anything, except in terms of how it changed us once we were outside again.

Adam cleared his throat, and I looked up sharply from my iced tea, into the depths of which I'd been gazing for some time. He ran his fingers nervously through his short-cropped hair and shook wearily, slumping back against his chair. "As I said a few minutes ago, I knew you weren't really interested."

I rattled my glass, looking into the ice for a response, then set it on the table with a quiet groan. "Look, Adam, I'm sorry. I'm making a mess out of this. We were friends once, weren't we?" I looked up at the question, but Adam wouldn't meet my gaze; he was focused on the window, on the world outside. I hesitated, then continued into the awkward silence. "I'd like to think we still are, but ever since Mitsuko, it's like... it's like there's this wall between us." I heard my voice rising, even as I tried to stay calm. "Every time I reach around it to shake your hand, you slam my knuckles into it."

Adam raised one arm, waving it irritably before dropping it back down, then turning to lean with his elbows on the table, his head buried in his hands. "I don't know, Johnathan," he said quietly, his voice muffled. "It's not Mitsuko. It's.... I just don't know how to deal with what you're doing. Everything I've ever learned about life and the delicate art of living tells me that your plan is a very fancy suicide." He lifted his head and spread his arms. "There, I said it."

I picked up my glass again and rattled the ice, draining the watery tea from the bottom. Then I looked back to Adam, trying to compose my expression. "What about Imogen Franklin? What about all the other successful uploads?"

"Yes, what about them?" Adam quipped tightly. "Wonderful emulations, all of them, but people? Living beings?" He stopped, then looked down at his hands folded in his lap, his voice suddenly very childlike and lost. "I don't know."

I leaned forward, elbows on the edge of the table. "They've beaten Turing tests," I offered with a faint smile.

Adam's eyes snapped up to mine, his frosty glare chilling the grin off of my face. "That proves nothing and you know it. The truth is, Johnathan, you *don't* know. You *believe,* and that's all well and good, but you're basing your fantasies on hope and faith, not on any sort of rational process." His voice grew hard. "You've fallen in love with a computer program. That's *fine,* Johnathan. People fall in love with all kinds of things. Buildings, cars, kitchen appliances. I've heard reports of a woman who fell in love with the Berlin Wall and even changed her name to be closer to it. She nearly died of grief, back when it came down. It explains a lot, but it doesn't make what you're doing any more sensible, and she at least didn't ask to be entombed in concrete to be with her lover forever!"

As he spoke, he shifted forward, rising up out of his chair as his eyes bored into mine. His voice rose, softening the chatter elsewhere in the Aquarius. Then suddenly, he dropped into his seat, making the legs scrape against the tile floor. He pressed his palms into his eyes, speaking barely above a whisper. "I'm done with you and Julia acting smug and superior because you're capable of seeing what others can't. Call them visions all you like, but from here, they sound more like hallucinations. You're not shamans; you're lunatics. You need help, not people telling you to rush headlong into madness."

I sat rock-still for several seconds, then motioned to the waiter who had quite sensibly been giving our table a pass. He refilled my glass, then set down a bill, onto which I threw a credit card without looking. Once he was gone, I regarded Adam across the length of the table. It might have only been a few feet, but the gulf seemed uncrossable. "No, really," I said quietly, trying to find it within myself to smile. "Tell me how you really feel."

Adam shook his head. He looked suddenly tired. Spent. "C'mon, Johnathan."

The waiter slid the final bill onto the table, and again I waited until we were alone to speak; it gave me a chance to sort out my thoughts. "I'm impressed that you haven't spent the whole meal trying to talk me out of it, but why only now? Why wait until the day before I move to tell me all this?"

"What was I to say?" Adam barked a weary laugh. "'I think you're crazy for being in love?' You wouldn't have listened. You'd have laughed at me, and rightly so. I thought... I don't know... maybe that you'd realize how impossible it all was and that it was time to move on. Instead you found a way to make it all work out, and suddenly anything I could've said was too little too late. And I did say something. Repeatedly. You didn't listen. You were so focused on the idea that I was telling you not to be in love that you missed everything else I said."

I scrawled a hasty signature on the receipt and tossed the pen onto the table as I stood. "So... is this 'good-bye', then? Or just 'see you later'?"

Adam turned towards the window again. "I don't know, Johnathan. I... I just don't know."

There wasn't anything more to be said after that. The drive to Tadashiissei was filled with a heavy silence, a fog of distrust and grievance that neither of us could pierce. I wanted to say something, but every pithy turn of phrase, every apology died in my throat when I remembered those angry, accusatory eyes. Several times, I turned to look at him, but from behind the wheel Adam held his face unflinchingly forward, only his eyes shifting to glance at the mirror, at the side of the car, and occasionally, at me.

I caught his gaze once. It seemed accidental, as though he didn't mean to do it but couldn't help himself. His eyes weren't hard, then; they were pleading. His jaw was set, his teeth clenched to stop himself from speaking, but the lift in his brows and the drop in his lower lids told me how much he needed to be the second person to speak, the one to say, *No, I'm sorry too.* His breath came in short spurts, his nostrils flaring, daring me to challenge him and begging me to break the silence. I looked away; I wasn't the one that needed to relieve him of his guilt.

The car stopped all too suddenly in front of my final destination. In the warm afternoon light, the concrete walkways that meandered through the tessellated tiles were a rich gold, like the path to the end of a rainbow. The luminous LED-board over the building invited everyone to Irokai and advertised the group and extended-stay rates. I knew my stay was a long one, but I would be going alone. The rest of my party was waiting for me inside.

As I got out of the car, Adam shut off the engine, then leaned over to the passenger side. "Johnathan?" His voice cracked as he spoke.

I stopped, then turned and squatted to look inside the car. "Yes, Adam?"

Adam hesitated, then held out one hand to me, his fingers trembling. "Good-bye."

I stiffened, but I took his hand in mine and shook it anyway. "See you later," I replied. Then I stood and, not turning around, walked inside the building. Behind me, Adam's car sputtered to life and then pulled out of the parking lot, taking him away from Tadashiissei, back into the real world.

12 | JOHNATHAN DART
RELOCATION

THE SPECIAL ASSISTANCE AREA OF THE BEAUTIFUL WORLD FACILITY looked more like a consular office than a service desk; only a few scattered preserved print-outs of Tadashiissei news articles and a single corporate logo on the wall suggested otherwise. Aside from that, native landscapes decorated the walls, complete with English and Japanese text identifying the views: *sunset over Kigiku Island from the main ferry*, or *Murasaki skyline at night.* The only clock on the wall was an analog disk, showing the time as just about six-and-three-fourths local, early morning. Next to it hung a thick frame in which was visible a real-time shot of the Tadashiissei headquarters within Irokai itself.

A large ebony desk took up the bulk of the floor space, with three well-stuffed leather seats covering most of the remainder. Most of the desk itself was covered in screens and printouts, organized into neat groupings. Behind it was a tan executive chair, in which sat an older woman wearing a rainbow scarf with her jade-green pantsuit. With her thick-rimmed glasses and her hair pulled back into a tight braid, she looked like someone's grandmother. A small sign at the corner of her desk said, "May Peters, Customer Relations."

As soon as I crossed the threshold into her office, Ms Peters turned to face the entrance, then stood and smiled, filling her face with laugh-lines. "Mr Dart!" she exclaimed, holding out her hands to take mine. "Come in, come in." She led me to a chair, then returned behind her desk and sat. "The day has finally come, then."

I nodded in response, her smile lifting my spirits. "Yeah, that's why I'm here. Emigration."

In response, she clasped her hands to her chest and lifted her face upwards. "Lucky boy. I'll be retiring there, one day. You mark my words. I've got an apartment and everything, ready and waiting." She turned to one of her screens and tapped at it quickly with a slender finger, then motioned to the one before my desk. "A few last bits of paperwork for you, and then I can escort you back."

As I sank into one of the overstuffed chairs, she spun one of the terminals around to face me and then sat down across from me, her fingers tapping rapidly across a keyboard. The screen flashed once, and then a text viewer opened, exposing an intimidating number of documents. "You'll need to read these and attach your approval to each, I'm afraid," Ms Peters apologized. "Take as long as you need, though."

The paperwork covered a dizzying array of subjects relating to both my employment and my emigration; I had to sign everything from a non-disclosure agreement to a list of possible side effects ranging from memory loss to mood swings. I hesitated here and there, trying to scrutinize the forms for anything suspicious, but by the third or fourth heavy block of medical jargon, my eyes had already begun to glaze. The clock on the wall was at just before eleven by the time I had finished attaching a digital signature to every file and saving everything. Ms Peters then handed me two small bundles of paper and a pen. "They're for Legal," she explained with a tired smile. "Some things, you just have to have in writing, even now."

I squinted at the headers, but my eyes were tired from staring into the digital screen. "What are they?" I asked.

Ms Peters adjusted waved away the question with one hand. "Nothing too serious," she explained gently, pointing to the signature box at the bottom of the top form with the other. "This one's just stating that you understand that your job with Tadashiissei isn't contingent on your emigration; you can change your mind on that and you're still hired." She flipped the page and motioned towards the header. "This one's to certify that your digital signature on all the other forms is really yours."

I wearily scrawled my name on the forms, a tight cluster of angles that might have been more at home in a foreign alphabet. Then I sank back into my seat, rubbing my wrist with my other hand. "That's it, then?"

Ms Peters nodded eagerly and rose, taking the paper and moving over to an old-fashioned filing cabinet. She riffled through yellowing folders, then dropped my signature into one of them, closing the drawer with a metal clang. "That's it," she agreed, gesturing towards the doorway. "Let's get you back to Emigration."

She led me past lines of visitors through the entryway marked, "Transit," and down carpeted halls with soft lighting. To the left and right, we passed single- and group-transfer rooms. Most of the doors were closed; Fridays were one of their busiest days, I knew from experience. At the end of one of the hallways stood a simple door marked, "Authorized Entry Only." A small badge reader sat on the wall next to it. Compared to the openness of the rest of the hall, the sign was austere, almost foreboding.

Ms Peters turned and smiled to me. "Ready?"

I took a deep breath and nodded, and she held a small card to the reader. It chirped softly, and the door clicked. She pushed it open, and motioned me inside. The hall was wide and brightly lit, so much more so than the rest of the offices that my eyes had to adjust. Small green signs in white lettering hung high on the wall indicated lavatories, theaters, and waiting rooms, all with small arrows pointing the way. Curved mirrors hung on the ceilings at intersections to give around-the-corner visibility. The door closed behind us with a click that echoed off of the non-skid vinyl floor; an old Irokai advert flickered on its back, reminding everyone that the infinite existence was their option.

Ms Peters brought me to one of the waiting rooms, an austere suite that reminded me of a monk's quarters, though thankfully intended for much shorter occupancy. Outside of a small clump of electronic equipment on a stand beside the bed, the only other contents were a single bed, a desk, and a chair, all in pale green plastic. A stainless-steel bathroom hid behind the door. While I looked around, my escort activated the medical terminal with her badge. "I've let them know you're here and ready," she said, reading from the screen as I looked around. "Your relocation's scheduled for tomorrow morning with Dr Whitehoff. No breakfast, I'm afraid, but dinner is complimentary tonight. A nurse should be by soon to help you with any last-minute preparations." She turned away from the screen. "Is there anything else I can do for you?"

When I shook my head, Ms Peters walked over and took one of

my hands in both of hers, smiling broadly behind her thick glasses. "Good luck to you then, John, and congratulations." She squeezed once, then let go, shutting the door behind her as she let herself out of the room. The light from the hall shrunk to a sliver beneath the door, leaving me alone.

Once she was gone, I pulled out my palmtop and popped it open, thumbing a quick message to Mitsuko. «Inside the waiting room. Not long now.»

«Wonderful!» came the quick reply. «I love you.»

Imagining the words in her voice made me smile. «Love you too, Mits. See you soon.» Then I set the palmtop on the desk. I dithered about on the terminal and found a Special Requests menu, a list of the dishes the company kitchen could prepare for its travelers. I scanned the options, selected the "fish with three flavor", and then tried to find something to occupy my time. The words of the novels blurred together and the scenes of the movies kept crossfading. I was bored and anxious. I kept thinking about Adam's words. I didn't want to believe him, but it was hard telling a biologist he was wrong about life. Actually, it'd been easy to tell him he was wrong; it was harder to tell myself.

A knock at the door interrupted my frustrated reverie, followed by a younger Japanese woman in a white pantsuit stepping into the room. She had a cart with her, on which were two trays. One held silverware and a covered plate; on the other sat a bowl of water, a towel, a small pressurized can, and two razors: one electric, one safety. She set the first on the bed, then brought the second over to the desk, setting it next to the terminal. "Shave," she explained, gesturing to the implements in front of her.

I rubbed my chin and shrugged. "No need; I'm—"

The nurse giggled and shook her head. "No, your head. For the procedure tomorrow."

Comprehension hit me, making me tense up. "Oh.... Yeah, okay."

She motioned for me to lean back in my chair, and I did so. The electric razor snapped to life, and soon my hair sat in shaggy piles on the floor. She switched to the plastic razor, and soon my stubble and eyebrows followed. I squirmed uncomfortably as she wiped down my freshly denuded skull with a warm, damp towel, then patted it dry. Once her hands were gone, I turned to see her gathering up my departed locks onto the empty tray. Once she had most of them, she stood again and gathered the rest of her tools and bowed, leaving dinner on the bed for me as she left.

Ignoring my last meal, I stood and looked at myself in the mirror.

Hairless, I looked even less like myself than I imagined. I frowned at the bags under my eyes, the slightly puffy lips. I closed my eyes, focusing on the image of self-in-Irokai that had come to mean me, golden-eyed and ring-tailed. Once I had a clear picture of myself, I opened them again, only to wince at my wholly human self staring unhappily back at me. I looked like an alien, a stranger in my own skin.

Turning away from the disconcerting image, I grabbed dinner and sat back down in front of the terminal. Time stuttered by while I ate; every few bites I felt the need to check the time. I tried to find something to distract myself, but the monochrome of my surroundings left me little on which to focus. I grabbed my palmtop and searched for something to read to occupy my thoughts, but all the words on my screen started to run together from the weariness and the stress. With a sigh, I tapped on the chat icon and then on Mitsuko's picture. «Miss you,» I sent.

«I miss you too, love,» my girlfriend replied soon after. «Is everything alright?»

My thumbs hesitated over the tiny keyboard, then tapped out, «Nervous. Wish you could be here.»

The screen was blank for several seconds, then lit up again. «You know I will still love you if you wish to stay outside.»

I bit my tongue and shook my head, then thumbed at the small keypad. «No, I want this. I want to be with you.»

«Then we will be together soon,» she soothed. «Relax. Deep breaths. Get some rest if you can.»

«Hai,» I replied. «See you soon.» I stretched out on the bed and pulled up an old familiar collection of audio recordings of Franklin shorts, then set the palmtop to playback while I closed my eyes and listened. Franklin's voice was full and rich, with a faint Southern accent like a dusting of sugar on a molasses pie. She tended her descriptions with loving detail, and soon visions of a Raleigh that never was danced in my head, haunted antebellum mansions juxtaposed against magical research centers, enshrouded on all sides by encroaching nature. Her characters came to life easily through her words, and I quickly became engrossed in their intrigues, this afternoon's ordeal and tomorrow's adventure fading to distant concerns.

Someone knocked at the door again, pulling me back to the present, and then a slightly heavy man in pale green scrubs stepped into the room. In his hands were a paper cup and a bottle of water, which he held out to me. "I brought you a sleeping pill. Most people prefer to get a good night's sleep beforehand."

I tapped on the palmtop as I sat upright, and Ms Franklin's voice halted mid-drawl. In the bottom of the cup were two small pink pills. "How many people have done this before, anyway?"

"Maybe a thousand? Maybe two?" He retrieved the dinner tray from the desk, then walked back over to the door, his shoes squeaking softly on the vinyl floor. "I don't think Tadashiissei's ever published the numbers."

I paused. "Has anyone ever changed his mind, at the last minute?"

The orderly set down the tray outside the room, then stepped back inside and pulled the door closed behind him. "Are you having second thoughts?"

I rolled my shoulders half-heartedly. "I had a fight with someone about it right before I got here. Mostly I'm just curious."

He smiled gently and sat on the edge of the bed. "I'll tell you this: nobody I know has ever been forced into this. If you don't want to go through with it, all you have to do is say something. You can say no, right up until the procedure starts, and nobody will think less of you for it."

I nodded again, then tossed back the pills and dry-swallowed. I downed half of the bottle in one swallow, then handed it and the empty cup to the orderly. "Thanks."

"Don't mention it," he said with a grin. "Sleep well."

Once he was gone, I stripped out of my clothes, leaving my shirt and tie hanging over the back of the chair, my pants in a puddle on top of my shoes. I picked up the palmtop again and sent a final message to Mitsuko. «Not long now. Good night.»

«Good night, John. I love you,» she replied. I smiled at the screen, then unpaused the palmtop and set it on the pile of clothes. I turned off the lights and slid beneath the sheets. The pillows were soft and cool against my bare head, and soon there was nothing to do but wait Ms Franklin's voice to lull me to sleep.

MORNING CAME SUDDENLY, IN THE FORM OF FOUR QUICK TAPS against the door of my suite. I startled out of dreamless sleep still foggy from the medication and called out, "Come in?" My voice was hoarse, my throat barren. I rubbed my eyes with the palms of my hands, trying to grind the exhaustion out of them.

The knocking repeated itself, and then the door opened to admit two orderlies with a gurney between them. "Mr Dart?" the taller one asked. "We're here to take you to Emigration." They brought the gurney up to the bed. "If you can help us get you onto here, we can be on our way."

I nodded and scooted to the edge of the bed. It took a coordinated effort, with me still half-asleep and trying to preserve some measure of modesty under my blanket, but eventually I ended up on the gurney, which the orderlies then escorted out of the room. I stared upwards at the ceiling as we travelled, laughing quietly; someone had taken the time to paint the ceiling a light blue, dotted in clouds and the occasional rainbow. Here and there a plane or a bird flew, as well. I was flying, floating through unfamiliar hallways on my way to a magical kingdom far away.

The journey came to a stop all too quickly with the bang of my cart hitting a pair of double doors that swung wide as I entered the room. Figures in white and pale blue drifted around a bank of intimidating electronic equipment, studying the lights upon them intricately and speaking to each other in hushed tones. One clamped something to one of my fingers. A second began drawing something on my forehead. A third approached with a tray and a wheeled stand with a plastic bag hanging from it.

"This is going to hurt just a bit," the last figure warned in a deep voice, and then I felt a sharp pinprick in the back of my right hand. I winced and looked down to see the spectral form taping a tube to my hand. "The IV's ready," he said before slipping away to attend to another console.

A shorter man, his face obscured by a cap, mask, and goggles, leaned over me. "Mr Dart? I'm Dr Whitehoff. I'll be leading the team that's helping you out today. How're you feeling?"

I blinked, trying to decide how I was. "Tired," I admitted.

The doctor nodded. "That's okay, really. We're almost ready to go, so just be patient for a moment." Then he was gone, off discussing something with one of the others. Another figure in off-white – almost a cream, or an eggshell – hovered nearby, tapping on the plastic tube. I watched her inject something into the line, then give a thumbs-up sign.

"Good!" Dr Whitehoff said again, his face suddenly before mine. A soft rubber mask slid over my nose and mouth, and I caught a whiff of something faintly sweet. "Now, breathe in deep as you can and count down from twenty for me."

This is the last thing I will say with this voice, I thought as I nodded. "Twenty," I said as I breathed out. "Nine... teen...." *These are the last breaths I will take with these lungs.* I managed as black tendrils swam up around me. "Ei— Eight... teen...." *These are the last thoughts I will have in this body.* Those warm dark threads wrapped themselves around me. *If something goes wrong, tell Mits—* "Sev...." Then they pulled me down into oblivion with them.

my forehead. I flinched, then batted lazily at the touch with a paw. I heard a gasp, then the sound of a splash and the cracking of a china teacup and saucer. "John? John!" Mitsuko's voice startled me, and I closed my fingers around hers as she tightened her grip.

Sensation came gradually back after that. I could feel the texture of the woven tatami mat beneath me, the warmth of the blanket over my legs and stomach. The window was open, letting in a cool breeze that ruffled the fur on my chest and muzzle. Strains of a classical music broadcast filtered from a terminal in the other room. I opened my eyes to see Mitsuko gazing into mine, the afternoon sun tinting her emerald eyes with softest gold. The fur beneath them was damp, but her ears were high and she was smiling.

With Mitsuko's help, I stood carefully, not quite sure I could trust my legs. One cautious step at a time, she walked me over to the open window, and I leaned on the bamboo sill and stared out at the warm, long rays of light. The broad roofs of the houses of Midori Prefecture glowed a rich yellow. In the distance, the long flat tram platform stood invitingly, and golden rails disappeared into the distance towards the other parts of Irokai.

I glanced around, pulling up my hardline and checking the interface. Everything seemed the same, except for one element. Buried deep within the menu structure was an option for a wake-up call, a warning to let me know a few minutes before being lifted out of Irokai. This time, the option had simply been greyed out. Trying to access it got me only an apologetic reminder that that function was unavailable.

I smiled back at her, pulling her down into a warm embrace, nuzzling into the fur of her neck. "Looks like I'm here to stay this time," I whispered in her ear.

"*Hai,* John," she breathed, holding me tightly. "Welcome home."

13 | JOHNATHAN DART
ASSAULT

THE APERTURE LEADING TO CENTRAL SUPPORT IRISED OPEN WITH A
beep and a hiss. As I stepped through, I gestured down the length of
the tunnel with a paw. "By default, the gravity in this area would be
turned off, as well as outside," I explained to my team. "Ideally, what
I would like to see is an accurate rendering of centripetal force pulling
people against the walls." I turned to one of my coworkers. "Hideaki?
How hard would it be to get a proper curve from the center at zero out
to one gee at the main ring?"

Hideaki, a tall grey wolf that peered out at the world through half-
lidded violet eyes, considered the question with his head bowed, tapping one claw against the dome of his bubble helmet. His tail wagged
slowly, then tightened reflexively against his back as he shook his
head. "We could do it, probably, but expanding the ring would then
mean a longer station or slowing the rotation, which would affect
other areas."

I thought about his response, holding one paw near the wall. The
magnetic pads under my fingertips pulled them towards the metal.
Hideaki had come to the design team from Customer Relations,
which meant his primary concern was less about *can* and more

about *should*. "We don't really have people measuring the sizes of the prefectures, do we?"

He nodded in response, smiling more with his muzzle than his tail. "Irokai Geographic Society. They tried to create a definitive map of the area and determine the scale of the world. It was in response to their efforts that we put in the random-paths borders on the defined spaces." He gestured back to the iris. "They will know if we change the rotational speed, meaning our sizes at least in some aspect will be fixed. If we have a ring, they will know its circumference."

I frowned. The idea of somebody deliberately trying to map Irokai, forcing structure onto something so malleable, seemed like smugly telling a child how a stage magician did his tricks. Still, if it was a concern, we could accommodate. "So, working design. Let's call our main ring a flat five kilometers in circumference, set our rotation speed to make the floor of that level just under one gee, and then make the story that resources are limited in space. That will drive up demand without really limiting our building capacity. We will also want a residential ring or a hotel at whatever distance amounts for half-gravity."

Hideaki nodded in response. "That sounds reasonable. We can also work on the design of the station to maximize our ring count."

I grinned at that, tailtip flicking in amusement. "Thanks for volunteering. Anyone want to design the outside of the station?" About half the team's paws immediately went into the air, so I tapped my wrist. "I'll schedule a meeting by the end of the week to assign that group; accept the invitation if you're interested. We need to balance realism and ease of development against our expected visitor load, and apparently their preconceptions, too. More on that later, though." I pulled up my hardline and checked the clock: almost eighteen. "Okay, that was everything I had to offer, and remember this is all preliminary design work, so anything you think you can improve, go ahead and make suggestions. Thanks, all, for coming."

I gestured back towards the iris, which opened not to a maintenance tube but instead to the conference room I'd reserved that morning. I held back, waiting for everyone to shuffle out, then shut the portal. I glanced at my account, watching the numbers slowly ticking down. I didn't have quite as much in it as I would have liked, but I really didn't feel like walking home. I flicked through menus with my eyes, hooking up the portal to my front door, then acknowledged the charge for linking a development system to production. My account dropped as soon as I did so, but the iris dutifully opened to reveal Mitsuko's and my front hall.

The front door closed behind me as though I had just stepped through it. I reflexively wiped my paws on the bristle-brush by the door, then shrugged myself out of the *uchūfuku*, letting the silvery weave slide to the floor. "Mits?" I called as I knelt, scooping up the puddle of cloth. The smoky-sweet scent of burning wax caught my nose as I stood.

"*Hai!*" she sang back from further within, her voice slightly muf-fled. "In here!"

I grinned and slung the garment over one arm, then walked nude to the bedroom. I nudged aside the sliding door with my free paw, the paper whispering quietly in its wooden frame, then drew in a sharp breath at what lay beyond. Violet forget-me-nots and cactus blossoms lay scattered about the room, with candles interspersed among them, their flickering flames filling the air with their scent. In the center of this, Mitsuko lay stretched out across the futon, a silk camisole of creamy jade clinging to her fur that didn't quite reach the top of the matching panties that hugged her hips. Around her neck was a choker of forest green, with matching ribbons tied about her wrists and ankles. Braided strands encircled her tail, at the tip of which jan-gled a small silver bell.

A few flower petals clung to her top and her fur, as she stretched and sat upright, they fluttered to the mattress beside her. "Tell me," she murmured, her emerald eyes shimmering in the firelight, "how may I be of service to you this evening?"

I stood transfixed, my next words stuck in my throat, a familiar tension stirring in my crotch. "Mits...." was all I could manage as I walked over to the bed, the spacesuit falling, forgotten, to the floor.

Mitsuko slid from the edge of the mattress as I approached, kneel-ing beside the bed, her arms outstretched to me. Her pads slid across my thighs as she embraced me, her muzzle directly in front of my crotch. Wordlessly, she opened her lips in a smile, then extended her tongue and caressed my sheath. Her eyes closed in an expression of bliss as she drew out my cock, urging back the covering skin with her muzzle.

I tensed, my tail flicking behind me as I gazed down at my lover, caressing the backs of her ears with my fingerpads. "You... don't —"

She drew back, looking up at me with the same smile as before, and lay a finger across her lips with a wink. Then she cupped one paw against my scrotum, carefully tugging back the sheath from the shaft, rapidly stiffening within. Once fully free of its protective cover, she leaned forward again to place a gentle kiss at its tip, then slid her lips down its length, taking me into my muzzle.

As her muzzle engulfed me, a shudder ran through me. I threw back my head, eyes shut tight, muzzle agape. My fingers stroked the back of her head, tracing through the short fur there, thumbclaws running along the edges of her ears. I panted in time with her strokes, out as she slid backwards, until my lungs burned and her muzzle just brushed the end of my cock, then in quickly as she dove down again, her lips touching my sheath and my cock slipping into her throat.

Even as Mitsuko went down on me, her attention seemingly focused on making my knees shake and my body tremble, her delicate fingers were busy elsewhere. One paw tenderly rolled the delicate orbs within my scrotum while a claw tickled along the sensitive skin behind it. The other she held against my rump, one finger teasing around the base of my tail, making it shudder along with the rest of me.

"Mits, I—" I half-moaned, helplessly rocking my hips in time with Mitsuko's ministrations. "I can't—" It felt like lightning running up my spine, from crotch to the back of my head and then scattering just behind my eyes. She did something, pressing with a finger in a place I didn't know existed, and my chest froze in mid-gasp.

Time halted for a moment, my whole body burning with need, and then Mitsuko withdrew her paw from between my legs, clutching at my rump as she hungrily drove herself down onto my shaft. She moaned against my cock as I plunged it between her lips, fucking her muzzle urgently, my legs trembling with need. Then, in the space between one heartbeat and the next, I came, crying her name as I shot my load between her lips.

Mitsuko's claws dug into my rump as I climaxed, holding herself against me, not a drop escaping her muzzle. Only after the aftershocks subsided did she help me turn, then let me collapse back against the bed, sending up a cloud of flower petals as the mattress shifted. She met my pleasure-sodden groan with a giggle, sliding up onto the futon beside me. "Oh, *hai*," she said quietly, resting a paw on my stomach. "I could help you with that."

"Oh, Mits," I groaned, turning my head just enough to look into her emerald eyes, meeting her smile with a weak grin. "That was incredible."

Mitsuko giggled again, resting her head on my shoulder, ruffling the fur of my stomach with her paw. "If you have found my assistance valuable, perhaps you would be so kind as to fill out a visitor survey?" Her green eyes twinkled, her tail arcing behind her in amusement. "Tadashiissei prides itself on exceeding expectations."

At that, I rolled up onto my side, unable to keep the frustration out of my voice. "Sure, which is why we have to restrict the station to one commercial ring and a space hotel."

At that, Mits' eyes instantly softened, the intensely pleased grin fading back to a gentle smile. "Hideaki, again?"

I sighed; she got it in one. "I shouldn't be pissed; he's doing his job, and he's good at it. It's just.... He's not an artist. His background's in Hospitality, which means he's worried more about what people think of the art than the art itself." I held out a paw. "I know, I know. So are you. But... you've got vision, Mits." I smiled when I said it, reaching out to cup her cheek.

She put her paw over mine, fingers curling around it. "You flatter me, John," she said quietly. "But I do not think it is his past career that bothers you, is it?"

I hesitated, then shook my head. "It's... Irokai Geographic Society?" I tried really hard to keep my tone even, but I could see in Mitsuko's wince that I'd let my irritation show. "Sorry. It's.... We've got an infinite amount of room to build, subject to memory availability and rendering power, and we're worrying about whether the trees on Kigiku are in the same place every day? What kind of person looks at a place like this and worries that the roads aren't straight?"

Mitsuko was quiet for a few seconds, her expression suddenly unreadable. When she did finally speak, she sounded hesitant... almost nervous. "Perhaps it is the same kind of person who expects to pay for basic services such as food and happiness?"

That thought made me grimace, tail kinking against my back. "I don't even want to go down that road. I'm sorry, Mits." I stroked my claws over her cheek and down her neck. "I should not bring work home with me, and being mad at Hideaki is definitely work. He means well; I just get mad at the pedantry sometimes. He will come around eventually. We just have to get out of final design with something he can approve. After that, the rest of the team can make adjustments based on artistic license and company revenue potentials. That will mollify him, even if it gives the Geographic Society mange."

That made Mitsuko laugh, which made me smile, the first really comfortable smile I'd had since lunchtime. I gave her a quick hug, nuzzling into her neck, then pulled back. "Let's go out for dinner. I'm sure there's a café somewhere in Beni we haven't seen yet."

"Oh, *hai*," Mitsuko agreed, rolling onto her back. "My coworker Momoko mentioned a *taverna* that I think you might like. She said their *dolmades* were quite good."

"Sounds good." I nodded, then pulled myself out of bed. A quick series of eye-flicks through the hardline and I had my wardrobe open and ready. I stood in front of the mirror, scrolling through options. "Blue polo or green?"

"Blue, I think," she said as she rose, her lingerie morphing into a gauzy sky-blue blouse and a medium grey skirt. "And your slacks."

"Works for me," I replied. A few quick filters and crops later, I had the exact shade of her blouse applied to my shirt. I considered, then darkened the whole outfit a few shades, leaving the pants just barely above charcoal. I nodded my approval, then spread my arms as everything whirled into place. I turned, trying to look at the back of my pants in the mirror, tail curling behind me. "Are you sure they fit these right? These always feel loose."

Mitsuko laughed and walked over, putting her paws on my waist. "That is because you never wore tailored clothing before. You expect looking nice to be uncomfortable." She lifted onto her toes and kissed the back of my neck, running one paw over the back of my shirt, tugging lightly at the hem. "Being attractive should always be this easy, *ne?*"

The only way I could respond to her lighthearted giggle was with a happy sigh. I turned and took her paws in mine. "Let's walk. It's a beautiful evening and I'm not in any hurry."

She nodded her approval, giving my paws a squeeze with her own. "I agree." She nudged aside the sliding rice-paper door, and we stepped outside. The sky overhead was a brilliant blue with long streaks of pink and gold stretching out across it as the sun slipped below the horizon. The walk to the tram station was a good chance to stretch out my legs and just enjoy the company of the woman I loved, and by the time we had arrived at the underground terminal in Beni Prefecture, I was really looking forward to a good dinner and the conversation that inevitably came with it.

The skies in Beni were perpetually overcast, but today the usual mist had strengthened to an actual shower, one that left puddles along the uneven sidewalks. We dashed from awning to awning, winding through curving streets lined with storefronts and tenements. A pair of wolves leading a small pack of cubs behind them peered in through windows. One of Mitsuko's coworkers, a mouse in a white blouse and black skirt with a rainbow scarf around her neck, led a small group of obvious tourists through the streets, gesturing to various landmarks while they snapped photos and gawked, muttering cheerfully about the rain.

Fat raindrops spattered off of broad canvas umbrellas set up over wooden tables in front of the Greek café, and we both sighed in relief as we ducked underneath one, taking a seat out of the rain. Almost as soon as we sat, a wolf in a black button-down shirt and slacks approached us. "Hello and welcome! Have you two been here before?" When we both shook our head, his smile broadened and then sent an offer for a local link to their menu. "Well, welcome to Timeus. My name is Rich; I'll be at your service today. We try to serve things in the traditional style, which means a lot of smaller dishes so you can try different things...." While he continued with his patter, I accepted his request, then started scrutinizing the code. It was a clever system, a manifested object that sent a request to their central system for the daily specials, accessible from anywhere in Irokai. I made a note to dig more deeply into it to see how they had set up their security.

The chatter stopped, and I realized that I'd been asked a question. Ducking my head, tail curling behind me, I took a guess. "Uh... tall glass of water and... what's retsina?"

The waiter grinned. "So, retsina's a traditional Greek wine that's sealed in flasks with pine resin while it ages, so the alcohol takes on a really distinct flavor and aroma. Some say it's an acquired.... Hey, that's funny." He blinked, then held out his arm, pads upturned. "It's stopped raining."

At that, Mitsuko and I looked at each other in confusion, then back to the road. Sure enough, the puddles on the ground no longer rippled with raindrops, and even the ever-present mist seemed to be clearing up. Then I looked up to the sky, and a sinking feeling spread through my gut as I watched the clouds drift apart. The sky lit up in an unnaturally vibrant blue, and the opening passages of Grieg's *Spring* from *Peer Gynt* began to play from nowhere. Then, for the first time since its inception, the sun began to shine over Beni Prefecture.

Mitsuko's paw found mine and squeezed it. "Something is very wrong."

The moment after she said that, my hardline snapped on, followed moments later by a priority summons: «All Hospitality, Development, and Security staff please prepare for relocation to the nearest Tadashiissei office. This is an emergency.» The signature on the summons came from Sasaki Rei, one of the security division chiefs.

I squeezed Mitsuko's paw in return, then looked at the waiter. "I think dinner will have to wait." Then I accepted the summons, and the world dissolved around me.

THE WALLS OF THE TADASHIISSEI'S BENI PREFECTURE HEADQUARTERS were an uncomfortable brownish-grey that wanted to be a taupe but just ended up looking dirty, and the carpet was an industrial-pile mocha that tried very hard to match, but failed. Outside of that, though, the interior of the facility was as modern as the one in Murasaki. A massive black glass-top table dominated the middle of the main room, with low-backed aluminum-piping chairs haphazardly placed around it. Over the table's surface, a scale map of Beni Prefecture hovered. Clusters of red and yellow dots flashed all over its surface, spots where people had called security about a problem. As I watched, more lights blossomed over the table. One of the younger staffers leaned against the long edge of the table, tapping the points as they flared to life, scanning the windows that opened in front of him, and then closing some of them immediately, consolidating others and flagging them with kanji that lit up on the map. I leaned in and squinted at them: *daiji*. Serious.

At the head of the table, a broad-shouldered tiger in a black silk Mandarin top with off-center buttons and matching pants loomed over the map, sorting through collections of flagged reports. He looked up as we approached, nodded and held up one massive paw, the other shuffling a collection of flagged red dots hovering over Beni Prefecture. He flicked three of the set aside, then drew the rest together and circled them with a paw, and they fused into a single larger light. "Open bug report. Description begin: building with doors connected to the outside have all exits randomly assigned to other interior rooms, teleport disabled as per local secure facilities, security override disabled as per local administrator, local administrator access returns non-existent user, description end. Attachment begin, security parent report one-one-eight-one-one. Send. Confirm report number." His claws tapped against the flickering dot, attaching the ticket to the security report, then fading from view.

Once finished, the paw aimed at us lowered, and he looked up from the map, bowing. "Dart-*san*, Ikanobari-*san*. Thank you for accepting the summons."

Mitsuko stepped forward, a faint smile on her muzzle despite the nervous flicker of her ears and tail. "Do not be so formal, Rei. It is good to know Tadashiissei has assigned its best to this situation. What is happening?"

For a moment, the tiger held curiously still, only his tail lashing behind him, but then he turned suddenly and gestured to the map. "Multiple large-scale disruptions. Visitors have reported everything from clothing and items randomly disappearing to unscheduled severe weather to the complete disappearance of geographic features.

The Nanakōsei building vanished approximately twenty minutes ago, starting from the ground floor upwards."

My eyes went wide, and my fingers tensed against Mitsuko's paw. "How?"

The tiger started to answer, but Mitsuko interrupted. "What of the occupants, Rei? Are they all right?"

Rei looked back to the map. "The travelers who were within the building at the time were caught by the system integrity verification routines and extracted from Irokai. Some are experiencing transition shock and are being treated. They are also being given a refund for their most recent visit and credit towards a future trip." He grimaced. "This will severely hurt Tadashiissei's image."

"I don't give a damn about the company right now, Rei," I replied, squinting. "You said 'the travelers', not 'everyone'. What about the *residents?*"

Rei paused, then adjusted the spectacles sitting on the bridge of his muzzle. "Residents?"

I gestured back to Mitsuko with my free paw. "You know, the folks like Mits and I?"

The security chief paused, looking from me to Mitsuko and back. "Of the approximately four-hundred individuals present within Nanakōsei at the time of its disappearance, all but two have been identified outside. The two missing are both permanent residents of Irokai; one is an emigrant, the other a native. Neither can presently be located." His voice was eerily calm, which only made the fur on my tail bristle all the more. "Checking their user account records show that both were archived as of fourteen local time, suggesting a minimum of loss when we restore them from backup."

"*Backup?*" My shout drew the entire room's attention. Mitsuko's grip tightened on my paw, but I ignored it. "You're telling me two people may theoretically have just died and that's all you can offer?"

Rei's voice remained infuriatingly level. "John, we are all doing everything we can to resolve this situation as quickly as possible. Right now an unknown number of hackers have managed to bypass all of our security and cause disruptions to Irokai's codebase on a level that we are simply unprepared to handle. Multiple large-scale structures have had their internals scrambled, three buildings have reported inverse gravity, and at least one apartment complex has had all external exits rerouted. No-one knows how deeply these intrusions run, or who is actually responsible. Most of the external development staff is currently attempting to rewrite the entire world on a live system as quickly as possible in hopes that most of the attacks will simply fail once they are done, and the remainder are presently verifying the state of the backup system, which is presently offline to prevent further corruption. I understand how much worse this situation is for you than most, but at present my entire staff is dedicated to ensure the integrity of the area and identify additional attacks."

He nodded in my direction. "Presently we are minimizing access to external communication to prevent wide-scale panic, and teleportation has been limited to recalls initiated by senior members of Security or Hospitality to prevent future accidents, but we can't maintain that forever. I'll ensure that you have a secured line to the outside so that you can coordinate with the rest of your team." Then he turned to Mitsuko. "Hospitality has been authorized to take any necessary steps to ensure safety. I would ask that you coordinate with those still available to ensure that we escort as many travelers out of Irokai as quickly as possible. The fewer people we have to protect, the safer we can make the remainder."

14 | HASH(0x8BE0F03480CB) GIRI ESCAPE

THE CLOCK ON THE WALL INSIDE THE LOBBY OF TADASHIISSEI'S Murasaki Prefecture office said twenty-one, but the light outside suggested early afternoon, the sun still bobbing just above the horizon as if trapped in a loop. *At least the sky is blue again,* I reassured myself. It had been blood-red earlier in the day, a dark crimson that oozed ominously around the clouds. The developers had reverted that quickly enough, but the memory of it still sent a ripple of tension down my arms. I balled my paws into fists, closed my eyes and took a deep breath. *Now to wait for the stars.*

When I opened them again, the sun was no closer to setting then before, but a fresh crop of user reports had blossomed across the map of the prefecture. Fingers tapping rapidly over the glass surface, I pulled some of them towards me, opened them all and scanned through their descriptions. Some included snapshots: a rain of winged toasters, a person's face reduced to an iconic yellow disk, a flame hanging in midair; those fell quickly into clusters of similar conditions. The ones reporting only in text took longer, scanning for keywords to add them to the growing collections. A few drifted back to the map, but the rest eventually sorted into five larger collections, each of which I tagged for the development team.

The crisis of the moment resolved, I opened my personal archive of all the security reports I had filed relating to *Irokai no Minshukakumei*. None of the present attacks shared any immediate similarities with past intrusions; in the past, they – whoever they were – had been more than willing to claim credit for their work, attaching their name and slogans to all of their assaults. None of the latest attacks, though, showed any sign of ownership. And yet, I kept seeing signs of common identity among them. The floating flames, for instance, reminded me of a past display of fiery *kanji* in a bonfire on Kigiku Island. Staring at the two images in their respective reports, it almost seemed that I could spot the places where the two used the same randomizing functions.

I copied the filed reports to my archive, then waved away the windows with a sweep of claws and shut my eyes. *Feel, and accept the feelings, but do not succumb to them,* I reminded myself. I felt anger, and fear. For months, if not years, I had reported threats to Irokai's security; Tadashiissei had done nothing. I had pointed out correlations between past assaults, suggesting a large and organized effort; Tadashiissei had done nothing. I had all but begged my superiors to open further investigations, to find the people who were breaking my world and to stop them; Tadashiissei had done nothing.

Now, I was reduced to sifting for patterns in apparent chaos, making connections where none existed, and hoping that Tadashiissei would do something. I was angry, and I was scared.

A touch on my shoulder brought me out of my reflections. "Giri?"

I opened my eyes, looking over my shoulder to Koneko's face; her wide blue eyes were squinted in concern, her ears and whiskers held back; in her other paw, she held a mug of hot tea, steam rising from its mouth. "You've been here over fourteen hours. You need a break."

I put a paw over hers and shook my head, looking back to the map. "I am taking breaks as time permits. I took a walk—"

"Five hours ago," she interrupted, thrusting the mug at me. "Orders from management. You're off-duty for six hours, minimum. Get a meal and a nap."

I held my gaze level as I took the tea from her, then rose from my chair. "Very well," I said after several seconds. I took an obligatory sip from the mug, then passed it back to Koneko with a minimal bow. "I will return in six hours, then. Thank you for the tea." Koneko returned the bow, her expression carefully neutral, then motioned me away from the table, sliding into the seat I had just vacated. As soon as she was comfortable, a fresh array of lights blossomed over the map, and her fingers began tapping across its surface, sorting through customer complaints.

I watched her work for a few seconds more, then turned and walked out of the front of the building. The skies were still a rich afternoon blue, streaked with pink and gold. Someone had put a human infant's face on the sun, constantly changing expressions. I watched it laugh silently for several seconds, then suddenly begin crying for no reason. The rapid change of expression sent the fur of my tail into a bristle, and I turned my gaze away, focusing on the sidewalk in front of me as I walked the short distance back to my apartment. The building, a glass-and-steel high-rise, looked thankfully free of infection, though I did not take the time to validate the entire system. I did, however, test that the front door would let me back onto the street and that the elevators had the same number of buttons as when I left.

I did not want to admit it, but I was even more tired than Koneko had suggested. Leaving the recovery efforts up to my superiors, though, seemed unthinkable. After all the times I had warned about this very danger and had my reports quietly ignored, the exhaustion was just one more thing to tolerate in the line of duty. Still, I was relieved for the order, despite the irritation at being interrupted. It meant that, at least for a few hours, the failure to protect Irokai no longer weighed on my shoulders. *You have done what you can, and you continue to do so,* I reminded myself. *If Irokai falls, it will be because they failed to listen, not because you failed to warn them.* It was a small comfort; the thought of my home disappearing was no more pleasant now than it was when it had occurred to me before.

I dropped heavily into the futon in my living room, covering my eyes with my paws. Such thoughts would get me nowhere. I felt mounting annoyance and aggravation, but I had no means to deal with either. For now, all I could do was as had been suggested: eat, sleep, and hopefully awaken to a steadily shrinking queue of complaints and questions. I summoned up my administrative window, and a few quick glances later, I had a hot meal on the way. While the menu was open, I glanced at my standing account, the numbers hovering in the bottom-right corner of my interface, and smiled wryly at the note hovering in its place: «All residence fees have been temporarily suspended while we resolve these ongoing technical difficulties.»

That resolved, there seemed to be little to do but wait. I had no interest on watching more reports of the disasters, and I was too tired to focus on other entertainment. Dinner arrived soon enough, and I quickly tucked into fried vegetables and shrimp over noodles with thick broth; the food was a welcome distraction from the rapidly compounding absurdities, and once I was done, the exhaustion I had been staving off hit me at full force. I stretched out on the futon, not even bothering to return to my bedroom. "Lights, off; windows, close." I told the room, shrouding the apartment in darkness.

THE HARSH BUZZ IN MY EAR SNAPPED ME TO A ROUGH APPROXIMATION of awareness, enough to realize that I had an urgent personal request. After a few seconds of my head ringing, I opened the hardline and glanced through to receive the message from... Briar? «How may I help you, Briar-*san?*»

«Giri, it's Briar.» The words came through in spurts, chunks of text followed by stretches of silence. «We need your help. Bad.»

I counted off three seconds, letting the last of the ringing fade. «I have another two hours of mandatory downtime, Briar-*san;* I am afraid there is little I can do at the moment.»

«FutureShock hit, Giri,» came the hasty response. «Some kind of lockout, can't leave. Got two uploads and a dozen analogs, some kind of deep object hack. Need your help.»

«*Usagi-san,* I appreciate your situation, but there is little I can do at present.» I responded. «I can provide you a list of contacts who have agreed to help me.»

Her next message was almost instant. «Please, Giri. Most here don't trust Tadashiissei. Some think this is a company plot as it is. I don't know who else I can call.» A moment later, she sent a second reply: «Please don't make me beg.»

I sighed, rubbing at my eyes. I wanted to insist she find a replacement, but really, could I in clear conscience ask that of her? I didn't trust most of my superiors to have the best interests of Irokai and its inhabitants in mind; what assurance could I offer someone who knew less about the situation than I did? I rose from the couch and stretched, trying to awaken the rest of the way before I left the apartment. «I will be there as soon as I can be. Please do what you can to prevent panic.» With that, I took a moment to adjust my coat and left for the tram station.

Finding the afflicted area Briar had described was easy enough; a few minutes' walk from the terminal, I caught wind of something that smelled distinctly of dust and mold. Following the scent another block, I found a patch of some kind of abnormal discoloration on the wall of a café, spreading slowly over the surface. As I watched, the rust-colored brickwork turned a mottled yellow with streaks of darker green. The white area then began to distend irregularly, taking on a slick, swollen sheen. Once it had bulged out like a pustule, a small cluster of filaments shot up from the building, arcing in semi-random curves back towards the surface. Where they fell more than a few feet, they withered and vanished; where they came into contact with regular brick, they spread their symptoms, fresh buboes bulging upwards from the surface.

I opened my hardline and scanned the spreading infection; it looked like someone had gone past virus and directly on to digital fungus; the whole city block appeared to be infected. There was no lockout; the door to the club that Briar had mentioned simply did not exist any more, nor did most of the buildings. The tendrils moved slowly, likely to ensure that no people were accidentally hit, but anything infected became defined as a host, losing all properties outside of spreading the disease, and the more hosts, the faster the infection could spread.

Studying the vector, I had to admit it was an elegant disruption: simple, thorough, and fast. Unfortunately, it had also spread further than I could repair on my own. «This is Giri of Tadashiissei Security,» I broadcast to the prefecture. «Is there anyone within Development or Hospitality currently available that can assist with resolution of an attack? I have two residents and several tourists trapped within a building; their only exit has vanished and tensions are rising.» I waited several seconds for a reply, then repeated myself, but still no response came. I closed the menu, then took a deep breath and let it pass slowly, trying to release the sudden burst of anger I felt.

Four or five seconds later, I opened my menu again, reaching out to Briar. «*Usagi-san,* I cannot get to the door; one of the attacks has blocked access. This will take me a few minutes to resolve; are you and the others safe?»

«For now,» came the quick reply. «The entry's covered in some kind of web and spreading into the interior. Slow, but we don't have a lot of space left. It got Wyth's cloak and Babel's suit when they tried to analyze it, but nobody's hurt.»

I wanted to ask who Wyth and Babel were, and why they would stand so close to an obvious source of danger, but those questions could wait until afterwards. «Stay away from it for now. Do you or anyone there have local administration access over your present area?»

Briar hesitated several seconds before responding. «I do, yes. What do you need?»

I considered, then shook my head. «Everything. Please grant me read access so that I can try to get you out as quickly as possible.»

«Giri, there's a lot here,» Briar protested. «This place is pretty custom.»

«Please, Briar-*san*. You asked for my help; I am attempting to comply. I am in Security, not Development; I can only access what I can see. You must trust me on this.»

It took almost a minute, but the next message I received from Briar contained the header record for something defined as FutureShock, and I quickly opened and began parsing the code. My eyes widened at some of the contents; they had to have deliberately broken the rendering engine in dozens of places: wall objects with references to nonexistent textures, symbol primitives invoked directly, disjoint spaces connected solely by teleportation, rooms in which every wall had been defined as "ground" to disable gravity. The entire area appeared to be either the worst programming attempt I had ever seen, or one thoroughly premeditated violation of Irokai's building code. I fought down the urge to simply let the virus wipe out the club and have them rebuild it according to the guidelines; the time for recriminations would be after the patrons inside were safe.

Something flickered out of the corner of my eye, and I turned, then dropped just in time for one of the viral tendrils to launch itself overhead. The reek of mold filled my nostrils in its wake, and I skittered on all fours out from under the tentacle as it arced to the ground. Suddenly this had become much more difficult; standing in one place while I focused would be impossible with that thing looking for new targets. I could not teleport them out directly, nor could I edit any of the privately-owned areas around, but I could define a new door in an uninfected area that led to the interior of the club, then allow Briar to connect back to it from the inside. It was an unpleasant hack, but it would resolve the problem in the immediate, assuming I could concentrate long enough to make the changes. «Give me a few minutes, *usagi-san*,» I sent to Briar as I stood and started walking. «You should receive a link request presently. Please accept and build a reverse link.»

«Got it, thanks, will be waiting,» she replied. As soon as I received her message, I closed down the communications window and willed the *katana* into place at my hip. Finding an unowned area of Beni proved difficult; the zone was a popular destination and many people had staked out claims to buildings, even if they had done nothing more than add construction signs and donation request links to the doors. However, surprisingly close to the prefecture's Transit Center,

I managed to find a tenement whose owner had improperly secured it; its front door was closed, but it had not been made private. Closing my eyes, I paced in a circle in front of the facility and ran through forms in my mind, then nodded to myself and stopped.

With a forward step, I drew the sword, opening the development menu. As the tip of my blade swung in a wide arc, I hashed and scanned the building's construction list. With a decisive thrust to my rear, I deallocated the previous owner, then claimed it for myself as I brought the katana back to my chest. Another loud pop behind me made me turn, and I had to remind myself to step aside to dodge the oncoming tendril. I made a quick downward slice and cut the old link between portal and building, then stabbed outward in front of me as I sent a fresh request to Briar. I held the point of my katana perfectly still as I waited for Briar's reply, then returned to a ready pose as I acknowledged it. Lastly, as I slid the sword back into its *saya,* I closed the access menu and stepped up to the tenement.

As soon I approved the link, the door jerked open from within and a dozen... forms... spilled through it onto the street. Some I could charitably describe as heavily modified; others seemed to be complete rewrites, so thoroughly altered that I could make no guess even as to original species. The first to leave the door seemed like an ordinary raccoon, but rendered in high-gloss plastic and enamel. The second appeared to be little more than a wireframe model of a wolf, lacking any internal structure at all. The parade of bizarre figures continued, each more vivid than the last. The last to leave was the most shocking; it might have once been a rabbit, or perhaps might one day become one, but at the moment it looked mostly like a collection of brass gears and rods with colored tubes interwoven, inscribed all over with glowing runes and covered in places with black rubber sheeting and small patches of fake fur. After that one left, I shoved the door closed again, then looked over the group, breathing slowly to keep my emotions in check. I hastily scanned them each for any sign of the infection I had seen on the buildings elsewhere, but each of them came up clean.

The clockwork contraption turned – to look at me, I presumed, though I could only guess based on the position of its ear-supports – and then stepped closer. "Thanks," it said in what might have been Briar's voice from within a metal box. "We had some time to spare, but not much, and we were all getting escape pod fever down there." It stood for several seconds, silent, then tilted its head to the side. "Giri?"

I shook my head, breaking my stare. "Yes, good," I said hastily to fill the silence, then addressed the group at large, raising my voice. "You all appear uninfected. Please, for your own safety, I would consider exiting Beni Prefecture as quickly as possible; the infection—" Another wet rupture interrupted my speech, followed by somebody's shriek. The summons was instinctive, as was the turn and throw, and then my katana hung in midair, halfway between a pink rubber mouse and the incoming tendril. As soon as they connected, the blade began to convert.

"As I was saying," I continued as I began escorting the group towards the transit center, "the infection here is spreading too quickly for me to resolve. If you can leave Irokai for the time being, I suggest you do so. If you cannot, Tadashiissei has established a shelter in Murasaki Prefecture to provide temporary—" I caught myself suddenly, then opened my hardline and began poring over each of the figures in turn. All of them showed extensive edits, most of which had no attribution at all. Few of the modules carried approval from the company, though none of them seemed at first glance to violate the rules any worse than the club itself. For all that they were aesthetically disturbing, they were well within the terms of service.

I spun to face the mechanical rabbit. "Who among you made all of these changes?"

The clockwork creature's brass antennae suddenly flattened against its head. "That's...." It stopped, then looked to the rest of the group. "I did," it said with a sigh.

I narrowed my eyes, then looked to the others. "Did any of you help?" They exchanged glances amongst themselves, then looked back to me, their eyes hard. I sighed, then held up my paws, pads out. "I understand." I took a deep breath, then let it out suddenly. "Irokai is under attack," I said bluntly, cutting through the delicate statements that Hospitality had been pedaling. "I believe that Tadashiissei is more intent on preserving its image than on protecting its creation. I am looking for volunteers willing to assist with reversion of past damage." Most of the motley mob visibly changed from reserved to surprised and, at the last, perhaps even a little eager. "Are any of you interested?"

One paw, grey-furred and decorated with glowing tattoos, rose hesitantly, and I nodded to its owner. "What do you call yourself, *koyōte-san?*"

He looked first at me, then to Briar, then to one of the others. He stepped forward, his tail bristled behind him, and folded his arms across his chest. His eyes narrowed, and the light from the designs in his fur shifted to a warning amber and began to pulse. "It's Sparks," he proclaimed, and an electrical arc leapt down one arm as a demonstration.

I nodded, then opened my hardline. Without the sword, it took me more time to remember the locations of all of the menus, but eventually I found the one I needed and set his administration flag. I had to limit his scope to Beni Prefecture and scale down his access in other ways, but once I was done, I nodded to him. "You should now be able to make at least some local edits. See if it worked, Sparks-*san*."

Sparks' ears flattened against his head briefly, but then after a few moments, he knelt and touched the ground, and a webwork of blue circuit traces branched out from the point of contact. His eyes went wide and the changes reverted instantly. His brow furrowed and he did it again, and the ground began to glow in a circle around his feet. He stood upright, grinning. "Wow. It... it worked. I don't know what to say."

At that, my tail flicked, the closest I would permit myself to a smile. "Please say that you will assist, Sparks-*san*. We cannot be everywhere; we need people we can trust."

Sparks nodded at that, and I turned to the mechanical rabbit, doing the same for her. "Please validate?"

The rabbit knelt and traced some sort of symbol in the ground. In the wake of her motions, glittering silver lines poured into place, forming runes that began to radiate warmth. "Looks like it's working. And of course I'll help."

I smiled. "Are there any others, Briar-*san?*"

Briar shook her head. "The last one was Jules, but he got banned." She held up one brass arm, her paw outstretched to block any criticism. "Not for hacking. He... got in a fight with Legal over access charges. You can look that up."

I shrugged. "If he is banned, he cannot be of help to us; that is beyond my ability to correct." I turned back to the rest of the group. "There is much work to be done, but it has been a difficult day for us all. I would ask that you all meet me here tomorrow at—" Before I could finish my sentence, a thunderclap sounded behind me that sent the crowd scattering. I spun to face the target, one paw moving to the hilt of the sword that was not there, but rather than a fresh assault, I found myself staring into the eyes of my manager. The tiger scowled down the length of his blunt muzzle at me, his arms folded across his broad chest. His tail lashed behind him in visible displeasure.

"Where do I begin, Giri?" Sasaki Rei's voice rolled its vowels like storms on the horizon. "I've been watching for several minutes, hoping that I was misinterpreting your actions, but it would seem I wasn't."

The few from the club who stayed began to grumble, but my attention was on my supervisor. My own eyes narrowed in response. "Perhaps if Tadashiissei were dedicating sufficient resources to resolve these incidents before they put our customers at risk, Sasaki-*san*—"

Sasaki cut me off with a wave of his paw. "Tadashiissei is doing what it can with the resources it has. The company does not have to justify its actions to you, only to its customers, and they, by and large, seem happy with how this unfortunate incident is being handled. You, however, have seen fit to violate a direct order to remain off-duty to rest, to alter private code without permission, to perform drastic edits to an environment without justification, and to grant tourists prefecture-wide administrative access without authorization." He paused after each infraction in the litany of my misdeeds just long enough to let its gravity take hold. "What possible explanation could you have for acting in so reckless a fashion?"

I closed my eyes. *Feel, and accept the feeling.* I struggled to keep my tone as level as possible. "Perhaps, Sasaki-*san*, if Tadashiissei had taken a single one of my warnings about *Irokai no Minshukakumei* months ago when these sorts of attacks started, we might not have found ourselves in this position now."

Sasaki's eyes narrowed at that, and I couldn't help but smile faintly in response. "Perhaps, Giri-*san*, if you had followed instructions I would not now be forced to take such drastic action." His tail-tip flicked, then held eerily still. "If I cannot trust you to fulfill the orders that you have been given, then I cannot trust you to be responsible with the authority you have enjoyed. Effective immediately, your position with Tadashiissei is hereby terminated, your security access revoked." I felt a wave of nausea pass over me, followed by a chill that settled into my spine and refused to leave. "Any personal effects that have been left at one of our offices will be relocated to your apartment within twenty-four hours. Good evening." Then, with a second flash of light, the tiger was gone.

"What a dick," Briar said anticlimactically into the uncomfortable silence that followed. Then, more quietly, she added, "I'm sorry." Mistaking my silence for refusal to answer, the clockwork rabbit stumbled onwards. "I shouldn't have asked you to—" My paw snapping up, pads towards her, stunned her into silence for a moment, but then she backed away. "I'm sorry," she repeated, lowering her head.

I took another deep breath, holding it deep in my lungs, silently counting off seconds. *Do not succumb to it.* When the moment of anger subsided, I let go and lowered my paw. "What is done, is done. I acted as I believed right; I would do so again. That this is the result only proves my point."

Briar was silent for several seconds, then muttered, "He's still a dick."

I opened my eyes and studied the mechanical rabbit for several seconds, tail flicking, but before I could respond, the sky above began to finally darken. I glanced towards the sun, watching it sink below the horizon, then turned my face to the heavens, watching for the eye of the Dragon to shine in the sky. Even as blue faded to indigo, though, *Seiryū* was nowhere to be seen, though there wasn't a cloud in sight. I turned to the far horizon, hoping to catch sight of the Tiger, but *Byakko,* too, stayed invisible.

Then the sky faded past twilight to darkness, exposing the empty, starless heavens.

Something within me broke in that moment, something indistinct and tenuous that simply let go at the sight of the void overhead. Suddenly, it no longer mattered whether Tadashiissei survived, whether Irokai endured... or whether I did. All of my pain, all of my struggle, and yet even this one thing was beyond my power to protect. "The stars...." I had nothing left to say. There were no words for what I felt, staring at the expanse of pure black overhead. The lights had been taken from inside of me as surely as they had been taken from the sky.

"Giri?" Briar's voice, subtly changed, rescued me from falling into space. I lowered my gaze from the empty sky and turned to face her, but everything I had meant to insist died on my lips. In the time I had stood stunned, the rest of the inhabitants of the FutureShock had dispersed, leaving Briar alone. However, instead of the half-finished automaton, she was again the rabbit I had first seen standing in the middle of the Sunny You. Her ear tips were black, as was a small patch at the end of her muzzle, but aside from that, her fur was so white that it gleamed. On her shirt, a stylized metallic gold atom whirled slowly, while the patterns of her skirt rippled through muted matching greens. A pair of bracelets clattered quietly against each other on her wrists.

All around her, swirling in lazy orbits, a small cluster of stars twinkled. They winked and fluttered, dancing casually around her figure. She smiled, then caught one in her paw and held it out to me. "I can't give you back what you've lost, but I can give you this. You did a good thing back there; you deserve recognition for that."

I took the star from her, glancing at it briefly. "You did copy it, *usagi-san.*"

Briar shrugged, still smiling. "You going to turn me in?"

"No," I admitted, closing my paw around the light, then held out the other to her. "I would rather ask you to join me."

The rabbit entwined her fingers with mine, some of her starlets hovering around my arm in response. "I'd be glad to."

Most of the trip to my apartment passed in relative silence. I was unsure of what to ask and half-afraid of the answers I might receive. I knew she had had a security record at one time. Someone she knew had been banned. The clockwork form, and in fact most of the other figures leaving the club, disturbed me. I wanted to know how, and what happened, and why. *What would you do with the information, though?* I asked myself as we exited the tram in Murasaki and I directed her towards my apartment building. *What* could *you do? Would you call Security?*

At that, I stopped myself at the door to the lobby, turning to face the rabbit. "My apologies, Briar-*san*; this has been a very—"

Her finger was across my muzzle in an instant. "You don't need the honorifics, Giri." She smiled, a tiny star floating in front of her eyes as she looked at me. "Just 'Briar' is fine. Or just *usagi,* I guess. We're equals now, aren't we?" Then, to emphasize the point, she withdrew her paw, opened the front door, and waved me inside.

"You are right... Briar," I agreed, heading to the elevator. "This has not been an easy day for me."

The rabbit giggled in response. "We were bodily assaulted by a macrovirus. I think everyone's stressed." She turned. "Listen, Giri, if you don't want this—"

It was my turn to silence her again. "I want this, Briar." I moved the paw in front of her to her cheek. "You have shown me multiple kindnesses, and for now, I would rather not be alone."

She smiled. "I never sleep alone if I can help it."

As soon as we entered the apartment, her fingers were at my shoulders, tugging the coat down my arms and tossing it over the back of my couch. The sweater followed quickly, and then her fingers were at the waist of my slacks, making short work of the zipper. "I want to see you," I said softly as she knelt, sliding her arms around to unfasten the button holding the flap over my tail.

"You will," Briar said, grinning up at me, still fully clothed. She tugged down my pants and underwear, letting out a giggle as she leaned forward to place her muzzle close to my groin and inhale deeply. "Nice," she breathed, making me stir. Then, before I could respond, she rose from her crouch and stepped back, lifting her muzzle to the ceiling and closing her eyes. The lights dancing about her dimmed slightly, drawing in closer. The rabbit drew in a deep breath, and as she exhaled, her top and skirt dissolved into a myriad of whirling, multicolored wisps floating around her. She smiled, then stood next to me, her stars enveloping us both.

My paws found her hips as hers rested upon my shoulders, and then she was in my arms, her muzzle pressed to mine, her legs around my waist. She was surprisingly light as I pulled her to me, walking slowly to the bedroom. Her white fur was thick and so, so soft, and her scent rich and full in my nostrils. I set her down carefully on the edge of the bed, leaning forward to kiss her; her muzzle tasted faintly sweet, and she trilled quietly in the back of her throat as I lay down beside her. Her paws roamed over my chest as I slid an arm under her head, then drifted down to my sheath, tenderly stroking the short fur with her fingertips. Soon, she had me fully exposed and breathing hard, gazing deeply into her eyes. Even now, they glinted like copper.

Briar smiled in response and wrapped one leg around my waist, guiding me to the entrance to her tunnel, then pressed herself to me. I held one paw one her back to steady her, and placed the other on her hip for balance. She hissed, arching her back as her heat engulfed me, sending a shiver down my spine as she embraced me fully. A slow moan escaped her muzzle as she sank herself to the root of my shaft. "Nice," she breathed again, eyelids fluttering as she held herself around me. "Please."

I nodded in response, then slowly pulled away, drawing in a shuddering breath as she clutched at me, then gently pushed myself back into her depths. She began to keen softly, moaning slightly with each stroke, while I held her to my chest, her breasts pressed against me. The stars that surrounded her pulsed in time with her breath, her heartbeat, flickering in response to her arousal. Her short tail flagged with each thrust, back arching as she met my motions with her own, rocking her hips, pulling herself against me.

I held the rabbit tightly, trying to take my time, to coax her slowly to release, but she was as skilled as she had suggested, and soon I was as eager as she, hips grinding rhythmically against her. With every thrust, I felt myself drawing closer, tensing, shaking. Her quiet moans were an aphrodisiac, the scent of her fur an inspiration. Stars swam in my vision, encircling us both. "Briar," I whispered through clenched teeth, "I cannot... hold out...."

The rabbit's only reply was a high-pitched whimper and a nod as she met each of my thrusts with one of her own. She relaxed herself as I drove myself into her, then tightened as I pulled away, milking me with expert control, and despite all my meditations and training, there was little I could do but give into her ecstasy. The longer I resisted, the more I shook with need, tension rising within. My sheath tightened against me, but I closed my eyes, determined to delay as long as I could. One more stroke, and another, and another, and—

With a grunt, I drove myself as deeply into her as I could, arms locked around Briar, her muzzle pressed into my shoulder as I came, pulsing within her warm, tight tunnel. My breath hung in my throat, body spasming, her sex fluttering against my cock, squeezing as much out of me as she could. For seconds, I lay rigid, buried hilt-deep within the rabbit, every muscle locked and twitching. Then, slowly, I sagged against the mattress, spent, and let out a groan of relief and release. "Oh, Briar... Briar...." My fingers slid gently over her back as I nuzzled into her neck. *"Arigatō."*

The rabbit moaned softly into my shoulder, muzzle pressed softly into my fur. *"De nada,"* she replied, her voice satirically formal. I blinked and pulled away, looking curiously at her, but her brass eyes glinted at me in humor as she snuggled against me. "Sorry, I had to. You don't have to thank me, Giri. I wanted that."

"As did I, " I sighed. "But still... I wish to. Thank you, Briar." With a groan, I withdrew, rolling onto my back, feeling the tension of the last day, the last week, the last few months, starting to drain out of me.

Briar rolled up onto her side next to me and rested her head on my shoulder. "So, I have to ask.... Why the sword?" She grinned. "It's so stereotypical."

I turned to look at her, giving a faint shake of my head. "It is, yes, but... since you ask, I will tell you." I leveled my gaze once more at the ceiling, letting out a long sigh. "Irokai has always fascinated me. I always wanted to know how it worked, why it worked. I knew, even from my *kaishi* – my... birthday, essentially – that this was a created place, a playground for others, but I saw no reason why that should stop me from wanting to understand it." I paused, then sighed. "They wanted me to be part of their security staff, but that was not my desire. So, I studied, earned a degree in software engineering, and applied repeatedly for a transfer to Development. Each time, it was politely suggested that my skills were of more use to them where I was. Never mind that I wished to do something different; they simply preferred letting those who could leave the world design it. When

I learned—" I stopped that thought; it was unnecessary to delve into personal politics.

"Eventually, I decided that if what they wanted was a toy soldier, that would be what they would receive." My muzzle twisted into a faint smirk as I continued. "I changed my name, took up *battōjutsu,* and practiced using it as a focus to improve my access times." I rolled up onto my side, looking into Briar's eyes. "We may be wholly digital, but I have no more awareness of my code than you do, and our models were based on human neural networks. My muscle memory is stronger than my base recall, but my recall tied to muscle memory is better than both. Simply put, I work better with it than without." That made me frown. "This is no longer an issue."

"Wow," Briar whispered, her eyes wide in awe. She spread one paw over my chest, entwining her fingers into my fur. "What was your name before you changed it?"

I hesitated a moment, then shrugged. "Chō." I considered. "I think... I may change it back." Then I smiled, covering her paw with one of my own. "As for stereotypical, would you not say that over-sexualized rabbits are just as bad? I recall an old saying involving breeding."

At that, the rabbit laughed and pressed herself against me, sliding her fingers lower down over my stomach. "Yeah, well, where I'm from, foxes have the same reputation."

As her fingerpads brushed over my waist, I lifted my voice slightly. "Lights, off. Clock... off." Once the room had gone to darkness, I pulled Briar to my chest once more. "I cannot guarantee your safety if you stay, or mine. If I am gone by morning, though, I will have left happy."

15 | JOHNATHAN DART
MEMORY

ON THE FOURTEENTH ITERATION THROUGH THE MOCK TURTLE'S soup song flashing before my eyes, I figured out the trick. "Debugger, stop, open window." The words stopped scrolling, and in front of me, a fresh window opened, the codepoint highlighted. "Add watch. Set step speed, one-per-second. Resume." Glowing green letters still rolled through my field of vision, much slower, but my eyes were on the small window, watching the source code dance. As a line of text faded out of my field of vision, the pointer suddenly jumped from user space to the environment. "Stop!" The words stopped, and I dragged over the debugger window to confirm.

The Voice of Irokai was a core function that could tap into any audio stream in order to deliver important system updates; it had permission to access anyone's audio system at any time. However, for deaf tourists and noisy environments, Tadashiissei provided an alternative: a scrolling text field, which again couldn't be disabled but could be resized or relocated for customer comfort. That hook was always present, even if the recipient of the message could hear! The hack bypassed the audio system, went straight for the visual interface, repositioned and altered the text to be as annoying as possible, and then began dumping chunks of Project Gutenberg passed through a fishbowler. The end result looked like a badly-written description of a drug trip.

"Debugger, abort run." The words vanished from my vision. "Open e-mail, title, quote, bug one-four-six-two-two, end-quote." I dumped a fast summary detailing my findings, suggesting that the visual hook be disabled as long as the audio one worked and access for the text interface be explicitly limited to the individual. It wasn't a cure, but the real fix would take locking down the Voice of Irokai, which was way outside of my scope. Ideally, I'd have never gotten this deeply into the core systems in the first place, but with the ongoing crisis, Tadashiissei needed all the help it could get.

I pulled my test results together, then attached them to the outgoing message. "Send to developers-internal. Close. Suspend." With that, the remaining windows faded around me, leaving me sitting in the back of Tadashiissei's Beni office, rubbing at my muzzle with one paw. "One down...." I glanced up at the wall, to a list of open issues, then shook my head. "Too many to go." I rose out of the chair and stretched. "I can't believe I'm up this early."

Mitsuko put a paw on my shoulder, smiling gently, her own deep green eyes tired. "You were not sleeping, John, nor was I. At least this way we are helping, ne? The outstanding crises are being addressed. Progress is being made."

I groaned, paws on the small of my back. "Yeah, but the overall list is still growing." I rolled my shoulders in a shrug and twisted, trying to pop my back. *Explain to me again the sense of giving people the ability to fly and then letting them have sore backs.* I wondered if it might be some function of the map from neurons to code that made me still think my muscles felt tight, when in fact I had no muscles to tighten. That got me thinking about the models they were using and how they got the tail to function so naturally, but before I got too far into that path, I felt something in my lower back give way and the tension melted. "Still, I wish the reason I couldn't sleep was 'busy' and not 'worrying about not waking up'."

"Do not worry, John," Mitsuko's other paw was at my side, and then her body was warm against my back. "I will not let that happen."

I reached back and hugged her against me, then turned and kissed her forehead. "I appreciate the thought, Mits, really." I stretched again, loosening up my shoulders. "I'm going to take a break and see if anyone is open for breakfast. I'd rather not just instantiate something."

"Oh, *hai*," Mits said, making a face. "One can only see the same plate of eggs so many times before doubting its sincerity. I will meet you in a bit; this meeting cannot last much longer." She slid back, out of my arms, then tapped her ear, holding one paw in front of her, waving me away with the other.

The skies over Beni were overcast, but the rain had yet to return. *At least someone got rid of the music,* I thought, paws stuffed into the pockets of my slacks. The streets were eerily empty, as were the store fronts. Pseudo-organic tendrils jutted and swayed haphazardly from buildings and road, spreading in a fibrous network across rooftops and across streets. Signs hung on the walls at regular intervals suggesting that tourists visit Murasaki Prefecture or the Bazaar at Hana while Beni Prefecture was undergoing emergency maintenance; it looked like most everyone had taken the suggestion.

One front door to a tenement building hung open, unlike all the others in the block, but even more oddly, it opened not to one of the stock building interiors but to an unlit staircase, leading down. I recognized the floor of the FutureShock as soon as my hinds touched it, that weirdly cool, slick feel of trying to process the sense of touching nothing. This, however, wasn't the Shock's entrance; there was no warning message and no sign. From a quick scan of the environment, it looked like somebody had hacked the door in place.

A quick review of timestamps showed that the edits had been put into place late last night, after the extended shift had gone to bed. The link out from the club had Briar's information stamped all over it, which didn't surprise me; she was the sort to make that kind of quick hack, but she had to have authority to link to a public area. The inbound link had a name I didn't recognize on it, but where the author's employee number would have been was only the single line: «Terminated, Sasaki Rei.»

That made me pause. Something very clearly had happened, but based on what little I had, I had no way to tell what, and the last thing I needed was more mysteries while I was already tired and hungry. I copied chunks of the relevant logs and databases to personal storage, then stepped inside the door. I wasn't interested in what the Shock had to offer at the moment, but it was the first sign of anything other than abandoned buildings and other people's tampering.

"Briar?" I called out as I entered the main room of the club, but the interior was as empty as the rest of the prefecture. Semi-fungal fronds covered large chunks of the walls, swaying and occasionally sending out a fresh shoot to cling to one surface or another. The sunsphere looked clean, as did the mirrors, but most of the rest of the hexagons had been obliterated by it. The Tree sported eerily organic curves in addition to its angular branches, and underneath it, most of the benches looked like they'd been completely overwritten. I squatted over my heels, pulling up logs and object models. From a first glance, it looked like it did some kind of space analysis, then did a massive property overwrite to spawn copies of itself, but where was it getting its environment? It wasn't calling any kind of environment model. Could it really be doing a fast location test? That seemed really inefficient, especially in open spaces—

Something electric slammed into me from the side, sending a spasm through my body and knocking me onto my side, landing on my elbow with a curse. A second later, some kind of thick vine shot through the space my back had just vacated, hitting the side of the Tree with a wet splurch. Where it hit, a fresh discolored disk began to spread, new nodules rising out of its surface. "You want to watch those force fields," a familiar voice called. "You'll have plenty of chances to get hurt, don't worry about that."

I scrambled to a sitting position, looking towards the voice in shock. Standing in front of one of the mirrors was a starkly white-furred wolf. His arms were folded across his bare chest, subtle shifts of his posture emphasizing the gold bars in his nipples and the matching chain that hung from his neck. He wore his pants baggy, covered in gold-toothed zippers, the wide hems sweeping the floor. His tail wagged behind him, matching his grin.

He walked over and held out a paw, which I took hesitantly, looking him in the eyes as he helped me back to my hinds. "Jules.... What're you doing here?"

Jules ignored the question, motioning with his free paw to the tendril that had almost hit me in the back. "That thing's nasty; cleaning it out of the zone's going to take work. I've spent the better part of a day deconstructing it, and you're not going to like it. It eats properties, fills space, clones itself, and that's about it. Oh, and it's unpredictable; it's doing some hash randomizer that tells it where to spread and how that I can't reverse-engineer. I've seen that spine-tendril trick before; I threw a chair and it got snagged in mid-air. It'd be a really cool screensaver if it weren't wiping out the place."

"Jules," I repeated, squeezing his paw more firmly to get his attention. "You got banned. What're you doing here?"

At that, he turned and looked at me. "I'm trying to clean up my club, but it looks like a lost cause. The back rooms are clean, though; it can't get through the mirrors. It can eat them, but it can't read the portal code." He smirked at that, tapping the edge of one and sending ripples across its surface. "These are still some of my best work."

I scowled, my tail lashing behind me. "Jules, quit dodging the question. Tell me what's going on."

The wolf rolled his eyes, letting out an exasperated sigh. "All right, fine. Follow me; I'm not standing around in here." He tapped on the mirror twice, then stepped into the quicksilver surface, pulling me behind him. I closed my eyes as it slid coolly over me, then opened them again as my hind again touched solid ground on the far side. The walls of this room were red, a deep crimson velvet interspersed with hardwood beams and brass. Gold dragon statues breathed a steady stream of smoke into the air, filling the space with a sweet herbal haze. The floor away from the edges of the room was recessed, with steps leading down to a thick carpet that matched the walls. Overstuffed sofas and bean bags lay strewn about the floor, next to tables on which a number of hookah sat. The whole place had the feel of a futuristic opium den.

Jules let go of my paw and spun as he popped out of the mirror. Walking backwards with practiced ease, he dropped into one of the bean bags built for two, snagging a hose on the way down. "Like what I've done with the place?" He grinned, slipping the filigreed nozzle into his muzzle.

"The dragons are new," I quipped, folding my arms across my chest. "Listen, Jules, I don't know if you noticed, there's a disaster happening, and last I heard, you were still banned. How'd you get back in?"

The wolf breathed out a cloud of faintly shimmering smoke, then stretched, crossing his arms behind his head. "I know people, okay? I caught wind that something bad was going to happen to Irokai, so I got with some friends and came to find out if I could help."

"Nice try," I replied. The grin vanished from Jules' expression, his eyes shifting away from mine as I continued. "Outside of Adam and I, you don't know anybody well enough to help you try to crack the security on Tadashiissei's servers. I wouldn't do it even if I could, but I'm not half the developer you are, and Adam wouldn't even know where to begin. Plus, I know you. You want to be here legitimately so badly that you wouldn't dare violate your ban, even if you could get an unregistered rig onto the network. Drop the patter, Jules. Just tell me the truth: why are you here?"

Jules started trying to look relaxed and confident, but the more I spoke, the more he looked like he wanted to crawl inside the bean bag on which he'd flopped. When I finally repeated the question I'd tried to get him to answer twice before, he sighed, ears flattening against his head. "Okay, fine, John, you caught me. Are you happy? Yes, I'm on an unregistered rig. I got the keys from a contact. I got tired of pretending this wasn't important to me. Ever since you moved, Adam's the only one left I see regularly, and he hasn't been the same since.

And he *still* refuses to call me Jules." The wolf sagged into the oversized cushion. "You know the ban's nothing but politics, John."

I sighed and shook my head. "I know, Jules. I said that from the beginning, but it was because you wouldn't let go of your crusade."

At that, his arms shot out wide. "Crusade? They're charging you by the second for the privilege of being alive! They're bleeding you dry, making you pay for stuff that should've been free, just for the sake of squeezing a little bit more money out of everybody's dreams!"

"My point, Jules," I said, putting a paw to the bridge of my muzzle. "Look, you're right, I agree with you. I always did, you know that. That doesn't justify you breaking and entering. Two wrongs don't make a right."

The wolf's eyes dropped, his body tensing. "How about three?" he breathed.

I cocked my head to the side at that. "Three? What—" His outburst and the quiet admission combined in my head with some of the things I'd seen over the last day, and my eyes narrowed to slits. "You *bastard.*"

Jules cringed. "John, I—"

"Stop." I cut off his protest with a sweep of my paw, and my eyes lit a deep and righteous gold. "Jules, you had better tell me the truth, and you had better do it right now. Did you have *anything* to do with what's been happening to my home?"

The only response I got was a nod, but it was enough. A chill ran down my back, the bottom falling out of my stomach. "Why?" It was all I could do to force the word out around a clenched jaw.

The wolf pushed himself out of his seat and jammed his paws into his pockets. His shoulders were stooped, his tail trying to curl between his legs. "Okay, yes, I was stupid. I was angry. After I got banned, somebody contacted me about an underground movement to protest Tadashiissei's policies towards Irokai. I joined. At first it was harmless pranks, leaving messages for people to find to make them ask questions, but Tadashiissei just kept it all under wraps. So... we escalated, and they just kept burying it. So, finally, after months and months of protests and trying to make ourselves heard legitimately, the group finally just blew up, hoping to make a scene that the company couldn't just hide. It worked."

I bit back the first reply, then gave up and let it out anyway. "Idiot. Do you really think they've heard a single thing you've said? All you're doing is proving that if you can't play your way, you're willing to ruin the fun for everyone else. Damn it, Jules, you're not this dumb! Since when did this kind of strategy ever work?"

He hunched further in on himself. "John, please stop yelling." His voice had gone very soft, taking that near-monotone I knew meant he was close to his breaking point. "I said I was wrong. I said I was stupid. I don't need you making it worse. I was angry. I was desperate. You're right; I want this. I want this desperately. I never expected Tadashiissei to ban me for trying to challenge their policies. I figured the worst that would happen is they would win and I would keep paying forever, hating it but doing it anyway because I need this. I need to *be* this. When they told me not to come back, I went a little crazy. I did some really dumb things. Now all I can do is try to fix them and hope for forgiveness."

I took a deep breath and let it out in a rush, feeling the anger sap out of me. I took a step closer to the wolf and put a paw on his shoulder. "You're forgiven, Jules. I couldn't stay mad at you. I just wish you'd thought this through before you did it. All of you. Two residents so far are confirmed deleted and the backup system is offline to prevent accidental corruption, so there's no pulling them back until everything's fixed."

Jules winced. "Oh, hell." He turned, his yellow eyes looking into mine. "Please, let me help."

I nodded. "I'll talk with Rei and some of the others I know in Security; they may be willing to listen to reason, and this will be a good way for you to prove that you're trustworthy, but you're going to have to come clean and turn over everything you've got. I mean it. And that means the rig, too, if he asks for it." His eyes went wide, but I pressed onwards. "I'm serious, Jules. I'll help you get back in, but you've got to go legit."

He sagged against me, but he nodded anyway, his arms wrapping around my shoulders in a hug. I returned the embrace, and suddenly he was clutching me to his chest, shaking, tears quietly rolling down his cheeks and onto my shirt. I ran a paw down his back, doing what I could to comfort him. "I've missed you," I said quietly. "I never quit loving you, you know."

That caught his ears and he withdrew enough to look at me, wiping at his eyes with one paw. "What? But what about—"

"Mits?" I smiled. "We were close, but it wasn't until after you got banned that we got together. I'd gone out of habit, but I was having a lousy time, and she happened to be off-duty. We spent the day just talking about Irokai, how much I loved it, how much you loved it. She told me she'd heard what happened and was sorry the company had responded as it had. We commiserated. Things went from there." I shrugged. "I wasn't the one who broke it off, Jules. I tried to tell you outside, but you were so set on it being a problem that nothing I said was getting through."

Jules chuckled quietly, his tail giving a half-hearted wave. "I wonder if Mitsuko knows how lucky she is."

I smiled. "She's got an idea. I've still got all your old avatars, you know. I kept them. We don't come here much, since you left, but we still reminisce about this place."

"Yeah?" The wolf's eyes lit at that. "Do you think... you could? Once, for old times' sake?"

I huffed, tail lashing. "Jules, remember that whole 'disaster' thing happening?" Seeing the look in his eyes, though, I sighed. "Okay, okay." It took a moment to scan through the interfaces to find where I'd archived everything, a few more to do a quick validation to ensure they were safe, but once I had them active, I backed out of the menu and then looked down at my paws. A quick internal command, and my pads began to glow. "Ready?"

The wolf nodded, his eyes focused on my paws. He licked his lips once, then waved away his pants, leaving himself nude in front of me. A fresh glint of metal caught my eye, making me chuckle; he'd put a barbell through his sheath, even knowing no-one would probably see it. "You really do need this," I said quietly, stepping closer to him. I knew the answer, but seeing him nod, watching the shivers of anticipation pass through him still made my cock twitch in its sheath. "Easy or hard, Jules. Pick fast."

Jules snapped his eyes shut, but not before I saw the hunger in them. "Don't be gentle," he whispered. His tail curled tightly against his back, his sheath stirring. He balled his paws at his sides. "Please."

I snapped open my hardline and enabled the pain transmitters, glimmers of pure white mixing into the golden glow. "Brace yourself," I replied, then grabbed his paws in mine, sending pulses of light up his arms.

Instantly, he clenched his jaw. "Hurts," he whimpered. "Don't stop." His tail lashed behind him as the light spread further up his arms and over his shoulders. I grinned, tightening my grip against his wrists, letting the light slide further over him, outlining his body in a radiant halo. His muzzle hung open, tongue lolling. He gulped air, letting out a gasp as the light enveloped him. As he dropped to his knees, he let out a high-pitched whine, flattening his ears against his head. "Please...."

I nodded, then pushed the light, baring down on the wolf's paws. Under my pads, the fur flattened, joints stiffening as his skin began to crystallize. His elbows locked as the change spread further up over his arms. "Please what?" I smirked. "Please stop? Please no? I could leave you like this, I guess —"

"No!" The cry was reflexive, thrusting itself out of Jules' throat with the force of a junkie begging for a hit. "Don't... don't stop." He opened his eyes, haunted and needy, looking down at himself as his shoulders froze. His expression locked into one of panic and bliss as his chest solidified, his ability to breathe gone but not the instinct to do so. Then the changes came faster, down over his stomach, his crotch, his stiffening shaft turning smooth as it turned to carved diamond. Light permeated the wolf's entire figure as the shift accelerated. He tilted back his head, muzzle frozen half-open. "Ye—" The word died mid-syllable as his muzzle became translucent, clear, his entire figure transformed into a crystal sculpture with a final flash of light.

I took a moment to validate that the editor had finished, then put my paws together, the light shifting from a deep gold to a bright blue. I put my fingers on his chest, and the glow suffused Jules' form, casting curious rainbows across the crimson carpeting. Deep inside, where the wolf's heart was, something sparked, then caught, an orb of cerulean lightning crackling to life. It flickered, then flashed, sending tendrils of current out through his frozen limbs. As it crossed joints, the crystal fractured, then broke. Metal plates grew to seal the shattered ends, with powdered gemstones providing lubrication. Metal shafts grew inward through the hearts of the crystals, forming rods to carry current from the central core out to the smallest segments. Fractal filaments pulsed with power as the ball in his chest throbbed. The last spark sent a wave up his head, restoring his neck and filling his eyes with St Elmo's fire.

"—es...." Jules moaned as he collapsed, his fall muffled by the thick plush pile. "Oh, gods.... Oh, John." The crystalline wolf shook, fingers clutching at the carpet. "Thank you.... I'd... I'd almost forgotten how good that feels."

"Oh, *hai,* John is quite skilled at that." I spun around, ears flat against my head. Mitsuko stood next to the magic mirror, her arms folded in front of her chest, her tail waving lazily behind her in amusement.

"Mits!" I ducked my head, a chill running down my back. With a guilty glance, I dismissed the glow around my paws. "How... how long were you watching?"

My girlfriend giggled. "Long enough to watch you give Jules-*kun* what he wanted?" She walked towards us. "I did tell you the meeting would be over soon, John."

Jules pushed himself back to his hinds, though he was still shaking from the rush of the change. "I'm sorry, Mits; it was my fault. I was the one that asked him to—"

Mitsuko put a finger over Jules' crystalline muzzle, silencing him. "I have no reason to be jealous, Jules," she said quietly. "I know John loves me. I know John loves you too. And I am glad to see you again, even under such circumstances." She withdrew her finger, then leaned forward and pressed her muzzle to the wolf's, eliciting a quiet whimper from him as they kissed. She withdrew, then licked his muzzle teasingly. "Perhaps when this is all over, we shall finally get to know one another, *ne?*"

Jules' tail wagged, though the wolf's cheeks still glowed with embarrassment. "I think I'd like that, yeah."

"Oh, *hai*, I do as well," Mitsuko murmured. "In the meantime, though, I suggest that we both show John how much we know about him, *ne?*" She grinned, and then as she arched her back, her clothing dissolved, falling around her in a flutter of leaves and flower petals.

"I think I'd like that, yeah," Jules repeated, turning his attention to me, his expression taking on an almost feral grin. Lightning flickered throughout his entire form as he took a step in my direction.

I looked from wolf to raccoon and back, reflexively taking a step backwards. "Hey, what about.... We just stepped out for food, Mits.... We don't have...."

Mitsuko advanced, grinning. "We should make the time. If Irokai is to disappear, then our final moments should be good ones; if Irokai is not to disappear, then we may continue our work afterwards. There will always be more reasons not to do the things we wish, *ne?*" With that, she smiled, kissed her paw, and blew it at me, enveloping my muzzle in a cloud of sweet-smelling pollen.

Reflexively, I tried to draw in a breath before the dust hit me, but by the time I knew she was doing it, it was too late to avoid pulling the pollen deep inside. Almost instantly, a warm tingle ran along my spine, tail shivering and muscles relaxing. My knees went weak, but thankfully I had a beanbag nearby to break my fall. I landed smoothly, feeling almost liquid as I draped across the overstuffed leather.

Jules grinned down at the other raccoon, dropping to his knees. "Nice one, Mitsuko." His eyes turned to mine, flickering with concern. "How you feeling, John? You can still say no."

I looked at the wolf, a warm grin spreading across my muzzle. My head felt clear, my body relaxed. The pain in my back was gone, as was the tension in my shoulders I hadn't even realized I had. I was still in control, still very aware of my surroundings, but all of the stress of everything that had happened over the last forty-eight hours just melted and poured out of me. "Good," I murmured. Watching Jules move so freely and so confidently, I couldn't help but remember how it used to be between us. I missed it. I missed him. I'd told him the truth, earlier, one I hadn't even really said to myself; I did still love him. "Very good. Please." I groaned and, with a bit of maneuvering, shifted the bag so I was mostly level, my rump over the edge, my knees spread.

The wolf let out an electric growl, positioning himself between my legs. His crystal shaft rose from its sheath, glittering and smooth. "It's been a while," he admitted. "Too long. I may need a little help."

At that, Mitsuko was beside him, smiling. "How may I help you this morning?" Before he could answer, though, she knelt, one paw ducking between her own legs. Her breathing visibly quickened as fingers shifted against her sex, and then she gently wrapped her paw around his shaft, spreading her nectar along his length. At her touch, his back arched, letting out a modulated groan. "Oh, *hai*," she breathed huskily. "I can assist you with that." Once his shaft glistened from her juices, she withdrew her touch, leaving him to crawl closer, his cock bobbing up as he moved between my legs.

The wolf's pads were as cool as I remembered as he spread my cheeks, nestling himself between them. The tip of his cock tingled with current as he cautiously positioned it against my pucker, then wrapped his arms around my thighs. "Ready?" When I nodded, he leaned forward, pressing himself inside of me in a slow, smooth motion. Almost instantly, the pressure and power and pleasure pulsing under my tail made me groan, bliss spreading over me in shockwaves up from my crotch. Jules slid his smooth crystalline cock as deeply as he could into me, then held himself against my legs, panting. "Forgot... how good it feels...."

I closed my eyes and nodded in response, trying to breathe deeply, senses overloading. "Keep going." I put one paw on my sheath. He groaned as he withdrew, then thrust forward again, achingly slow, visibly relishing every twitch and spasm of my pucker against his cock. I did my best to match my strokes to his, and soon we had established a rhythm between us, his crystal-and-lightning form moving against mine, arousal surging every time his hips came to rest against my rump.

Mitsuko giggled above me, and I opened my eyes again to see her standing over me. "Excuse me, but is this seat taken?" Without waiting for a response, she knelt over my muzzle, legs parted. At the cleft of her crotch, rather than the delicate folds I knew, a vivid blue-white magnolia blossomed, its petals unfurled. As she neared, her scent, rich and heavy mixed with floral fragrances that overwhelmed my nose. It filled me with the urge, like an insect, to explore her depths. As soon as I could reach her, I parted my jaws and flicked my tongue out to savor the taste of her nectar as she rocked against my muzzle. With each breath, that teasing, aching desire burned more fiercely, and I tried to slide my tongue further into her.

"Wow." Jules' voice was distant and panting. "You got him." I felt Mits arch her back above me, glanced down to see the wolf's paws at her breasts, then focused my attention back to her floral depths. We all of us moved together, my girlfriend above me, my ex-boyfriend below, each of us shifting and moaning and panting in time to the others' movements, driving each other to higher and higher depths of joy.

The wolf was the first to break the pure sounds of lovemaking, whimpering against clenched teeth. "Not... gonna last." I nodded and started squeezing him as he thrust himself into me, tightening as much as I could given how out of practice I was and how devoted I was to licking each and every petal from base to tip and back, tongue circling Mits' stubby stamen at the base of her cup. She keened quietly, driven closer to release by my actions as well as Jules' eager caress at her chest, but it was the one between my legs whose rhythm was breaking. His whole body shook, paws moving back to my hips to pull himself deeper into me, struggling to hold out one more, thrust, another, and then with a warbling howl he drove himself into the top of his knot, sending not spunk but a wave of pure electricity deep into my guts. The surge of power sent its own spasms running along my spine, down to my tail and up to the top of my head, and my paw tightened around my shaft in time for me to come, sending spatters of my own juices across my chest.

As the last aftershocks of his release passed, Jules pulled out of me carefully, a last zot of his charge leaking against my pucker and making me jump. He grinned, then sprawled back on his back. "I needed that," he groaned. "I can't tell you how much. He doing okay for you, Mitsuko?"

The moment my orgasm had left me, I had turned my attention back to Mits' petals. At the wolf's comments, though, she rose and then bent down to kiss my muzzle, flicking her tongue across her juices soaking into my fur. "Always, Jules, but I am afraid that something urgent has arisen."

She held out a paw to me, which I took, rising and shaking my head to clear it. "What's up? Sorry you didn't finish, Mits."

The raccoon smiled at me, but her eyes were hollow. "It is okay, John. For now, we must go." She tapped her ear. "While we were engaged, I received word from the head of Hospitality. The decision has been made at the highest levels to increase our efficiency in handling the ongoing issues. With most critical system disruptions resolved, senior management has opted to declare the crisis averted and handle the remainder as maintenance issues."

Jules' eyes flashed, baring pointed teeth in a growl. "Hello? Metafungus? I don't think this counts as resolved."

Mitsuko turned to the wolf, arms folded across her chest. "Oh, *hai,* you are correct, but nor is it an emergency if the zone is empty. All available personnel have been asked to locate and escort anyone remaining within the area to the transit station for Murasaki. In one hour, Beni Prefecture is being taken offline until further notice."

16 | IKANOBARI MITSUKO
FRUSTRATION

TO MATCH THE STYLE OF MIDORI PREFECTURE, I DREW INSPIRATION for the interior of the house from the Edo period. In deference to Tadashiissei design guidelines, the walls were bamboo, not wood, but fashioned in the traditional styles with a wide deck that encircled the property. The interior walls were traditional paper in sliding frames to maximize utility of the space and provide privacy to those who needed it. I could, if I chose, light the entire area with but a few candles, even in the middle of the night.

Unfortunately, those same translucent screens did little in their native form to block sound, and John's voice had steadily grown more impatient and terse since placing his first call. Not wanting to interrupt him, I eventually had to use my interface to block all of the external sound from the room. That, however, sank the sleeping area into a deep quiet even more disturbing than his barely-constrained shouts. Even on calm days, a breeze blew through Midori Prefecture, and I had a pair of small traditional wind chimes that hung near the window to inspire relaxation. With the isolation, that comfort was gone, along with the steady whisper of the wind outside.

I tried to sleep, but the stillness made it difficult, as did the knowledge of John's anger. Even not being able to hear him, I could imagine his voice in my mind, rising and falling as he paced. Reserved even at his most enthusiastic, to hear him actually upset was a shock, one I was glad I had not had to encounter before. I sighed, rolling onto my side, folding one arm beneath my head. I knew before this entire matter was resolved, he would be again. I wanted to comfort him. I wanted to tell him it would all be resolved and soon. I wanted to tell him it was all just an accident and that come morning he would have an apology. I could do none of those things; all I could manage was to keep the bed warm and wait for his return.

I shifted onto my back, folded my arms behind my head, and gazed upwards at the ceiling in the stifling silence. It could have been minutes or hours that I lay there, waiting. Without the cadence of his voice, I had only my own sense of time to measure. I knew that, if I wanted, I could check the exact moment, but it was less important to me than John's mood would be upon his return. He had gotten so little rest since the attacks started, only to be woken out of his first night of sound sleep. When he first stirred, he was quiet, even apologetic. Quickly, however, his tone turned to frustration, then to anger, carrying him out of the bedroom into the front area. The first strains of righteous indignation had crept into his voice just as I was muffling the room, leaving me to anxiously await his return, my eyes closed, attempting to feign sleep.

Fingers at my shoulder made me stir, and I followed them back to John's face, looking down at me. His golden eyes were distant, looking through me into the distance; beneath them, the fur was dark and slightly damp. His ears arched forward, but his tail lay against the ground behind him. He sat over his heels, resting his elbows on his knees. As my eyes touched his, he smiled, but his gaze remained unfocused. He glanced away at the walls, then back, cocking his head to the side. I nodded and restored the ambient sound, taking in a deep breath and letting out in a sigh as the wind chimes gently rang outside the window.

He blinked, then removed his paw and wiped at his eyes with his pads. Immediately, I reached out and lay a paw against his arm. "John —"

John shook his head, covering my paw in his other as if to remove it. "Please, Mits, I...." His voice trailed back into silence as he stopped, fingers sliding up along my arm. "You're beautiful, Mitsuko."

More than his tone or expression, his use of my full name chilled me. I tensed my fingers against his arm reflexively, trying to keep my expression neutral. "Something is troubling you," I murmured. "I have not heard you call me that since we began dating."

John's brow furrowed at the comment, but the corners of his muzzle pulled back into a smile that did not quite reach his eyes. "I've got an idea," he said, cupping his other paw over mine. "Let's head out to Kigiku Island for a while. I haven't gotten a chance to gaze at the city lights in a while."

My ears pulled back against my head and the tip of my tail flicked in concern. "John, you have gotten very little sleep; are you sure this is a good idea?"

At that, he relaxed, squeezing my fingers gently against his arm. "I'm sure; maybe we can curl up on the beach and get a nap together."

I smiled gently at that, carefully keeping my concern from my voice. "Oh, *hai,* that does sound enjoyable." I rose from the bed, motioning a light jacket and skirt into place around me. "Though, you will want something to block the chill, I think," I chided when he moved to follow me.

John's ears reddened slightly and he nodded, but then a wide grin crossed his muzzle. He lifted his head towards the ceiling, his arms spread, and a flash of light erupted from his back as golden-feathered wings emerged from his shoulders. As their tips passed his fingers, a shudder ran through him and his eyes began to glow. He batted at the air around him, whipping up tiny cyclones that sent the wind chimes jingling as he pushed himself off of the ground. *Problem solved,* he sent wordlessly, holding out his paw to me.

I took it, my muzzle agape. "But... John, I thought this had not been approved!"

It's not, but— He stopped, a frown flitting across his features, his eyes dimming for a moment before he gently squeezed my fingers. *Right now, I don't care. Just come with me, please, Mits?*

After a moment, I nodded, and he gestured to the window, sweeping it open with a flick of his wrist. Outside lay not rows of bamboo houses in Midori Prefecture, but the tops of a vast and unkempt forest. Leaves rustled in the wind, accompanied by the steady gentle patter of light rain. The sweet hint of fresh water blew into the room, riding the stiff breeze that stirred the thin blankets on the mattress.

I had not thought my eyes could go wider. "A portal to Kigiku? John, what are you doing?"

John's smile faded slightly. He took my paw in both of his, bringing it to his muzzle, pressing the pads softly against his cheek. His eyes closed, and he drew in a deep breath, only his wings moving. *Please, Mits, I promise I'll explain. I just.... I need to get out of here for a bit. I've never seen Kigiku, and I've always said I should. I'm exhausted, but there's no way I'm sleeping right now. Just... come with me. I want*

*to sit on the beach and gaze back at the lights and be with you for a while
and experience something I've never gotten to do here. Please.*

I cupped my fingers against his muzzle, stroking along his cheek
with my thumb. "Of course, John," I said softly. "I would love to come
with you. I am just concerned; this impulsiveness is unlike you."

He shook his head at that. *Yeah, you're right, but I need to get this
out of my system. Okay?*

I nodded again, and John took me into his arms, lifting me off of
the ground. Supported by his embrace, I wrapped my arms around his
neck, entwining my legs with his, and then we were soaring through
the sky, skimming the tops of the trees. The wind whipped around
us, rippling my skirt around my ankles and tugging at the hem of
my jacket; wrapped in his arms, though, I could barely feel the chill.
Overhead, the starless sky was an empty span of black, devoid of
depth or distinction. I shivered and buried my muzzle in the nape of
his neck, hugging myself to him, feeling his wings beat the air around
us as we sailed just above the forest crown.

John shifted his legs, then kicked, arching his back to pull us
upwards, rising higher into the air. We twisted as we rose, spinning
slowly to get a panoramic view of Irokai as we sailed aloft. Behind us,
rows and rows of Midori's low bamboo houses stood. At the edge of
the residential area, taller and taller buildings began to appear, until
Murasaki seemed to erupt from the ground, rising in columns of
steel, its towering skyscrapers holding aloft a corner of the sky. The
Bazaar at Hana, beside it, spread out in apparently endless sea of tents.
Despite everything that had happened, lights glittered against the
backdrop of the night, from streetlights to shimmering neon signs,
reflecting like stars off the deep, dark waters. Where Beni Prefecture
should have been, however, was only emptiness. Not even barren land
remained to show where the clusters of converted warehouses and
tenements once stood. At a point past the Bazaar, the ground simply
disappeared, empty ocean stretching out to the horizon. I shuddered
despite myself, and John's arms tightened around me in response.

John's legs bent, tipping forward at the waist. His wings flexed,
and we turned, twisting in space, until we were upside-down, facing the ground. Craning my neck, I could see the narrow curve of
a rocky beach, and the slow and steady ripple of waves against the
edge of Kigiku Island. Then we were falling, diving, one powerful
pump of John's wings sending us hurtling towards the ground. The
impact would not kill us, even if we hit the ground at speed, but we
could still feel the pain. That sick giddiness washed over me and I
smiled despite my terror, closing my eyes and clinging to John as we

plummeted. One second passed, then another. As the third began, my training asserted itself and I opened my hardline, swiftly navigating through windows to halt our momentum and return us safely back to the portal to our home.

John pressed his muzzle to my neck, and I hesitated, my eyes not making contact with the override. *Don't be afraid, Mitsuko,* he projected into my mind.

On the count of four, we slammed into the water, sending up a plume in our wake. Instantly, the cold surrounded me, but the glow extending outwards from John's fur enveloped me in its warmth. I opened my eyes, turning to look into John's. He smiled, his own shining, and I flashed emerald at him in response. He laughed, sending up a fresh cloud of bubbles, then pulled me against his chest for a last embrace before letting go and turning to kick his way back to the beach. I nodded, then swam upwards, breaking the surface of the water with a laugh.

Clapping echoed from the shore. I turned to see Jules standing on the beach, arms in front of him. "Very nice," the wolf called when John's head reappeared beside me. "Only a four from the technical panel, but a nine-seven on the artistic." He smirked. "Next time, keep your back straight when you hit the water. Hey!" He jerked back as John threw water at him. "Splashing the judges is a foul!"

"What are you doing here, Jules?" I asked as neutrally as I could as I rose out of the water, wiping my paws down along my arms to push most of the water from my fur.

Jules smirked. "Glad to see you too, Mitsuko." He hooked a thumb in John's direction. "He called, said he wanted me to meet you guys here." The wolf turned to the other raccoon, who was busily shaking out his fur. "Didn't say why, though. Maybe you want to explain? As well as—" He folded one arm across his chest, gesturing towards one of John's wings. "Weren't you the one who told me to build the Shock so there'd be a place for those kind of convention-breaking mods that wouldn't cost everyone a fortune?"

At that, John froze. His face dropped as he took a seat, crosslegged, his wings and tail drooped behind him. *I was, yeah.* He drew in a deep breath, then sighed, wrapping his arms around his knees. *I got a call from Tadashiissei Support. I'm on the employee rolls as a member of Development, but when I immigrated, my account got reclassified to Resident. The guy on the phone rattled off a lot of numbers I didn't feel like following, but the bottom line was that everything I did at work over the last week to try to fix things that got broken during the assault got billed wrong. Now my bank's throwing a fit about some of the charges.*

He looked up into my eyes. *I've got until the end of the week to get things straightened out.*

I did not remember closing the space between us. One moment, I stood on the beach, trying to squeeze the water out of my clothes. The next, I knelt in front of John, my arms around his shoulder, my muzzle pressed into his neck, my body shaking. No tears fell, but they were superfluous. John embraced me with ferocity, squeezing me to his chest.

Jules' tail visibly straightened out behind him, bristling, and his lips pulled back in a grimace. "I suppose it's too late for me to say, 'I told you so'?"

I spun my head around, glaring. "Jules!"

The wolf shrugged; his tail started to relax, but his ears remained flat against his head in anger. "This is why I told him I couldn't move here in the first place. This is *exactly* what I feared would happen, this kind of bureaucratic disaster." He shrugged. "When I tried to fight it last time, I got told not to come back. I'm only here now because of a cracked account and some bad decisions. So how much do you owe? I'll start pulling the money."

I let a faint smile cross my muzzle. "I am surprised you did not call it a ransom."

The wolf's tail darted back out at that. "I'm surprised you didn't kick me in the shin," he riposted. "Still, what else am I going to do, let him get zeroed and then go beg to have him restored from backup? When's the last time anybody even got backed up? And what about those folks that got blanked when Nanakōsei vanished? How many was that, ten? Fifteen?"

"Jules, with respect, it was two, and one of them was a native with an archive that predated the first attack," I corrected firmly, trying to keep my voice level. "The other was a resident. Every effort is being made to restore then both as quickly as possible."

Jules growled at that. "Every effort, after they admit the backup system might be corrupt and they take it offline. For all you know, they could come back in several discontiguous pieces. Frankly, I'd rather pay the extortion fee."

It's not the money, John replied, finally. He squeezed, then let go and rose, spreading his wings. *It's... it's just been everything. This was supposed to be better than reality, and it is, when it doesn't feel like the death of a thousand cuts. That's what this whole disaster has been, from the attacks themselves to Beni going offline to this whole mess with my account. This—* He turned, gesturing to encompass the whole of

Kigiku Island and Irokai beyond. *This could all be so much more than it is, but it's like the people who own the place just want a money machine and a tourist trap!*

"Yeah, well...." Jules shrugged. "Might have been good for you to figure that out before you decided to get a 'Property of Tadashiissei' tattoo on your ass."

I shook my head. "Jules, I understand that you are upset, but please try to be constructive." I looked back to John and put a paw on his shoulder. "This truly is an intolerable situation. I wish I could do more."

You know, I think you can, John replied, his eyes brightening. *Who else do you know at the company that would agree that there's something really wrong with this mess with my account?*

I considered, then smiled. "Giri has been speaking of laziness within Security's management for months. He would probably not be surprised to hear that Financial is the same way." I opened my hardline and pulled up an employee roster, scanning for the line noise of his last name. After a second pass without success, I checked the Security roster, but all I could find was «Chō Giri: Terminated» with yesterday's date. "Oh my."

What is it? John sent, cocking his head to the side.

I closed the window, turning my attention back to the others. "It appears that Giri has been removed from the company, but I do not know why."

Jules smirked, folding his arms and shrugging. "Makes sense. They get rid of their squeaky wheels, just like everyone else. I went freelance for a reason."

Except they can't get rid of all of us, John replied, his eyes shining. *Jules, page Briar, Sparks, everyone you can from the club. Love, contact everyone you can that will listen, including Giri, and have him start calling anyone in Security who's read his reports. I need to get back and start whipping up a graphic for people to spread.*

The wolf frowned. "John, I hate to say this, but we tried this, and it didn't work."

John's smile spread from ear to ear. *No, you tried to take down the company by destroying everything it built, and in the process you probably alienated every single person you wanted on your side. Now we do it my* way. He motioned the wolf to join him, then slid an arm around my waist. *We tell everyone what's going on in here. We show them what's at stake. We stop playing by their rules, and we force them to play by ours.*

I hesitated a moment, then spoke, softly. "I do not wish to dampen your enthusiasm, love, but what happens if they simply decide to shut down Irokai in response? Then we have lost everything."

They can't, though. That would be murder! John's tail flicked as he laughed, motes of light dancing around him. *There's an old saying: 'If someone owes you a hundred dollars, you have power over him; if someone owes you a million, he has power over you.' Right now, because we're completely dependent on them, there's only so much they can do to us. They're bound by their own contracts!*

Jules rolled his eyes and put his paws on John's shoulders. "I think the upload scrambled your head, hon. All they have to do is promise to archive you someplace safe and transfer your bits to your legal next of kin, and then they can do whatever they like. They don't have to do a thing to you; they still own Irokai."

For a moment, John froze, and it looked as if Jules' words had broken John's spirit, but then his voice dropped to a fervent whisper. *Then we have to ensure that Irokai doesn't belong to them any more, don't we?*

That sick giddiness struck me again, and I counted the seconds of silence: one, two, three, four, five. "John.... You are proposing attempting to steal the company's primary product from them. This will not look good on your quarterly review, *ne?*"

No, love, I'm only proposing asserting the rights I still have as an independent, thinking being. I don't remember anything in the immigration paperwork asking me to give up any of those when I came in here, and they couldn't make it stick even if I did. I'm still the same person I was before I uploaded, even if Adam says otherwise. You, Giri, everyone that's uploaded, we're all still people, *even if we're running on silicon and not carbon. We all still have rights as people, and if Tadashiissei isn't going to enforce and protect them, then we have to make sure that everything belongs to those who can and will.* He kissed my cheek, wrapping his wings around both of us. *This, my loves, is the Democratic Revolution of Irokai.*

17 | CHŌ GIRI
RESISTANCE

THE LAST TIME I STOOD ON THE SKYBRIDGE BETWEEN EVEREST AND Nanakōsei, I had the distinct impression of standing in space. The streetlights below glittered like stars and the moon shone in the sky above. The glass floor leeched the heat from my pads, and the wind outside made me shiver despite the warmth of the corridor. The illusion of being suspended in mid-air was almost perfect. Unfortunately, the matte black square that sharply split the transparent tunnel was an all-too-real reminder of where I stood. Glowing letters hung in front of it, apologizing for the inconvenience in English and Japanese. Aside from that, though, the walkway was all very much as I remembered it when I had summoned Mitsuko here.

I felt a flash of anger at the memory. It was hard not to draw a direct line from this place to the makeshift entry to Briar's club and the events that occurred there. Had I not gone to someone else for help, I might never have had the chance to put a stop to the attacks on Irokai. I could have continued indefinitely, cleaning up the petty messes and complaining to my superiors. When the real assault happened, I could have simply ignored it all, followed my orders, and told myself that nothing more could be done. I could have simply done my job as I had before, willfully ignorant but happy.

I balled my paws into fists and jammed them into my coat pockets to try to stop my fingers from shaking. None of these ideas was true, but it was hard not to believe that it could have happened that way. I almost wished it had; I would have felt less disappointment. I wanted to say that Briar had more than offset the frustration, anger, and resentment I had felt towards both the company and myself. In truth, she made more of a difference than I could have thought possible. She, however, was but one bright point, and I had been in a very dark place for a very long time. I was glad for how things happened, to be sure, but not because of her. I was still unsure how comfortable I was with her. One night of pleasure after shared stresses was no reason to be interested in her, and her other interests made me nervous, to put it politely.

Really, I had been getting desperate for some time, and the orders I had received were only fueling my urgency. I had not wanted to be where I was, but I had seen no other way to go. Helping Briar and the others had meant defending my principles as well as protecting my home, and what, truly, had it cost me? I no longer worked for a company I disrespected in a position I did not enjoy. I had gotten the best possible outcome I could have reasonably expected, and far better than I could have received.

Neither of those lies gave me any comfort, either, while I sat alone in my apartment, staring out the window at the Murasaki skyline, wondering what to do with the rest of eternity. Back before all of this had happened, I asked myself in the past what I would do with myself, if Tadashiissei had not been in my future. Each time the question had arisen, I had pushed it aside. Now, I had no choice but to admit I had never answered the question. I knew that finding a job would become a necessity in the near future, but who would hire a security agent fired for negligence? After his public confrontation and dismissal, I doubted that Sasaki would be willing to give a positive reference.

A quiet voice spoke from behind me. "Perhaps formal reintroductions are in order; your family name was different, the last time we spoke."

I shrugged. "It was my name at incept. I thought it more fitting than what I picked before."

"Interesting," Mitsuko replied. "Why did you change it back?"

I smirked and turned to face the raccoon, leaning back against the black warning sign. "Unimportant; it was no longer me."

Mitsuko stood silently for several moments, considering my words. Her eyes remained half-lidded, masking her thoughts, but her tail twitched behind her in confusion. "I was not sure you would be here; you did not accept my invitation. I was not even sure that I had invited the right person."

I took a deep breath then sighed, resignation returning to my expression. "I was not sure I would come. Still, here I am." I had not wanted to respond, but I felt obliged to do so. It had not been a summons; I no longer worked for Tadashiissei and could not be ordered to attend. Yet, after making such a demand of her so long ago, I had never apologized. The least I could do was treat her request with the same urgency.

The raccoon nodded in response, then bowed slightly. "Please, allow me to explain my request. My lover, John, is facing suspension of his account over some financial discrepancies. He is organizing a protest at the Tadashiissei plaza for tomorrow morning starting at eight, local. He hopes to continue it until someone else within the company responds to his requests for help."

I frowned. "I have little interest in further hurting my chances at gainful employment by participating in a protest against the company from which I was just fired."

The corners of Mitsuko's muzzle turned up in a faint smile. "With respect, Giri, you worked in Security, not Hospitality. More importantly, though, I have heard about your final exchange with Sasaki Rei from multiple sources. I suspect that attending a public rally in support of those actions would do more for your reputation than avoiding it."

"Multiple sources?" I tilted my head to the side. I had Briar's support, I knew, but she had said nothing of anyone else commenting on my actions, nor had she mentioned telling anyone else. "From whom?"

The raccoon's smile broadened. "It is not important from whom I heard which detail; some of the names were certainly aliases unwilling to admit that they were members of the FutureShock." She folded her paws together in front of her. "What I may say with certainty is that more than one person has publicly praised your actions. From all reports, you acted in a swift and decisive manner in response to a customer safety complaint, took creative steps to resolve a large problem, and that you were terminated without regard to any mitigating circumstances." She paused to give her words some weight, then continued more softly. "I am asking you to lend your voice to a protest, not to publish security flaws."

I folded my arms across my chest. It was hard not to feel a swelling of pride at her words, but it was not enough to overcome my frustration at myself and at the whole situation. "It will not be much of a protest if only present and former employees of Tadashiissei are in attendance," I replied.

The tip of Mitsuko's tail hooked in amusement, and her eyes flashed with pride. "With some generous assistance from some mutual friends, we have generated a fair bit of interest in this rally. I suspect that a significant percentage of the resident populace and a fair number of tourists will be present to hear what we have to say, and to share their own stories. It would seem that there is a great deal of frustration with a large number of corporate policies: billing practices, terms of service, ownership of modifications, and so on. It would take only a reason for this disapproval to transform into dissent."

I held still a few moments, considering my next words. "And you believe that your lover and his story can provide that tipping point?"

"Perhaps not," she admitted. "His situation is... extreme, but he is not well-known in his community." Then she looked into my eyes. "I do, however, believe that you and your controversial termination could."

Her words stunned me. I slowly returned my paws to my pockets, shifting my weight against the wall. It was difficult to believe, but if her other words were true.... "Does anyone else within Tadashiissei know of the protest?"

Mitsuko shrugged. "I have seen no reason to inform anyone else in Hospitality of its coming. As to whether anyone else within the company knows, that I cannot say."

I lowered my head, looking down through the glass floor to the streetlights below, watching them twinkle like stars. "I still do not understand why you think my situation will attract more attention than his. He is a dedicated and respected employee facing suspension."

The tip of the raccoon's tail hooked as she held up two fingers. "First, I agree that my mate's situation is the more dire, but it is also the more... abstract." She blushed, ducking her head in an apology to her absent lover. "Financial matters are difficult to explain and are easily lost in details. Not everyone can conceive of why suspension of his account is such a problem for him as a resident, and explaining it cannot easily be reduced to simple concepts. Meanwhile, everyone should be quite capable of empathizing with someone who has lost a job for political reasons."

I nodded on response to that. "And the second?"

Mitsuko's ears rose. "As I said before, my mate is popular within a small segment of the populace and within the company proper, but in the larger community he is not so well-known. He is doing this in hopes to call attention to his situation, but he is not a public speaker. Others have volunteered to share their situations, but I fear that their problems may be overshadowed by their open enmity towards Tadashiissei itself. You are accustomed to dealing with the public, your plight is easily understood, and it seems you have a small but dedicated support group, some of whom have a great many friends across all sectors of Irokai." She paused, then laced her fingers together once more. "Also, before the attacks on Irokai began, you did ask for our assistance, did you not?"

I lifted my head and tilted it to the side. "I did, yes, but that was in response to the rogue edits from Minshukakumei. This is a matter of corporate policy."

"And yet, a direct connection could be drawn from one to the other, could it not?" She tilted her head to the side and smiled. "Had Tadashiissei responded to you when you first suggested there might be an issue, this matter might have been resolved by the time Johnathan moved. Had you not assembled such thorough notes on past attacks, Johnathan might have had far less information on which to work, preventing him from resolving nearly as many hacks. Had he not been so instrumental in the recovery effort, he would not have been forced to activate as many special functions, and thus his bank and Tadashiissei would never have come into conflict. Thus, without your engagement, we might not now be in this situation, having to organize this protest."

The raccoon's smile slid to a mischievous smirk. "You asked us for assistance, Giri. We are assisting you, exactly as you feared we might need."

At that, my eyes went wide and my ears flattened against my head. "You are suggesting rebellion."

Mitsuko's expression returned to a careful neutrality. "I am suggesting protecting my lover. We have an open admission from Financial that the matter is not one for which Johnathan should be punished, and yet they insist that they are powerless to stop the suspension. As part of my duties as a member of Hospitality, I am authorized to use any administrative authority necessary to protect the well-being of residents and visitors to Irokai. If Tadashiissei cannot or will not correct this, I will be forced to do so." Her golden eyes glinted. "If this happens, I fear there will be repercussions, which will lead to an escalation, and from there sides will quickly be chosen whether I wish them to be or not. I am asking you now, Chō Giri, whether you will help me avoid this unfortunate outcome."

I stuffed my paws back into my pockets. This was a side of Mitsuko that I had never seen before, and some part of me wished never to do so again. Even having hinted at open warfare against Tadashiissei myself, I had never wanted the conflict; I only ever wanted the attacks to stop. Now, here was someone dropping more than hints, and she was offering a very narrow window of opportunity for me to act. My fingers closed around the flyer for the protest that Briar had sent me earlier in the evening, and I closed my eyes, nodding once. "*Hai*, I will attend."

18 | SASAKI REI
| CHALLENGE

THE TALLEST STRUCTURE IN MURASAKI PREFECTURE NATURALLY
belonged to Tadashiissei. Rising from the center of the district, opposite the main square from the transit center, the Jewel of Irokai served
as both in-world headquarters and symbol for the world itself. Much
like the pictures I had seen of their physical buildings, a multicolored
tessellation of translucent tiles surrounded the building itself, transi-
tioning from the grey concrete that surrounded it. Instead of ending
at the base of the tower, however, the tiles themselves curved upwards,
rising as facets of a rainbow spire that seemed to hold aloft the center of the sky. Separated from others by a wide plaza and unique by
design, the tower demanded that all who came to the district gaze
upwards at those who had brought them Irokai.

Almost as impressive as the tower was the crowd that had gathered around it. The clock had not yet touched eight, but already over
a hundred people stood on the tessellated tiles, milling about slowly,
murmuring. I scanned faces and accounts as I walked through the
crowd. Many were nervous or excited. A few people were visibly
angry. Many in the audience had had at least one encounter with
Tadashiissei's terms of service and account access policies. I kept my

expression carefully level, but inside I was smiling; this was precisely the type of audience I hoped would come.

At the opposite side of the plaza from the transit center, a waist-height platform stood near the main entrance to the Tadashiissei Tower. Whoever had placed it had chosen its location well; it stood too far from the doors to be considered an obstacle, but it forced the crowd to stand close enough to the building to be an implicit barrier. A small group clustered behind it, talking amongst themselves. The rabbit I didn't know, but she struck me as familiar. The other two, however, I recognized as soon as I saw them. John stood with his arms crossed defensively across his chest, his tail lashing and his ears against his head. Mitsuko rested one paw on his shoulder, her eyes full of concern but her tail held low and her shoulders hunched. All of them were dressed in professional wear, as if for a job interview.

As I stepped out of the crowd, a voice behind me spoke. "I do not believe you are welcome here."

The smile that I had attempted to hold inside let itself out in a smirk. "Giri." I turned to look at the fox. He stood relaxed, his paws jammed into the pockets of his coat. He had replaced his usual sweater, though, with a simple button-down shirt. His muzzle was expressionless, but his tail wagged behind him in amusement, almost wolf-like. "I would like to say I'm surprised to see you here, but I suppose I shouldn't be."

Giri half-bowed, but he kept his muzzle lifted, his gaze locked with mine. "I would say the same."

I returned the gesture, even though there was no respect in his. "I work for Tadashiissei Security. It's my responsibility to ensure the safety of Irokai."

The words hurt me to say, but that was nothing compared to the pain visible in Giri's response. His tail brushed out behind him. His eyes narrowed in a squint, and the corners of his muzzle tightened. He raised one paw to his waist, hesitating a moment before grabbing his belt. "I suggest that you leave, Rei. Have Security send someone else to cover this event."

My own tail lashed; it was hard not to respond to his anger. Before I could do more, however, the rest of the gathered group had joined him. The rabbit put a paw on Giri's waist, while Mitsuko and John interposed themselves between us. "Giri, go keep an eye on the crowd for me; I'll call you when I need you." As the fox nodded and walked away, the raccoon nodded to me. "Rei. I'm glad you could make it."

I folded my arms over my chest. "Are you the ones who organized this event?"

John shrugged. "They organized themselves; I just put together the flyers. It's more like a flash mob than anything else."

"And your reason for the flyers was?" I asked, narrowing my eyes in suspicion.

The raccoons exchanged glances, then Mitsuko said. "I believe that will become apparent in a moment. John, I believe it is time."

John nodded back, then turned to me. "Excuse me, Rei." With that, he hopped up onto the platform, raising his arms over his head. He closed his eyes for a moment, and then when he next spoke, his voice boomed out over the crowd. "If I may have your attention, everybody?"

The crowd fell silent, turning to face the podium. "Thank you all for coming out here so early; I know most of you are probably just thinking about sleep." He paused, letting a brief chuckle pass through the audience. "I also want to take a minute to thank the folks who run the FutureShock for helping me get this together so fast." He paused to let the applause run its course, then lifted his arms again, projecting his voice out over the whole of the plaza. "I don't want to bore you or waste your time, so I'll get to the point. There's something wrong with this place, but it's something we can fix."

He stopped a moment, looking down to Mitsuko, then back out over the crowd. "When I first came to Irokai, I did so because I thought it would be fun, a chance to be something else, somebody else for a while. I came back afterwards because I found something more. I found a place where I could do things I just couldn't do outside. I found a place I could experience things that simply had no analog equivalent." He brought his paws together overhead. "I moved to Irokai, uploaded myself and became a resident, because I found a place where magic could be real. I found a place where the old rules just didn't have to apply any more." He spread his arms wide, and a pair of pigeons flew from the space between his cupped fingers.

He paused a moment, letting the crowd applaud in response, then dropped his voice. "That, however, didn't mean that people wouldn't try to make some new rules. Different rules. Less popular rules. Outside, the rules you simply couldn't escape were things like gravity, the speed of light, or your own heartbeat. In Irokai, they're rules like subscription fees and access charges." The light around the podium began to dim, as if gathering the shadows from the corporate tower over the stage. "Sure, they're small. A nickel here, a dime there, a dollar somewhere else. It's never too much to ask, but is it too much to pay? What's the difference between walking and flying, if gravity's just a number in a database? What's the difference between raccoon and rabbit, between wolf and weasel, when you can change your body as easily as your clothes?"

The people in the audience began to murmur, with scattered claps, but John continued to speak over the swelling throng. "I took a job with Tadashiissei because I wanted to help make Irokai a place where anything was possible. Where anything *is* possible. When the attacks started, I pitched in and helped as much as I could, figuring out what was wrong. When that required me to make changes to the environment, I made them. I did what I had to do to make Irokai safe again. Now, Tadashiissei's told me I have to *pay* for everything I did in the line of duty!" He paused, then broke into a shout. "They're threatening to suspend my account – to turn me off – if I don't agree to pay!"

The crowd, already grumbling, broke out into a full-throated growl. "It gets worse," Giri called back to the stage, his own voice even but matching John's in pitch.

"Giri!" John motioned for the fox to join him. "Come up here, tell everybody what happened to you that night in Beni Prefecture."

Giri nodded, the crowd parting as he approached the platform. "I worked for Tadashiissei since my inception, in their security department. I saw the signs of the coming assault and tried, time and again, to warn them, to investigate, to take steps to stop it, but they did nothing." As he spoke, he stood straighter, lifting his head, visibly projecting the pride he took in his work. "When the attacks began in earnest, they acted surprised that it would happen. After working almost two complete shifts consecutively, I was ordered to take a break. There were still emergencies to resolve, but I was assured they would be. So I went home to sleep, only to be woken by a request for help that no-one else could answer, from several people trapped in a building in Beni Prefecture. I did what any decent person would do, and I went to help. My intervention saved two residents from the virus currently keeping Beni offline."

He paused, letting the crowd absorb his words, then sighed, visibly slumping on stage. "No sooner had I finished, than my manager arrived to fire me for disobeying an order."

"It's not right!" The rabbit from earlier cried out, and suddenly the growl became a rumble of discontent. "If you hadn't acted, at least two of those people would *still* be stuck waiting for a restore. And who knows how many other residents got hit when Beni got taken offline."

"No, it isn't right," John echoed, talking over the rumbling crowd. "If we were just customers, maybe they could get away with it. *Caveat emptor,* sure, but for some of us this isn't a game any more. This is our home. These are our lives, and we have rights, and Tadashiissei can't take those away from us just because we can't leave! We have a right to live without worrying about getting deleted because they can't secure their systems. We have a right to know why Beni Prefecture's still offline. We have a right to not have to pay just to live!"

Hearing his words, I couldn't contain my smile any further, but I knew my part to play in this even if they didn't. "Excuse me," I called up to the stage, letting my voice carry over the crowd as the others had. "I am here as a representative of Tadashiissei Security, and—" The crowd turned ugly, hurling jeers and threats in my direction. I raised my voice to be heard over the mob. "And I feel it necessary to remind you, John, that as a fellow employee of the company, you're obligated to abide by certain rules and regulations governing public conduct. I think you'll find that this event is clearly in violation of them."

"Oh, you're still here?" The raccoon's tail hooked, and he smiled, but his eyes were dark. "What're you going to do, fire me?"

I chuckled. The whole of the event could not have gone better had I planned it myself, right down to the dialog. "No," I conceded, gesturing towards the building. "But surely you must be aware that by now, your demonstration has not gone unnoticed, and no doubt your department manager is aware of your actions against Tadashiissei, and she will have many questions."

John folded his arms across his chest and motioned for me to join him up on the platform. "She already does, and she supports me. Since you're here, though, I've got a couple of little favors to ask of you. They're simple; they won't take you long." Once I was standing beside him, he held up a paw, then started ticking off points on his fingers. "One: go back to human resources and you tell them I quit. I can't work for a company that treats me like this. I wouldn't put up with it before and I refuse to put up with it now. Two, tell my old manager and my team that we demand that they make Beni Prefecture their top priority."

As the crowd burst into applause, he turned to face them and grinned, then motioned for quiet. "Three," he said as he faced me again. "Tell the board of directors that the residents of Irokai demand a seat at the negotiating table, not as employees, not as customers, but as citizens with inalienable rights, to collectively renegotiate our terms of service and account maintenance fees. Four, tell them that regardless of whether they meet with us or not, we demand an end to the user-level environment charges for residents. I'll pay my taxes, but no more micropayments, no more death of a thousand bills."

I crossed my arms and scowled, whipping my tail behind me. "They will be unlikely to listen to you. You did sign a contract with Tadashiissei before you came here."

"As a tourist, yes, but not as a resident," the raccoon countered with a smirk. "So, let's put this in terms they'll understand." He closed his eyes, drew in a deep breath, and opened them again, lifting his voice to the crowd. "I just pulled my bank account information from your database. Five: you tell the board of directors that until Tadashiissei meets with us on our terms, they don't get another dollar from me."

I let myself laugh, knowing John and the rest would think it directed at him. "Do you really think that one rebellious resident will change corporate policy?"

A strong tenor rose out of the crowd in response. "No, but maybe two might." A tall white-furred mouse in a sleeveless top, vest, and denim skirt stepped forward, her hairless tail whipping behind her.

I turned, raising one brow. "And who might you be?"

The mouse grinned. "Imogen Franklin." The author adjusted her glasses, then put her paws on her hips. "Maybe you've heard of me. I've written a few books that folks seem to like, and your company's been bragging for the last few years about saving my life. Maybe if they get a cease-and-desist telling 'em to stop using my name, that'll make 'em listen." She grinned up at the platform. "Give 'em hell, John!"

In the wake of her words, a chorus of numbers rang out from the crowd as people rushed to be next to disable their payments. A flurry of cheers rose from the crowd as more and more people cut off Tadashiissei from their banks. Then the rabbit I saw earlier yelled out: "No more payments just to live!" Her words were infectious, and they too spread through the crowd, until the whole plaza was filled with people chanting *Irokai no Minshukakumei*'s slogan.

John turned to me, a wide-eyed smile on his muzzle, his tail waving slowly behind him. He had the look of an artist, stunned by his own creation. "Do you think you can handle those for me, Rei?"

I smirked in response. "Perhaps Mitsuko will be telling them herself." I gestured down to the empty space behind the platform where she had been standing some time ago. "While you were enraging our customers, she was summoned inside." John's eyes widened even further as his gaze followed my open paw. "Nevertheless, I'll deliver your requests. Good morning." Then, before he could reply, I bowed, opened my hardline, and teleported back into the tower, leaving behind a thunderclap and the echo of my smile.

19 | IKANOBARI MITSUKO
ESCALATION

FROM THE TOP FLOOR OF TADASHIISSEI TOWER, THE PLAZA BELOW looked like so many pixels arranged in seemingly random patterns. They spread out from the base of the building, following a set of infinitely elegant rules that unfolded in ever-increasing complexity. They stopped abruptly at the edges of the park, cut off mid-tile by a concrete sidewalk that surrounded the building. In the past, I had always imagined it as a wall Tadashiissei had built around its vision, to make room for others in the world that they had built. This time, it seemed more that Irokai had imposed it as a barrier to protect itself.

Much of the plaza itself was blocked by the rising swell of protesters. Most people gave the tower itself a wide berth, and a clear strip of tile ran from the front door of the tower to the edge of the sidewalk, but even that space had people crossing it on their way to or from the gathering. Judging by the movement of people crossing the concrete divide, though, more people were still arriving, coming in from every prefecture still online to give voice to their frustrations. My access panel confirmed that, since the protest had begun, most of the residents of Irokai were either at or on their way to make themselves known. A majority of the remainder were inside this building.

A voice behind me pulled my attention away from the scene below. "It is an impressive sight, isn't it?"

I turned away from the window and bowed to the chairman of Tadashiissei. "Oh, *hai,* sir, as always."

He returned the gesture, a deep bow from the waist, his hands held together in front of his chest. He remained bent for several seconds before rising again, gesturing to the glossy black boardroom table like the ones in the security offices. "Please, Mitsuko, sit."

I hesitated a moment, then did so, cupping my paws together on the table as I bowed again. "Sir, with respect, by now Johnathan will be frantic in his search for me."

The chairman held up one taloned hand and shook his head. "I have always appreciated your decorum, but please, this is not a time to stand on formality. You may call me Kūsō if you wish."

I lifted my head, unable to repress my wry smile entirely. "If it would put you at ease, Kūsō, I would be glad to do so. How else may I be of service to you this morning?"

The irony of attempting to put the chairman of Tadashiissei at ease within the world that he had helped create was not lost on Kūsō; he smiled broadly in return, showing rows of needle-sharp teeth. "I have a number of questions for you, Mitsuko. It seems that your lover's gathering has turned out to be popular." I nodded, and he continued. "I've heard that even Imogen Franklin put in an appearance. Is that correct?"

I nodded again. "She directly challenged Sasaki Rei in support of Giri, yes."

Kūsō stood quietly for a moment, stroking the white wisps of beard on his chin, then took a seat at the table opposite me. His fingers tapped rapidly across the surface, and soon several pages hovered in the air between us. The first said, «Why do you pay to live?» in bold letters across the top, asked several other leading questions, and then displayed the date in one bottom corner and the Minshukakumei logo in the other. "Did John put this together?"

I considered how much to explain, but I could think of no reason not to tell him everything. The decisions were likely made at this point; it was my role to facilitate them. "It was a suggestion from Giri and our mutual... friend... Jules, that he take advantage of past visibility to spread his message. I opposed the idea, because of how the organization had sought to spread its message before. However, neither seemed convinced by the argument, and it does not seem to have hurt their popularity. This seems to confirm the suspicions of many within Hospitality, that our actions have created a wellspring of antipathy towards the company. Fortunately, that does not seem to have extended to Irokai itself."

The chairman leaned back in his chair, steepling his talons. "Tell me about him. John."

I took a deep breath. "Tadashiissei lost a brilliant developer when he presented his separation this morning." I paused a moment, considering my words. "His visions are inspirational. His dedication is phenomenal. He may hesitate on which course of action to take, but once he has committed himself, he will see it through to its conclusion."

"Interesting." Kūsō tapped on the table, shuffling papers until he came to Johnathan's – Minshukakumei's – list of demands. "Do you believe he's committed to this?"

I held my tongue, considering. I wanted to believe that he did, but I remembered all too well the times he had proclaimed that something had to change, only to return to old habits once he had to fight someone for his beliefs. He stopped advocating to have Jules' account access restored once the company legal department began asking difficult questions. He abandoned his friendship with Adam rather than risk confrontation with one of his oldest friends. He gave into Hideaki's design requests rather than defend his vision. In all honesty, I expected this, too, to be a temporary fight for him.

Thinking about his anger on the beach at Kigiku, though, overshadowed those memories. His eyes were filled with a fire that I could not recall having ever seen before. He stood with his back straight, his head held high. His words burned with barely-contained passion. A fresh shiver ran down my tail as I remembered John insisting upon his rights. I smiled to the chairman. "I do."

Kūsō rose again, slowly walking around the table that dominated the boardroom. He stopped at the window, gazing down upon the crowd below. "This entire situation must be very difficult for you," he offered.

I shook my head. "My responsibility as an employee of Tadashiissei has been to perform my duties to the best of my ability, Kūsō." Then I smiled, rising from my seat to join him at the window. "In addition, my duty as a member of *Irokai no Minshukakumei* was always to further our cause by any means necessary. It has been difficult, *hai,* but I suspect that it will be over soon."

At that, the chairman turned to face me, grinning broadly, but hints of sorrow held in his eyes. He looked back to the window, tapping the talons of his hands against the blue-white scales of his arms. "I used to think this would never happen. Now that it has, it's hard to follow through."

I smiled and rested a paw on Kūsō's shoulder. "It is difficult for any parent to deal with a child that insists on independence."

Kūsō opened his snout to speak, but then looked past me as the door to the boardroom opened. I followed the chairman's gaze, facing the door as Rei stepped into the room. He bowed contritely at the waist, holding himself prostrate for several seconds. "I apologize for my tardiness, Kajō-*sama*. Word of the protest has reached the outside, and I was needed to reassure some of our department heads."

The chairman nodded on response. "Do we know the source of the information leak?"

The tiger's tailtip twitched. "At this point, I think it would be impossible to tell. All it would take is one person that opted to speak with the press. We've attempted to identify who it was in specific, but I lack the additional resources to both follow up on that and continue preparations."

"Yes, preparations." Kūsō looked from the head of Irokai Security back to me, his eyes burning with a familiar light. "What is your status? How soon can we proceed?"

Rei rose, his back straight and his arms held stiffly at his sides. "I've conveyed the plan to everyone outside in my division, and the heads of Hospitality and Operations. We have some last-minute validations to perform, but I'm confident that we'll be ready to begin in an hour."

The chairman folded his arms across his chest, glancing to the clock. "That's more of a delay than I'd like, but I would rather this go smoothly. How confident are you of that hour? Is that forty-five minutes or ninety?"

The tiger hesitated, then nodded sharply. "I'm confident that it's sixty, Kajō-*sama*."

Kūsō nodded, then took a seat at the head of the table, folding his arms. "Mitsuko, what do you think John's response will be?"

I leaned back against the window, closing my eyes. "John purchased a licensed development environment some time ago from Tadashiissei, and he has continued to maintain it out of his personal salary separate from his professional work. In addition, one of the members of Minshukakumei, Jules, is on a custom induction rig specifically built for him from components slated for replacement but not actually broken. I suspect that John will retreat to there, then send Jules for help. They may try some kind of physical action."

The chairman leaned back in his chair, then turned to Rei. "Identify the data center hosting John's environment. Find four specialists that you trust in the area and have them waiting on-site for any arrivals.

Get final confirmation from all departments involved, and then tell everyone to be ready to commence at—" He stopped, then looked at the clock. "Fourteen. You have sixty-seven minutes. Go."

"*Hai!*" Rei bowed sharply, then rose and walked out of the boardroom, pulling the door closed behind him.

Once the head of Irokai Security had excused himself, I looked back to the chairman, crossing my arms. "He does not know, does he?"

Kūsō's grin threatened to split his snout. He leaned back in his chair, putting his hinds on the boardroom table. "Know what, Fuki?" His thick blue-scaled tail thumped against the ground.

I shook my head and smiled wanly. "Never mind, Kūsō. We all do what we must in this."

"Indeed." He stood, then bowed to me. "You have proven yourself invaluable to Tadashiissei, Mitsuko. May I leave the rest here in your control?"

I drew in a deep breath, but bowed in response. "Oh, *hai,*" I agreed. "I understand my instructions."

With that, the chairman walked out the door, leaving me alone in the boardroom. I rose and walked to the window, gazing down to the protest below. *I hope you will forgive me, John.* I opened my administrative access, flipping rapidly through menus until I came to the Hospitality access to the Voice of Irokai. Opening the menu, I drew in a deep breath, then spoke, all too aware that my words were being broadcast to everyone in the world. "Attention, please. Due to ongoing system instabilities, Tadashiissei has decided to perform a system rollback. At fourteen, we will be bringing Irokai offline, then restoring to a previous validated snapshot. All residents, please cancel all personal backups. All tourists within Irokai will be escorted out over the next half-hour. Thank you for your cooperation."

20 | JOHNATHAN DART
EVACUATION

AS THE VOICE OF IROKAI'S WORDS FADED, THE CROWD OF PROTESTERS collapsed into a mob. Tourists started running for the transit station or the tram platforms. Residents started whispering, gesturing among themselves. A few stood in shock, paralyzed by indecision. I knew I didn't have a pulse, but I could still feel my heart pounding and my fingers going numb. *Tricks of perception,* I told himself, but that didn't stop the dry muzzle or the need to wipe my paws on my pants to dry the nonexistent sweat.

Imogen looked up at the podium, then nonchalantly adjusted her glasses. "You sure got their attention," she quipped sardonically. "Think maybe you can get everyone else's?"

I nodded, then lifted my arms to my sides, amplifying my voice to boom over the plaza again. "Everyone, please! Calm down!" If the crowed noticed, nobody reacted. "This is an intimidation tactic to get us to disperse; it's harassment, and it's illegal. Everybody, relax; we'll take care of it."

The mouse pulled the pince-nez from her muzzle and breathed on them, then polished the lenses with her vest. "Nice. Here's some free advice for you, John: don't go into politics; stick with advertising." She closed her eyes for a moment, then opened them and let out a piercing whistle that rattled the windows and turned the heads of everyone standing in Tadashiissei Plaza. "Everybody, sit tight! They're playing hardball. Don't let 'em see you sweat and we'll get through this just fine!" At that, the crowd started to stabilize, and the shouts faded back to a dull roar. Imogen then grinned up at me. "All yours, John. You've got about ten minutes before people start cracking again."

As much as I appreciated the help, I was fighting my own rising panic. I held out a paw to her, pads out. "One sec, please." I opened my hardline, then snapped through menus to send a message to Mits, asking her where she was. She hadn't answered the last five times I'd paged, but I had to try again. This time, as with all the others, the only reply I received was, «The person you are attempting to reach is not presently available; please try again later.»

"Damn it!" I swore, pounding one fist against the other. "Where is she?"

The mouse cocked her head to the side. "Who, thin raccoon that was with you when you arrived? Green blouse, white pants?"

I nodded. "Mitsuko. She's a resident, too. I have to find her, make sure she's okay."

"Ouch." Imogen grimaced, then looked around the crowd. "Doesn't look like anyone's okay right now, though."

I nodded, but my eyes were back on the crowd, scanning for Briar and Giri, but they weren't hard to find. The fox and rabbit were clinging to each other like lovers in a life raft, his arms around her shoulders, hers around his waist. I glanced back to the mouse and said, "Let me check on them first." Then, punctuating my words with a sharp whistle, I called out to my co-conspirators. "Briar! Giri! Get up here, please?" The two looked at each other, then back to me. As the pair approached, I grabbed the fox's arm to help him onto the platform, then started talking fast. "I need you to run interference on the crowd and get people calmed down. I have to go find Mits."

I made it one-and-a-half steps before Briar grabbed one arm, Giri the other. "I can't let you do that, John," the rabbit said. "We need you."

"Mits needs me," I growled back, my tail lashing. "I have to go find her."

Giri shook his head. "I must agree with Briar, John-*kun*." The fox's grip tensed against my fingers. "This situation is of your... our... making. We have a responsibility to protect them from this."

My eyes went wide. "Protect them from a rollback?" I blinked.

"They're going to revert the whole damned database and we're inside it! How can we protect them from that?"

Despite the gravity of his expression, Giri's eyes twinkled. "You work in development; you tell me."

I shook my head rapidly. "No, listen, I don't have time for this; I have to go find Mits and make sure she's safe." I turned away from the two of them, but neither one would release their grip on my shoulder or arm.

"For æther's sake, John," Briar sighed in exasperation. "Start thinking digitally already!" She tugged on my sleeve, spinning me to face her, then gripped the sides of my head in her paws. "Mitsuko is fine. Yes, she might be panicking now just like you are, but consider. Either the rollback works as planned, or it doesn't. If it does, you're both restored to pre-disaster versions of yourself. Your relationship's older than this crisis; it'll survive. If it doesn't, you'll be back as you are now without any perception of the intervening time. Either way, you've got no reason to panic." She looked at the fox. "It's you I'm worried about; we only got together after this whole mess started."

"That is untrue," Giri replied, a faint smile spreading on his muzzle. "I arrested you for shoplifting before the attacks."

I rolled my eyes. "Touching, very touching. Now let go, or I'll delete you both myself."

Briar grinned. "You can't; you don't have access."

I sighed. "Not here, but if you were – that's it!" I snapped my claws sharply. "I've got an idea. Let go already; we don't have time for this. I said I'm not running and I meant it." The two hesitated, looking at each other, then stepped away from me. "Thank you," I continued. "So, I still have my old development server hooked into the system. The shutdown probably won't take that offline, and any code running there is probably safe."

"Probably?" Giri folded his arms across his chest, looking skeptical. "You do not know?"

I shrugged. "I doubt it; too many people have bought them and spent way too much money on them. My account's paid out through the month, and I can pay that one manually for a while. If we need, we can probably take up a collection to keep it active. Besides, do you have a better idea?"

When the fox shook his head, I opened my hardline. Some of my options were already grayed out, but the messaging system still worked. «I need your help,» I sent in a meeting invite to Jules. «Can you meet me at the transit station?»

The reply came quickly: «Weren't you the one saying being seen around the HQ was a bad move for me? I've read the transcripts from your spat with Security; nice job giving away the farm.»

I let out a groan. «Not now, Jules,» I shot back. «I need a portal to my server. We need to move people.»

«What for? It's just a rollback. At least it fixes the problems.» I could hear Jules' shrug in his text.

I sighed and snapped out a fast reply. «And makes more. Last known-good backup means before the attacks. Means before the revolt. Means none of us inside remember why we were fighting. Means you stay banned and we don't know why you're so angry again.»

Jules was silent for several seconds, then shot back, «Be there in three, hon.» Then his icon went grey.

I laughed and shook my head. "He never changes." I looked at Imogen, then Briar and Giri. "Jules says three minutes."

Imogen glanced upwards, then back to me. "You probably got two. Who is this guy, anyway?"

The rabbit's ears had already perked. "Jules? He's one of the founders of the FutureShock. Guy's a genius coder, if a little fast and loose. I thought he'd gone native when I first met him; I only found out he wasn't when he got banned for making a stink about uploading." She hesitated a moment, then mused way too innocently, "I didn't know he was back. Did they lift his ban?"

I couldn't keep the faint smirk from my muzzle. "Somebody sent him an induction rig and a hacked account. Somebody on the inside with ties to Minshukakumei."

That got Giri's attention; the fox snapped his head around, his eyes narrowed to slits. "Are you saying that someone within Tadashiissei was working to destroy Irokai?" His tail lashed, and I saw one of his paws reflexively go to his hip before clenching into a fist.

I shook my head. "I think somebody on the inside is playing double-agent, and Jules got caught in the middle. Tadashiissei destroying its own creation makes no sense. No, I think the company found out about a group of active dissidents, they tried to deal with it quietly instead of admitting they had security holes, and things ended up getting out of control." I grinned. "They fell victim to their own hubris, and they awoke a sleeping dragon." At Giri's puzzled expression, I explained. "The populist backlash. They made people angry enough to fight back."

The fox nodded, tail waving behind him. "It makes sense, though it still makes me angry. So much of this could have been avoided."

Briar shrugged. "Yeah, well, hindsight has perfect vision, so they say. Now they've got a bunch of angry residents and they're about to try to clean up their mess by wiping everything back to how it was, which means if Jules doesn't get his tail here soon, they're going to get away with it."

"They won't," Jules replied.

The rabbit whipped around, one paw on her chest. "Don't *do* that! Are you trying to get me to jump out of my pelt?"

The wolf grinned, his ears perked and tail waving. "That'd be kind of hot, but —" He glanced to the side, at Giri's glare. "I don't think your new boyfriend would approve." He turned to me, his paws jammed into the pockets of his oversized pants. "So what's the plan? I heard the Voice. And where's Mitsuko?"

I nodded in response. "We've got about forty-five minutes, and Mitsuko is... not responding to my messages. Is your account still wide open?"

Jules' tail lashed once. "Really." His eyes flicked about in his skull for a few seconds. "Yeah, everything seems to be there, why? Are you really going to try to crowd everyone onto your dev box?"

I shrugged. "It's the best option I can provide right now. Once I'm on there I should be able to make room for everyone."

"John, love, that box isn't sized to hold that many people." The wolf's eyes tightened around the corners and his voice dropped to a low whisper. "I don't think you understand the load you're asking to put on that thing, and its support system's about to get bounced. You're talking about...." He visibly snapped through menus, fingers tapping against the air. "Two-thousand people on a server maybe sized for a quarter of that. It's a development system, which means not ready for production. You overload it, it goes down in the middle of the rollback.... I don't want to think about what happens."

My chest froze. "So do you have a better idea?" I asked in the same tone.

He shook his head. "No, but I don't see how you're going to make this work."

I grinned, tail hooking. "You get me a public portal and get everyone here and then we'll worry about that."

Jules' grimace deepened. "No, you'll worry about that. I'll be calling Adam once you're up and running and then taking off."

"Taking off?" I blinked. "But... Adam? And what about all of this?"

Jules ticked off points on his clawtips. "One, I'd just be one more person on the system, and I have no idea what I'm doing to the local environment coming in from the outside. On Tadashiissei's boxes, I didn't care so much. On yours, right now, that's a risk I won't take. Two, great job sidestepping the rollback, getting out of their environments, but now you're on an isolated system that'd be way too easy to unplug. Somebody with physical access to the box needs to go guard it until they're finished. Three, I need Adam to come unplug me because I'm on an intravenous line and my disconnect function's on a hard timer that's not set to go off until some time Sunday night when the bag runs dry."

My eyes went wide, accompanied by Briar's gasp. "Jules!"

The wolf's ears went flat. "John, don't start on me," he growled. "I said I wanted to live here. Give me some credit, here. I'm not doing anything they don't do in the pods, just with homebrew equipment."

"They don't turn off people's safety switches!" I shouted back, then immediately caught my voice and lowered it. "Jules, assuming I survive this, we've got to have a talk about boundary-setting."

Jules winced, but his grin returned anyway. "If you make it through this unchanged, then it was a good thing I did this. If you don't, you won't remember it anyway. If you don't make it, it won't have mattered." He brought his paws together and cracked his knuckles. "Let's get this started." His eyes closed, but beneath the lids they shook rapidly, and he put his paws in front of him as if resting them on a table. "I don't see a teleport-enabled door around here I can borrow; I'll have to make one." The Voice of Irokai started to announce unauthorized local edits, then suddenly fuzzed into unintelligible static as a rippling liquid silver mirror poured into place, hanging vertically in midair. "I always hated that voice," he muttered. "Now, John, I need a door on your side. Object reference, database name, something."

I scanned my notes and documentation, then passed the wolf a reference. "Main airlock to the station."

"Station?" His head canted to the side. "Right, right. This ought to come through any minute. Send me a back link, and whatever you do, don't delete this door. I don't care what else you purge, but leave this one intact. Once it's gone, I won't be able to put it back." His connection request arrived and I approved it. "Good, now go through and send me back a remote link request; different zone, so you'll have to—"

I waved off the rest of the explanation. "I remember how to do this; I've got one in my office. See you..." I stopped, then looked at the wolf, my ears drooping. "I'll see you after this is over, I guess."

Jules nodded. "I'll hang around until the request comes in, then call Adam. It'll take him about ten minutes to get to my place, and fifteen to get to the data center, so figure half an hour and we should be in place. If they're going right at fourteen, that's five minutes of leeway. You better hope we don't hit traffic. Take care." One paw snapped out and grabbed the collar of my shirt, then tugged me into a rough kiss before shoving me towards the portal. "Now move."

I broke the kiss roughly, then turned to the others. "Once I have the place pared down, I'll contact you and you can start sending people through. We're going to be cutting this close, but we should make it. Everyone ready?" When they all nodded, I dashed through the portal. As soon as I was on the far side, my feet left the floor, sent flying from the force of a step in the local microgravity. Behind me, the iris of the airlock hung open, a hack Jules must have put in place to keep the connection back to the main servers alive.

It took me a few moments to sort out my bearings, but I quickly had the development panel open and started flipping through server statistics. With everything set as it was right now, the server could safely hold about five-hundred people, with another fifty pushing it into the danger zone. I grimaced; the station had to go if I wanted to fit everyone onto the system. First, though, I could de-allocate the biggest wastes. Space went first, as did everything else outside the station walls; that doubled my available memory. The physics engine governing orbital mechanics got me another hundred. I glanced out one of the portals at the black emptiness beyond; no stars glittered, no suns burned.

I shivered; this was about to become a really desolate place. Walls and doors started disappearing. Shops and pylons vanished. Every chair, table, and detail that didn't have to be there rapidly went into the trash and was purged. Soon I was down to the outer walls, a few textures, and the airlock; the server cap sat stubbornly at 1900. I closed my eyes and shook my head. A few finger twitches wiped out everything but the doorway and defined a single featureless rectangle of space, three meters tall, a hundred on a side. Everything else I reverted back to system defaults, as blank as the day I got it. Then I started scanning the base code and wiped everything I could think to remove. I hesitated a moment on the checkbox for the archive system, then disabled it as well.

I glanced at the capacity meter: 1970. It would have to do. I opened my communication window and sent a message to Briar and Jules. «The server is ready. Have Imogen start sending people through.»

21 | ADAM WATSON
EXPLANATION

THE FOURTH TIME THAT MY PALMTOP BUZZED ON THE PLASTIC counter in front of me, I set down my burger and wiped my hands on my napkin. The blue attention light on the front of the case incessantly blinked. I flipped open the cover and thumbed through menus to my chat sessions, but all of the recent messages came from an anonymous source. I had my thumb on the lid, but then the phone rattled in my fingers and a window opened: «New message from <unknown>: Adam, pick up; it's Jules.»

I frowned, then checked through my contacts list; I had several entries for Julia already, mostly e-mail or some messaging service or other that she'd used once or twice, then forgotten. I hit reply, then thumbed, «Julia? What account is this?»

«Long story,» came the quick response. «Please answer.» A few seconds later, the palmtop began to buzz once more, showing an incoming call.

I snapped the cover closed and held it to my ear, looking at it curiously. "Julia?"

"Close enough," an unfamiliar voice – quite distinctly male, deep and rumbling – replied. "Listen, Adam—"

"Who is this?" I demanded.

"Adam, this is..." The voice suddenly dropped to a whisper. In the background I could hear some kind of muffled commotion. "This is Julia. I'm stuck in Irokai. I need your help."

"Irokai?" I pulled the palmtop away from my ear, looking at it dubiously, then brought it back. "That's very funny. Who are you and what do you want?"

Whoever was on the other end of the phone growled menacingly. "Damn it, Adam! I need your help!" The caller's voice started rushing. "I'm running a hacked account on a grey-market rig, I've got an iv jammed in my arm, I can't wake myself up, and I need to be at the Infinicom building in half an hour! I don't have time for guessing games! What do you want? You're allergic to uncooked tomatoes, you hate mayo, and you've got a birthmark on your left shoulder. If you want a detailed list of your eleventh-grade teachers, I can do that, too, but I don't have the time."

I looked at my handset again, then said more quietly, "It's on my right shoulder, and who did I have for physics?"

"You didn't take physics in eleventh grade," Julia snarled. "You had Reidel for Chemistry II. Are you happy now? Twenty-nine minutes."

"That's cutting it close," I said as I rose, motioning to the waiter for my bill. "What is it you need me to do? Come and unplug you?"

"Yes, thank you." Julia's voice sounded infinitely relieved. "Call me when you get to the front door of the building. I'll walk you through it from there. Use this contact." Then the phone went dead.

I exchanged my phone for my wallet, then shifted impatiently from one foot to the other as the waiter took his time in returning my credit card for me. My eyes kept snapping to the clock on the wall, but the numbers didn't change that quickly. I had twenty-seven minutes to save her from herself on the way to whatever errand was so vital.

THE DRIVE TO HER APARTMENT BUILDING WASN'T ANY SLOWER THAN normal, but my breath caught in my throat every time I tapped on the brake. Julia's building had visitor parking, but of course today of all days the lot would be full; another three minutes vanished as I searched for a place to leave the car, then jogged back to the front door.

I pulled my phone out of my pocket and hit redial, then tapped my foot as I waited for the answer. "You're late," Julia replied as soon as she answered. "The code is two-two-three-six-one." I punched in the numbers, then tugged open the door when it beeped at me. The elevator took its time getting to the lobby, disgorging a gaggle of housewives on their way to lunch. The ride to Julia's apartment was an uncomfortable silence, punctuated only by the occasional noise in the background of the call.

"Julia, what's going on in there?" I asked as I watched the light at the top of the car tick slowly upwards.

"I'll explain when I'm out," she replied. "My front door code's one-six-one-eight-oh-three; mind the table in the dining room."

When I entered her door code, the deadbolt clicked open. "Lights, on," I said, and the room lit with LED lamps. Discarded clothing lay strewn across the floor, and an unsorted pile of mail sat on the corner of the table on my left, directly past a kitchenette. To the right sat a glass sliding door out to a thin balcony. Directly in front of me lay the bathroom, but next to it on the right was a closed door. "Is that the bedroom?" I asked as I walked to it.

Julia grunted. "Yeah. Come on in, but don't yell at me."

"Julia, why would—" I stopped dead as the door opened. Behind a giant mahogany desk that seemed impossibly large for the space, Julia's body sprawled, nude and corpse-like, in a leather executive chair that had been locked in a recline. Her head was at least supported by a thin pillow, but her right arm and legs hung over the arm rests and the end of the seat. Her left arm, she'd secured with cloth tape at the wrist and elbow, and a strip of gauze covered the back of her hand where she'd inserted a needle. A length of clear plastic tubing pinched with a garden clamp ran from Julia's hand to a hot water bottle hung from a coat hanger on a portable clothes rack. A plastic mesh covered her head, sending a rainbow of wires slithering under her desk. Her eyes twitched rapidly, and she was breathing, but a thin sheen of sweat covered her skin, giving her a ghastly pallor.

"What the *hell* were you thinking?" The words burst out of me as I stormed over to her body.

"I wasn't," she replied, "and I told you not to yell. It was a fuck-up. John's already screamed at me, and double jeopardy's against the law." She'd gone into pedant mode, artificially calm and reasonable. "Are you going to help me or what?"

"Yes, but not because of you; this is a travesty of medicine." I switched my phone to speaker and set it on the desk, then started loosening the tape on the back of her hand. "Where did you get all this?"

I could just hear Julia ticking off the words on her fingers as she spoke. "Sixteen-gauge needles online, along with instructions for the solution. Tubing for a tank aerator at a pet supply store, enema bottle at the pharmacist's. Hangers and the rack at the boxmart. Stop messing with the meat and look at the screen. I need you to shut down the induction rig."

"One moment; first, I— Hell! You've blown the vein! Where's the rest of this gauze roll?" I pressed on the back of her hand as the puncture site began to ooze, grimacing at the way the swollen flesh dented under my touch. "Did you sterilize *any* of this before you embarked on this little escapade?"

"Boiled everything but the gauze and tape," she replied, her voice even more distorted over the palmtop's speakers. "I'm no tyro, but it's been years since I had any reason to practice. Now look at the screen. Just jiggle the mouse; it'll light up."

"Spare me," I grumbled as I worked the tape from around her elbow. "Don't tell me you used to do more than smoke."

"Back off, Adam," she snarled in reply. "Now, will you *please—*"

I'd had enough. Not bothering to look at her computer, I snapped the chinstrap loose with my other hand and yanked off the nylon skullcap. Instantly, Julia's eyes snapped open and her body spasmed, sending her and the chair crashing to the floor. Her right arm flew up to her head as she started to swear, her left trying to follow but jerking tight against the tape I hadn't yet removed. That set off a fresh round of curses interrupted sharply by a gagging noise, then Julia's stomach inverting itself.

I put one foot on the casters and hauled Julia back upright, just in time for her to send another batch of vomit down her front. Then her eyes blearily met mine. "Don't... ever... do that... again," she managed to cough out around a mouthful of sick.

"I paid your body as much respect as you did," I sneered. "Besides, aren't you in a hurry?"

That stunned Julia into silence for a few seconds. "Okay, I deserved that," she mumbled. "And yes, I am. Oh, man, what a stink. Here, almost done." We finished extracting her from the chair, and then she was scrabbling for clothes, mopping the mess from her face and chest with a discarded towel. "Damn it, I can't make a fist; help me dress?"

I put my hands on my hips, struggling to keep my voice level. "That's because of the swelling. Julia, would you kindly tell me what the hell is happening?"

She stopped, took a deep breath, and sighed. "Irokai got hacked; you heard about that. John helped out from the inside, but his account got botched in the process. They gave him until tonight to pay his identity bill, and he organized a protest instead. When things got out of control, they announced a global rollback, no exceptions. John's moving everyone onto his dev system so they're not stored on Irokai's database when the shutdown hits, but that box isn't sized for that many people and I'm worried about hardware failures with that kind of load, plus he's exposed since he's now on an isolated server. I know where it is, but I have to get to it before Tadashiissei does so they don't pull his plug. Again. And for the last fucking time, Adam, it's *Jules*, not...." She looked down and raised an arm, gesturing downwards at herself. "Not this. Now hurry up and help me dress, damn it; we don't have time for this!"

I crossed my arms, standing stock still. "When you actually come out to me, it'll be Jules. Until then, it's Julia. I dislike diminutives, and I hate taking things on faith, two things that you and Johnathan seem to enjoy far more than I find comfortable."

Julia's eyes went wide, thrown visibly off-balance by my remarks. She stared in open-mouthed shock. "But I... you knew?"

I scowled and grabbed one of the shirts that looked vaguely presentable off of the floor. "No, I didn't *know*, because you never *told* me. I guessed, certainly; I'd have had to be an idiot not to see the signs, and you wouldn't have suffered an idiot this long. Like Johnathan, though, you just assumed I would run with the guess and hope it all worked out. You hinted, prevaricated, and threatened, but not once did you actually tell me why it was so important to you that I use Jules instead of your legal name. Arms up." As she complied, I pulled it on over her head. "Damn it, how can you both be so smart and still be so bloody *stupid?*"

Julia turned towards her dresser and pulled out a pair of Y-fronts; her voice was very quiet when she next spoke. "After all your crap about not having proof for things, I didn't think you'd listen."

I sighed. "Yes, well... *mea culpa.*" I nodded as I took the underwear and held them out for him. "Sometimes there isn't any proof to be had, and you have to go with your best evidence. In Johnathan's case, that would have been research on others who'd been uploaded before him, which still hasn't been done, mind you. In yours, you could have just said something, instead of all this bloody hint-dropping."

"There has been research," Jules snapped. "Imogen Franklin's been studied intensely since her conversion, and nobody's reported anything broken yet. As far as anyone cares, she's alive and well, just living inside a computer. As for the rest, well...." He gestured towards the ground with his injured hand. "Maybe it's not so easy to just say, 'I'm a guy.'" It's not something that comes up in casual conversation, you know?" Jules admitted. Then he grinned weakly. "Besides, I was going to upload instead of transition. The surgical options still suck, and I don't get the fur or the tail if I stay out here."

I grinned and snagged a pair of his jeans. "That's close enough. No time to bind, I'm afraid; you've got seventeen minutes to get to Infinicom and I'm parked three blocks away."

Jules shook his head. "I don't bind; hurts too damned much and I can't breathe when I do it. Gets in the way of my smokes."

"Filthy habit," I muttered as I pulled two pairs of socks from his dresser. I tossed one to him and knelt to help him step into the other. "I don't even want to think about what else you've put in your body."

Jules rolled his eyes and tossed the socks over my shoulder, back into the drawer. "I don't bother packing, either. Anyway, when you hate your body, it doesn't really matter what you do to it. Now c'mon. We've got to move."

22 | JOHNATHAN DART
CORRUPTION

WHITE. WHITE WALLS, WHITE CEILING, WHITE FLOOR. THEY WERE white because they had no texture, no color, almost no properties at all beyond their orientation. They had size, at least, six rectangles defining a space. They didn't really enclose one, though. Enclosing implied an inside, which in turn meant an outside; there wasn't an outside in which anything could exist. Where did that put this space, though? If there was no outside, then where were we? We existed, and yet we existed in a finite space. An inside, with no outside. Thirty thousand cubic meters of empty space, surrounded by absolutely white walls; that had been the universe, for the last twenty minutes.

Into that space, though, something had just entered that clearly didn't belong. It was.... I couldn't tell what it was. One corner was squared, sharply, like a building block. The opposite faces were irregular, rippling and jerking like some kind of living thing. Its surface shifted colors rapidly, along with its shape, though the three edges of it remained consistent. Fragments grew and shrank in the air, fingerlike projections or completely separate objects that vibrated slowly before fading out or merging with the underlying structure. It didn't even announce itself; one moment it wasn't, and the next it was, letting out chirps and warbles seemingly at random.

"So what is it?" Imogen asked, her paws on her hips. "More to the point, where'd it come from? I thought you said this place was closed."

"It is," I insisted. I hesitated a moment, then added, "It was, anyway." I opened my hardline and scanned through menus, looking for intrusions or malware, but each check came back clean. "I'm not seeing anything. Giri, any ideas?"

The fox shook his head, his tail lashing behind him. "I have checked it twice; even with your added permissions, it has no properties, no structure. It does not actually exist." He scowled. "It reminds me uncomfortably of the FutureShock."

I nodded at that. "Yeah, but Jules isn't here, and he did the real hackery on that place." I looked back at Imogen. "Let people know we're poking at it, but truth is I don't know." I glanced at Giri, but the fox shook his head. I sighed; I wanted to tell her more, but Giri was right to advise against it.

The mouse nodded, then walked back towards the group she'd been addressing before. "C'mon, folks. Let's go somewhere else and let these guys work. C'mon, everybody, make some room. Soon as these guys have things figured out, they'll let us know." She motioned, and despite the collective groans of about a hundred weary people, they rose and began to shuffle away, towards another part of the space. Before they'd even gotten a few steps, though, Imogen was back into her story, and it sounded like the others sank quickly back into the rapture of her narratives.

As soon as Imogen's voice was down to a murmur, I looked back at Giri, voice low. "Any clue? I'm at a loss."

Giri shook his head again. "The server is failing; that much is certain. Could this be a side effect?"

I stared at the shifting block and shrugged helplessly. "I have no idea. I can hack a bit on back-end stuff, but my job was always front-end components. Aesthetic, not functional. I'd need somebody like Jules or Briar for details, and even they might not know." I sighed. "I'm afraid this is out of my league."

The fox stared intently at the shifting image, a frown spreading on his muzzle. "It is growing." He motioned with one paw to the object. "It has a second corner now."

I looked where he indicated, tailtip hooking in frustration. "You're right, it does. That still doesn't tell us what it is, though."

"You know as much as I at this point," Giri said. "I would have to do a deep dive to determine more, but I am not sure I would know what I am seeing. It does not appear to have definition, yet it is there. It is not anything, yet it exists. And it is still growing."

I watched with fascination as a square, about a foot per side, slowly filled the space. The chattering and clicking that it emitted changed in timbre, and the shapes that it filled rapidly took on the edges and corners. It looked almost as though someone were pouring luminescent, light-and-sound-reactive goop into an invisible mold that hung perfectly still in the air. It ratcheted up to the top of the space, and then, as if meeting an invisible lid, it leveled itself and then formed a perfectly shaped rectangle, about four inches tall.

As if cued by its completion, a shout rang out across the space. Heads turned, and Giri and I broke into a sprint towards the voice. Imogen beat us to the site and was already asking questions of a visibly-upset black cat as we approached. "What is it? What happened?" She spread her drawl thick, resting a paw on the other girl's shoulder. "It's okay now. Everything's gonna be —" She stopped, then followed the cat's pointing finger to a space in front of her in which letters and numbers hung in midair. "Ah, hell."

"It just showed up out of.... Hey, is that my —" She stopped, as the block started to echo her speech, but a scant moment before she spoke, as if it knew what she was about to say. The same words scrolled in space, in a vivid violet, starting cleanly at one point then disappearing off raggedly off of another. Perpendicular to that, code fragments flickered. The area between them filled in rapidly as the cat spoke. "What's it.... It's writing down what I say!" She looked at Imogen, then me. "Why's it – it's hard to... to talk with... with that. How is it... doing that?"

"I have no idea," Giri said, spacing his words evenly. His words showed up a deep blue calligraphic script. "I find this even more disturbing, though."

I nodded. "Me, too. It's like it's—" My own speech came out in angular gold text, blocky and monospaced. "It's... reading out of the—" I stopped, head snapping to Giri.

The security expert's head canted to the side. "What? What is it?"

Imogen leaned forward and adjusted her pince-nez. "Yeah, you look like—" I made a quick cut-it gesture, dragging my paw across my throat, and she snapped her jaws shut, her teeth clacking audibly; the sound showed up as a splat of red in the air.

I put a finger over my muzzle, then motioned for Giri and Imogen to follow me. They exchanged glances but did so, stepping away from the fresh distortion. I looked back at the block of text, then squinted and whispered, "Test, test." It flickered as I spoke, and I sighed, returning to full volume. "Damn, never mind."

"What?" The word was simultaneous from three muzzles. A cacophony followed as they sorted out who spoke next, but Imogen easily overpowered both of the others. "Don't leave us hanging, John. What is it?"

I pointed to the space as it swelled. "It's a chunk of the speech engine. It's... it's how the graphics engine is rendering the speech engine."

Imogen and the cat just blinked in confusion, but Giri's eyes shot open in shock. "Are you sure?"

I nodded. "Pretty sure. I can't think of any other way it would be getting that information."

Imogen held up a paw. "You two lost me at 'chunk'," the mouse said. "Try again, in English."

Giri jammed his paws into the pockets of his coat. "If John is correct – and I hope he is not – it is... a piece of the underlying software that another piece, the display system, is attempting to render."

"Okay, I get that," the mouse said slowly. "But why? And what's so bad about that?"

I looked at Giri, then back at Imogen. "It's.... Listen, this plan.... The server can't hold everybody on here right now. I deleted everything I could, but I've still got more people on here than my development box can sustain at the same time. Everything we do, it all takes memory. Computer memory. Every thought, every action, it's all computer code. It takes memory to execute, to tell who's doing what. We're running out of it. It's—" I barked a laugh. "It's the only limited resource we have... and we're running out."

Imogen blinked and canted her head to the side. "How do you run out? Nobody new is showing up. Nobody's running anything, right?"

Giri shook his head. "It is not so simple. There must be a time delay between when a bit of memory is allocated to record that someone has done something, and when the bit that marked the past state is freed, to ensure that all systems have the new state. The more people, the more things are present, the more complex the interactions, the longer delay that must be to ensure safety."

I nodded at the fox. "Jules explained it to me once, but he's the genius on this stuff. The short form is that the system's out of memory, and it's out of backup memory, and there's nothing left for it to use to store people's actions... so it's using whatever memory it can."

The cat blinked. "You mean it's..." She looked back at the block of code, then burst out, "It's bigger! Oh my god, it's... there's another one!" Her finger shot out suddenly, and I followed it to another patch of flickering graphics hanging in mid-air, some distance away.

I groaned. "It's run out of everything else, so it's using *this* space. And because it is, everything that happens on the back-end that shows up is rendering, and we're all seeing it, so it's changing the environment that much faster!" I looked at Giri. "This... this beats the Beni hack, by a long shot."

Giri smirked. "I believe this is where Mitsuko would say, 'Oh, *hai*.'"

Imogen put a paw on each of our shoulders. "Okay, bad. What do we do? How do we stop it?"

I blinked. "Stop it? We *can't* stop it. Anything we do makes it grow faster!"

The mouse's eyes hardened, "John, that's – damn it!" The cat took off at a run, over to a group of people, pointing and jabbering agitatedly at the distortions. They turned, then approached, and the volume spread as their words were echoed, then spread as they went to show others. "I swear, nobody learns around here," she grumbled, putting her muzzle in her paw. "You and Giri work on this; I'm gonna go stop the deluge." Then she clapped us on the back and followed the others. "Hey! Hey!"

I tuned her out, then looked back to Giri. "This is going to go to hell fast if we don't do something. Ideas?"

Giri shrugged. "I do not know. I wanted to understand the way that my world worked, but... now I am not so sure."

I shook my head, then popped open my hardline. "There's got to be something." I started scanning menus. "Change the garbage collection speed."

The fox shook his head. "Desynchronized actions and corrupted accounts."

I scowled. "Cache dump."

He shook his head again. "That would make the problem worse; we want fewer misses, not more."

"Damn it, Giri, I want help, not —" I caught myself mid-outburst. "Sorry, sorry, this is... stressful. Suspend the whole system, wait for Jules."

Giri nodded. "I... am unused to being afraid, myself. If we trust that, we should have trusted the rollback. Plus, we have no way to know if he will be able to restore us, regardless of whether he wants to do so."

"Right. Damn it. I'm running out of options here." My eyes flicked over hovering menu choices. "What about—" A scream cut me off, followed by another. I turned, then gaped. The cat that had run from the conversation had one paw on her other elbow, shaking and crying as she tried to pull her fist out of a silvery box shot through with multicolored lightning streaks. One person had her by the shoulders and was trying to extract her; another was backing away quickly, then suddenly turned and bolted.

"Help me!" the cat shrieked, blubbering. "Help me, please!"

That was the only spark the room needed. What had been a crowd instantly became a mob, people running in terror from the alien blocks and from each other. Some tried to help; others tried to escape. Of course, with all that commotion, the system needed that much more memory to render it all, and the only place it had left to find it was in here. Alien spires and fractal fragments began to materialize across the universe as the graphics engine seized more memory to try to display what was happening.

I looked back at Giri, eyes hard. "Space partition; cut the ceiling in half, buy us some more time." The fox didn't respond. "Giri, I need your opinion here. What about – Giri? Giri, what're you doing? I told you, no loading!"

The fox had a sword in his paws; I hadn't seen him with it when he'd arrived. Come to think of it, I didn't remember him having one, but he held it balanced across his pads, his head bowed. "I... am sorry, John. It is the right thing to do. Please... give my apologies to Briar."

I blinked. "Giri? Giri, what the hell are you— No! No, no, no!" I ran over to grab the fox by his lapels. "Don't you dare quit on me!"

He smiled. "This is not abandoning the fight; this is giving you a little more time. It is... fitting. This is the role Tadashiissei wanted me to play, so I will play it. Good-bye, John-*kun*." He drew the blade in a graceful arc from its sheath, then turned it in his wrist and, with a solid thrust, rammed its tip into his gut. There was no blood; he must've been too conscious of how much rendering power that would take. Instead he just... froze in place. He didn't even crumple or fall. His body just stopped moving. His eyes were squinted tightly closed against the shock and pain, but on his muzzle was an almost beatific smile, his head upturned and his tail held high.

"Damn it!" I swung at the statue of Giri in front of me, but as my fist came in contact with it, a black square shot with angry red lines materialized around his head, wiping the smile off of his muzzle and catching my fingers in mid-air. "Shit!" I felt my heart leap into my throat as panic tried to set in. Screams and cries filled the spaces around me, interspersed with static and pure-tone beeping. Music rippled across the panel in front of me, notes making the lines wink on and off. A wolf grabbed my arm. Her eyes were gone; in each socket, a pair of luminescent letters glowed. She opened her muzzle to say something, but only the smell of violets and shift >> 2 && call_ function(vox, TRUE, #0xA1830128725E); came out.

Make or break(); *time.* There had to be something I could do. I wasn't going to let this be LOOKUP_FAIL(memory()); NO_ SWAP(memory());. I froze. What wasn't I going to let this be? I tried to remember what I was going to compare it to, but my mind felt empty. Why couldn't I think of anything? "Imogen!"

"Little busy, John!" the mouse shouted in response. "Trying to keep the panic down! What is it?"

"Giri's gone," I replied. "I can't think. I need your help."

The writer snorted; the sound echoed and twisted around itself in grey-brown whorls. "This is your field, not mine."

I shook my head. "My memory's corrupting. I need help to call_ function(vox, FALSE, NULL);." Golden letters scrolled across my field of vision. «There has to be something we can do. The rollback has to be almost done. We just have to hold out a little longer. The system should resync itself and the database will offload its —»

Imogen threw up her paws. "Don't have time for this! Just do something!"

Time. Timing. open_menus(admin()); Scan down to the system statistics. Find the Irokai services. *It is a shame he could not come back, Mitsuko said.* Lower priority. Lowest priority. Garbage collection. *The scent of rotten eggs, the feel of something unpleasantly moist, and a charnel taste, overwhelming.* Highest priority. Less action per time unit. More time for sync. Time.

I had to hope it would be TRUE;

23 | ADAM WATSON
ULTIMATUM

"WE'RE NOT GOING TO MAKE IT," JULES SAID FOR THE FOURTH TIME since getting in the car. He hadn't taken his eyes off of his palmtop except to glance at freeway exit numbers or look out the window for other landmarks. "Right at the bottom of the exit ramp, two blocks, turn left."

"So you've said," I sighed. "Look, wasn't there anyone else you could call to watch the server? Someone closer?"

He shook his head. "I've called Infinicom; they've got extra monitoring on the box, but they say they can't physically stash somebody in front of it. John or I could; we're both cleared for access to the hardware and the box belongs to him, but John's not exactly capable these days. So, guess who? Right turn."

"I heard you, Jules," I said, signalling and then weaving back across to the left lane. "So, they'll let you sit in front of the hardware but then what? You could stop them from pulling the server off of the shelf, but you can't stop them from pulling the shelves down. They could cut the power. Hell, Jules, if you really want to explore these paranoid ideas, why not imagine that they've changed all the clocks? It wouldn't even take that; they could have just lied about the time.

Even if they didn't, all it would take is one nervous operator hitting a switch too soon and—"

Jules' right fist slammed into the window, making it rattle. "Damn it, Adam, I know you're the voice of reason and logic and John and I are a pair of emotional freaks, but right now you're *not helping!* I'm worrying about John's survival and you're telling me all the ways in which he might already be dead. Not cool."

"As far as medical science is concerned, he died on the operating table three weeks ago." The words were out of me before I really thought about them. "If whatever passes for Johnathan is still running in there, then...." My voice trailed off when I glanced over and got a look at Jules' expression. "I'm... sure he'll be fine."

Jules didn't respond to that; he just looked back down at his palmtop. "Parking garage on the right. We've got two minutes." His seat belt was off as soon as he heard the parking brake engage, and before I had the car locked he was jogging towards the front of the Infinicom building. I had to sprint to catch up with him as he grabbed the door handle. Just as I approached, he jerked the door open, took two steps forward, and then froze. "Shit."

Inside, four people in dark suits and visitors' badges stood in the lobby, conversing and checking their watches. As the door swung wide, all four turned to look, staring directly at Jules and at me. They glanced back at each other, then turned to face us. The first, an older woman, took a step towards the door, her hand outstretched. "Miss Pennrose? I'm Sarah Bellwether, Tadashiissei Security. Would you—"

That was all the prompting Jules needed. He started forward, his head down and his shoulders squared, trying to barrel past four security guards. "Ninety seconds, Adam."

"Excuse me," I said to Ms Bellwether, stepping forward to run interference while Jules continued walking. "I'm Adam Watson, a friend of Jules'. He's a little busy; can I—" One of the guards moved to cut Jules off as he went around me, and I jumped to interpose. "Can I help you? Excuse me, but—"

Tadashiissei Security immediately started flanking, voices jumbling as everyone started trying to have the last word. "—don't know who you are but – can't let you – with us, please – out of the way!" Someone's hand landed on my shoulder. Like Johnathan tried to show me, I grabbed it and stepped back, tugging the guard off-balance, then shoved forward. Instantly two more hands were on my elbows, wrenching them behind me, and one of them called out, "Grab her!"

"Jules!" I shouted, trying to wrest an arm free. "Run!"

Jules' rapid footfalls were his only response, followed by another set as the last guard broke after him. I heard the beep of the door, and then the snap of the latch. A hinge creaked, and then Jules burst out swearing as the door slammed closed. "Get your.... Damn it.... Let go! Adam!"

Ms Bellwether tried again, firm but patient. "Miss Pennrose, would you—"

"No, you fuckers!" Jules' outburst was instant and unrestrained; something had finally snapped inside of him. "And it's *Mister;* now let *go*—" I heard a slam, and then a muffled curse. "—no right to hold me, I'm trying to—" A deep artificial chime resonated in the air, followed by another a few moments later. "Ow, watch the—*Damn it! Adam!*" He jerked his right arm free, then tried to elbow the guard holding him in the ribs. The security agent grabbed for him again, and the two ended up tumbling to the ground.

"Oh, c'mon!" I shouted, my words echoing off of the walls. "You can't *do* this! You've got no right to hold us! Where's Infinicom security?"

"They issued us the badges when we arrived," Ms Bellwether said, her voice tightening. "They were quite eager to help us, given our long-standing business relationship. We had probable cause to suspect both interference with contract and fraudulent conveyance. Don't prove those assumptions correct; you're smarter than that, Mr Pennrose."

"Now you get it right," Jules grumbled, barely more than a grunt. "I get it. You win, okay? I give up. Just... let me go check on the server, please. I've got some people I really care about in there."

Ms Bellwether's expression didn't change, but at least her tone softened. "Of that there's no doubt, but my orders are clear. I'm to escort you to a conference room on the eighteenth floor if you're interested, or out of the building if you're not. Those were the options given to me, and I'm afraid that's all I can offer to you. It's your choice."

"Conference room?" I asked, straightening. I tugged once, and the guards holding my arms let go. "But why?"

Jules followed suit, pulling himself free. "Does it matter? The rollback's started."

"Jules, I'm about fed up with your attitude," I sighed, throwing my hands up in the air. "You don't know the server's status right now."

He reached into his pocket and pulled up his palmtop. "Memory's at a hundred percent, swap's at ninety-eight, and disk operations are pushing the limits of the hardware. There's nothing more I can turn off or disable that doesn't put the box at risk. Somebody getting bored and trying to load a sparkler in there could bring down the whole damn box, and I hope nobody tries to see who else is online. I need to hot-swap some RAM into it so that doesn't happen, and some more disk would be really nice, too. That enough status for you, Adam?"

My eyes went wide. "Okay, so... that might have been good to know before."

Jules smirked. "Why? They're all just simulations, aren't they? They're not real."

"Excuse me," Ms Bellwether interrupted. "We should either take this conversation up to the eighteenth floor or out to your vehicle. Our security staff is monitoring the health of the server as well, Mr Pennrose. Now please, either follow me or have a nice day." With that, she turned and started walking towards the bank of elevators. The other guards withdrew as well, one standing by the elevators and the other two taking up position near the badge-coded door.

I walked over to Jules and offered him a hand. "We might as well follow her."

"Why?" Jules glared up at me but took my hand in his good one, then hauled himself to his feet. "What's the point? They won. We lost."

I threw my hands up in exasperation. "Jules, will you stop being so bloody *digital?* Look, is the server down?"

He pulled out his palmtop. "Ninety-nine percent. If it hasn't gone yet, it will soon."

"Oh, for God's sake, Jules!" I grabbed him by the shoulders and spun him forcefully towards the elevators. "It's still running; that means you can do something. You don't know what they want; if they wanted us gone, they'd have escorted us out by now!" I shoved him towards the open doors. "You're just running on blind faith again! I swear, you and bloody Johnathan, both of you." As I pushed Jules into the elevator, I turned to Ms Bellwether and forced a smile. "He's not normally this stupid, I assure you. He's just angry."

Ms Bellwether didn't respond; she just pushed the button for the eighteenth floor. The elevator filled with awkward silence; Jules either glared at the floor or the security guard, who stood gazing impassively forward, ignoring both of us. I watched the light display as the numbers counted upwards, then glanced to the guard. As the door opened, she motioned to the hall. "This way. Hurry; you're late." Then she was walking quickly down the corridor, leaving me to half-urge, half-drag Jules behind me.

The conference room looked like any of the ones on campus, with a large table in the center and wheeled chairs around it. A wide display hung on the wall at one end of the table, with a camera mounted above it. A laptop sat on the desk, to one side of the monitor. As I guided Jules into a chair, Ms Bellwether punched something into the computer, then quietly excused herself from the room and pulled the door closed behind her. The screen flickered once then came to life, dominated by an animated Tadashiissei logo. The color-panels winked in and out in sequence for a few seconds, and then they faded, replaced by a remote signal from some other office. The window in that room was dark, and sitting too close to the camera was an elderly Asian man. He'd long since gone gray, his hair cut short in a Western part. A faint mustache sat on his upper lip, and he wore a soul patch beneath it. His glasses were thick, and a faint reflection of the camera glinted off of them. He wore a severe grey suit with a dark green tie. As the camera focused on his face, he smiled warmly and raised one hand in a wave.

"Good evening," the elderly man said. His smile was unnervingly broad. "I believe you wanted access to one of my servers."

Jules shook his head wearily. "I don't have time for this shit. Who are you and what do you want?"

It took a moment for Jules' words to get to him, but once they did, his face darkened considerably. He sat upright, adjusted his tie. "My name is Kajō Kūsō. I own Tadashiissei, and by extension Irokai. You and your friends have been quite the nuisance."

"Nuisance?" My voice rose, incredulous. "I can't believe this! You let a major security breach put thousands of people at risk, you're threatening our friend with deletion if he doesn't pay your extortion fees, you're threatening to wipe everything that's happened just to stop the revolt your own policies started, and you're calling us the nuisances?"

Mr Kajō was visibly unimpressed. "I have no need to justify my reasoning to you, but you may rest assured that I hold the future value of my company above all else. That means doing what I think is best for Irokai. We found a number of collaborators within Tadashiissei who are being dealt with at the highest levels, and after extensive review from our database and maintenance teams, the rollback was seen as the best way to protect overall system integrity. Your friend is presently obstructing our ability to protect our creation."

"He's too busy trying to protect his memories!" Jules burst out, jumping to his feet, his chair skittering backwards across the floor. "Everything he's done since he uploaded himself.... You're talking about wiping it all out!"

"We must be sure there are no residual effects," Mr Kajō riposted. "Any one of them could be harboring viruses or malicious code."

"So you're saying you want to force them all to lose three weeks or more off their lives, just because they might have some kind of virus? You can't just scan them or something?" I shrugged helplessly. "Is this really the only way to do this?"

Mr Kajō made a faint shrug. "It's the fastest, and the one that will get the system back up and running the fastest with the least number of long-term side effects."

I smirked. "It won't stop the protests; it'll only make those worse."

The smile that Mr Kajō wore in response sent a chill down my spine. "With no-one inside who remembers, who will protest? Irokai will be on new software immune to the old attacks. Security has already been increased. For the residents, it will be as if none of this had happened."

I folded my arms. "Mitsuko will remember, when Johnathan's account gets suspended for non-payment of debts he won't remember owing."

Mr Kajō's smile faded slightly. "We are prepared to remove those debts from the record."

Jules grinned. "Giri will remember, when he goes to work and finds he's been fired."

"His position will be reinstated," Mr Kajō replied. His eyes were narrowed again, and the smile was gone from his face.

I shook my head in response. "We'll remember, because we're not in the system having our minds wiped alongside the residents." Mr Kajō's mouth opened, then closed again. "Not looking like the cleverest answer now, is it? Do what you want with your ones and zeros, but you can't touch us."

Jules' eyes darkened as he pulled his palmtop out of his pocket, looking down at it. "Adam, the box is screaming. We don't have time for this."

I nodded at Jules' comment, but I kept my focus on Mr Kajō. He tried again to speak, then caught himself. He let out a tight chuckle, then smiled once more. "You realize that, by locking themselves off from the main system during the upgrade, they will be unable to return to Irokai. Their authentication codes will fail. Their accounts will be rejected as fraudulent. Until they accept the database rollback, they will be unable to leave that tiny, tiny box. How close is it to dying? The drives are over capacity, the memory is running out. Soon it will come down very gracelessly, and if the backup system is offline...."

"You're a damned monster!" Jules shouted at the screen, slamming both hands down on the table with a grimace. "You're a lunatic and you're playing god with people's lives! Tadashiissei's done for at this point! If they don't go down this time, they'll go next time, or the time after! You can't keep Irokai forever! One day it'll—"

"One day Irokai will go offline, and not return," Mr Kajō interrupted, his voice sharp. "It is the way of all corporate services, is it not? Those who wish to build alternatives have nothing stopping them from doing so. Now, if you have nothing further to say, I should check on the rollback." His hand started reaching for the camera.

"Wait!" I burst out, waving at the camera. Mr Kajō paused, looking at me, silent. I was stunned by my own outburst, but then I swallowed heavily. *This is it. Make or break time.* "Look, you could let that server go down. You could've let the hacks do their work. You could've let it all be wiped out, but you didn't. You and Tadashiissei didn't. You tried to save it, and now you're trying to save it again, but you're not asking the people you're trying to save. They deserve a say in their own lives."

"You forget," Mr Kajō faintly sneered. "I *own* Irokai."

"Yes," I admitted, "but you don't own *them*. The residents. I'm not a lawyer; I can't argue for the digitals. I know, though, that Imogen Franklin's been ruled alive and well in there, and isn't she one of your big celebrities? You'd hate to see something happen to her, wouldn't you? Especially after all those efforts to promote her as a successful test case." Mr Kajō's eyes remained dark and impenetrable, and I continued. "Please, this... this is *real* to her, to all of them, even if it isn't to you. They've all got to be scared out of their minds in there. If that box goes down... if what you did to Johnathan three months ago wasn't murder, then letting that server fail surely will be."

For several seconds, Mr Kajō was silent, then leaned briefly off-camera, exchanging words in Japanese with someone I couldn't see. When he came back into focus, his eyes were still narrowed, but he seemed eerily calm. "I have received word that the rollback has completed, and I have some things to consider. I will speak with my legal team. In the meantime, I recommend that you go to the server room and install whatever upgrades will stabilize that development server. I will meet you within Irokai in an hour."

I shook my head. "No, I'm not going in there until I have some—"

Jules was already heading for the door. "Then you can be the one to guard the box; my hand's still shot for now. For now, though, I need you to hold parts for me. We're running out of borrowed time."

24 | JOHNATHAN DART
RELEASE

UNSUMMONED, THE HARDLINE FLASHED OPEN, DEEP INTO THE administration menu tree. «The operating system has detected a change in hardware and recommends rebuilding core configuration files. Proceed? Y/N.» "No" was simply missing, a hole in the world. "Yes" was there, but unidentifiable, a failure in rendering engine: NO_ SPACE;. Blinking at it, when it didn't really exist, took an act of existential judo. *How do I look at what I can't see?*

As soon as I did so, the window snapped closed, to be replaced by another one: «An error has occurred in the configuration subsystem: Unknown error occurred; The operating system recommends restoring from backup. Proceed? Y/N.» Somewhere, somebody was shouting my name. It sounded like Giri, but that wasn't possible; he'd deleted himself, hadn't he? Maybe he'd just wiped his header blocks, and the rest of his code was trying to execute somewhere without a process table. I wanted to laugh, but I was tired. So tired. Tired and LOOKUP_FAILURE();. My gaze hovered over the null-space where the Yes would've been if it had existed. If I closed my eyes and didn't open them again, it didn't count, but it was so much easier.

I blinked, and the world froze for a few moments. A third window opened on top of the second, visually overlaying it. I had to squint to make out the text: «No backups have been found! The operating system will now attempt to reboot to correct possible memory errors. Proceed? Y/N.» My eyes tried to stick to what would've been the Yes, but they wearily slid away from the undef();. *We tried, Mits,* I thought. We tried.

«Johnathan!» The name in full flashed under the window, rich brown in some Gothic font. It snatched my attention away from the admin window. *What? What's causing that? Nobody calls me that but....* A second sentence, this one pulsing with urgency, joined the first. «Exit the menu! Jules can't force a reload until you're out!»

I looked up – cautiously – at the interface and closed the window without picking either option. "I'm out!" I tried to yell, but no sound came out. Was I deaf, or had I been silenced? I had no way to test it, and no way to see if anyone had heard me, or if I'd made any noise at all. I couldn't turn my head any further; my arm was still stuck, as was one foot. I'd lost track of Imogen, and the others. I'd lost track of everyone. It felt like the lessons, centering my breathing and keeping my mind clear. The less I thought, the less memory I needed, the less feedback I generated, the fewer errors I spawned. Sure enough, the shouts – I assumed that's what they were, sent to me visually because of the hearing loss – were already rippling across the universe, sending fresh spikes, spires, and flashes through the spreading memory faults.

Something in front of my eyes twisted, a delicate, fragile tear in the universe, and then—

—the world went white, a complete and endless void, even beyond the defined borders of the server before. This was a pure emptiness, a lack of sensory input because there was nothing to sense, a world before the world had loaded. The hardline snapped open, displaying a fresh warning: «Your user account appears to have sustained some level of corruption. Shall we attempt auto-repair or would you prefer to flag the damage for manual review? Fix/Flag.» Blue monospace text rippled across the bottom of my vision: «Everybody, pick ‹manual›; the auto-repair system's offline. You'll look a little freaky but we'll get you sorted out.» I did as the Voice of Irokai directed, and—

—I fell forward, the momentum of my swing pitching me off-balance. Giri was gone, but I wouldn't have hit him anyway; my fist was missing, too. So was my left foot, for that matter, and the end of my tail. I opened my muzzle to cry out, but I was dead-silent as I twisted and slammed into the ground. All around, people were starting to pick themselves up off the ground; text scrolled rapidly in a dozen fonts and colors. I pushed back onto my knees and carefully turned. The white walls had returned; the distortions were gone. Imogen – bright red sans-serif letters twice the height of anyone else's – let out a whoop, her arms in the air. Everything from her waist down had vanished, but she shook her fists in the air triumphantly, whipping the people around her into a frenzy of applause.

I looked back to the point at which Giri had removed himself from the process list, but not even an afterimage marked his passing. I snapped open the admin panels and scanned through settings, looking for name lists. Most of the entries showed glitches in them. Number 1996 was completely missing; the list cleanly jumped from before to after. The only note for the missing entry said "unrecoverable." I bowed my head. *Briar's going to be livid,* I thought. *I don't know how much we'll have to rebuild, but somebody's got to have a backup somewhere. I bet Jules can—* A tap on my shoulder pulled me out of my reverie, back up to a wolf and stag kneeling beside me, looking concerned.

The wolf's muzzle opened, but when he spoke, more blue text scrolled by at the bottom of my field of vision. «You okay, John? Say something, please.» Jules quietly clicked his claws at me, then looked at Adam. «Any idea what's wrong with him?»

The stag raised a brow ridge and smirked, folding his arms across his chest. «How should I know, Jules?» scrolled by in more brown Gothic. «I'm not a programmer. This is your field.»

I held up my right arm, trying to put my paw out before I remembered it wasn't there. That got my ears flat against my head. «I think my audio's dead,» I texted back in blocky gold monospace. «Where are you guys? What's with the server? The door got hosed; did they finish the rollback?»

Jules and Adam looked at each other, then back at me. «One thing at a time, John,» Jules sent. «Let me.... Here, I have an idea. I've got your local backup system online in recovery mode. So much of the core code's corrupted in here that I think you're going to have to wipe and reinstall, but I think I can get the base species templates online if you don't mind rebuilding your mods. Want me to give it a shot?»

He didn't have to ask me twice. I nodded eagerly, and his eyes unfocused as he worked. His fingers began to twitch in front of him as he typed on a keyboard only he could see, and then a minute later, he nodded. «Go ahead and tell it to reset to default species settings.»

I took a deep breath and let it out slowly, then nodded again and opened the hardline to search for the reset. I had to manually add the option back to the administration menu; under any other circumstance, I'd have never wanted to use it. When the dialog asking me if I was sure I wanted to lose all my customizations, I hesitated for several long seconds before approving, and then suddenly I was back to the me I'd been when I first stepped into Irokai. I blinked and called up the template profile, scanning it wistfully; all of my updates were gone. Every last mod I'd ever built had disappeared. *It's okay,* I told myself. *I've got most of them saved some... damn, no, I had to ditch them with the station. Hang on, Jules has an offsite for that; it's old, but—*

Adam's voice snapped me out of my introspection. "Johnathan, did it work?"

I looked up sharply at the stag. His liquid brown eyes were wide and blinking, and he looked like he was trying hard not to show too much concern. "I'm fine, Adam," I said with a smile. "It worked."

Jules sat back on his haunches, visibly sagging with relief. "Great," he breathed. Then, with one finger to his throat, he spoke in a broadcast across the server. "Everybody, if you're experiencing any kind of personal data loss, try resetting to default; you'll lose all your mods, but it's better than losing an arm. If you're suffering from memory or other discrepancies...." He stopped and sighed. "We'll try to help you when we're back on production hardware." He stood and stuck out his arm to me. "Sorry we're late," he said with a sheepish grin. "I had to get a few things out of my system."

Adam rolled his eyes. "He had to go piss off a squad of security guards, is what he means. Speaking of which...." He looked down at a nonexistent watch, then frowned at his wrist and scratched behind one ear with his blunt fingers. "He should be here by now."

"He?" I blinked, then looked back at Jules. "He who?"

The wolf grinned from ear to ear, tail wagging behind him. He helped me back to my feet, then put a paw on my shoulder. "The head of Tadashiissei. He said he wanted to meet us here once he had a few things sorted out with Legal."

My eyes went wide and my tail lashed. "Legal? Kūsō Kajō's coming *here?*" When Jules nodded, a grin split my face. "We did it. I can't believe we may actually pull this off."

Jules cleared his throat, then hooked his thumb at Adam, who was looking around the area. "Thank him. He's the one who made the last-minute plea bargain. We just...." He stopped, then looked down. "We wanted it really badly, John. Too badly to think about it clearly. You refused to think about the legal angles, and I... I couldn't wait to be a test case. We made it work, but we both went about it all wrong from the start."

I blinked. "How should we have done it, then?" I glanced at Adam, who turned to look at Jules as well, a smile on his muzzle and one hand under his chin.

"The way you did it at the end, only all the way along." He looked at Adam, then back at me. "*Irokai no Minshukakumei* was a mistake; it just pissed people off. I probably turned off every person I could've counted on to help me out, throwing my tantrum. You screwed up, too, though; you should've understood your rights before you got here. When Adam pointed out that you and Imogen were still legally your own people, Kajō's eyes turned six shades of angry. He knew he'd lost, and Adam didn't even have to raise his voice to do it."

I blinked again, then turned to the stag. "Adam, I — Wow. I don't know what more to say. Thanks."

Adam shrugged. "I dislike taking things on faith. That includes an assumption of ownership for things that clearly don't belong to you."

I chuckled and grinned. "So, now what? How much longer do you think we'll —"

A sudden gust of wind and a flash interrupted my question. In the middle of the room curled a long, snake-like dragon. His body was covered in hexagonal sapphire scales, like faceted jewels in a flexible mesh, with individual opalescent white panels at various points. White hair streamed back from his long snout, tipped in a wispy mustache that fluttered each time its head bobbed or moved, and his eyes gleamed like diamonds lit from within. Four-toed feet ended in ivory claws that fluttered and clacked against the ground, and its entire length twisted back and forth, coiling and uncoiling on itself.

More important, however, was the raccoon in the green shirt and white pants that stood stoically beside him. "Mits!" Her name was out of my muzzle as soon as I recognized her. Her arms were warm and comforting and I sank against her shoulder, tears streaming out of my eyes as I pressed myself to her. "Thank God you're all right, Mits, I was so worried."

Her breath was sweet when she kissed me softly. "I am here, John," she whispered. "I will not leave you again."

The dragon twisted, hissing his irritation. "Hopefully not, Ikanobari-*san*. I've already lost one designer; I can't afford to lose one of my best Hospitality agents." His eyes focused on mine, shining down on me. "Dart-*san,* you've made Tadashiissei's legal experts very unhappy. I have brought her here as a sign of good faith; please accept this in the spirit in which it's given."

I couldn't help but grin at that. "I will, sure. I wasn't the one that made the rules, Kajō-*sama*. I'm just playing by the ones I was given."

"And you have played them well," Tadashiissei's CEO admitted. "They've issued a *preliminary* ruling accepting your terms while they review the matter more fully, but it comes with a condition."

I narrowed my gaze and my tail lashed, but as I opened my muzzle to speak, Jules put his paw gently on my shoulder. I glanced back to the wolf, who shook his head slightly. I nodded in return, then looked down at Mitsuko, who just smiled back in response. "What's the catch?" I asked, without looking back to the dragon.

Kūsō Kajō, the chief executive of the company that owned Irokai, was silent for several moments before quietly replying, "They refused to re-negotiate terms with every individual, citing a lack of resources and time, and have politely requested that you assemble a collective bargaining association in the next ninety days with whom they can negotiate new contracts for Irokai and its residents."

I stood stock-still for several seconds. My jaw hung open and my tail went limp. I looked back down at Mitsuko, then back at Jules; the wolf's tail was sticking straight out behind him, fur frizzed. "Let me get this straight," he said, looking up at the dragon. "Your legal team wants us to assemble a union, so they can cut one contract for everybody?"

Kūsō managed to look even less comfortable after that, his eyes narrowed and his claws clacking against each other nervously. "Not as such. To retain legal ownership of Irokai would give the appearance of coercion, and they fear any such contract could not survive a court challenge." He hesitated, then snapped his claws together irritably. "Upon review of the business model as it is presently established, in light of these new opinions, the only path to continued profitability is for Irokai's residents to collectively assume ownership of their environment, while Tadashiissei remains contracted to provide access and support services." He paused again, longer, then lowered his head. "Among other possible options."

I couldn't believe my ears. I spoke very carefully, just to make sure I was understood. "Mits, translate for me, would you?" She nodded, and as I spoke English, she converted to Japanese. "Correct me if I'm wrong, Kajō-*sama*, but... you're saying that Irokai needs a government. An elected government."

Kūsō's eyes came back to mine, brilliant white stars blazing in his skull. "*Hai.*"

Silence fell over the group, held painfully still for several seconds, until Jules whispered, "Holy shit."

I swallowed hard and looked down at Mitsuko; she was smiling, but her eyes were wide and her ears were flat against her head. "Did you know?"

She shook her head. "No, he said only that he had gotten word; he would tell me nothing else."

I nodded. "Are you okay? Did they hurt you?"

"I am fine, John," Mitsuko replied. She smiled gently, hugging me and resting her head against my chest. "I was scared for a time, but everything will be better now."

For a few moments, I stood in quiet awe, running a paw down Mitsuko's back, until the dragon cleared his throat. "Is that a yes, Dart-*san?*"

I looked back at Jules, whose grin threatened to split his head in half, then to the dragon once more. "It'll take more than ninety days to do it right. That can't be rushed."

The dragon nodded. "A provisional representative will be acceptable if an elected representative is not available within the time frame." He gestured to the space beside him, and an ornate door winked into being. "The rollback has been completed; you are free to return home. Your accounts will be marked as pending until the contract question is resolved. If you need assistance with any other data loss, please contact file a support ticket with Tadashiissei Security; someone will be assigned to help you. We will need to transition the ownership of such difficulties to Irokai at some point, but that will be part of the negotiations." He smiled coldly. "From now, your data integrity is your own concern, not ours."

I held up one paw. "First, Chō Giri. He... didn't make it through the server glitches."

Kūsō nodded. "I will have Sasaki look into it for you. If there is nothing further, I have other matters demanding my attention." He bowed his head, a move echoed by everyone around, and then disappeared with another pop and rush of wind.

I gave Mitsuko a gentle hug, then looked at Jules with a smile. "So, you ready to move yet?"

Jules grinned back, then cupped one paw to his chin and shifted his weight in mock-indecision. "Well I don't know give me a chance to think about yes."

I laughed and turned to the stag, then held out one paw to him. "I guess this is good-bye then, Adam."

Adam just smiled as he shook my hand. "See you later, John."

As he stepped back to go, Mitsuko suddenly pulled away and held up a paw. "One moment, please. Take this with you." She closed her eyes, then drew out a small glowing sphere – the transcendus mod from my simulation. She smiled, then projected to everyone, "All of you, with our blessing." She held up her paws, and dancing motes of light rose into the air, then settled across everyone in the room, blanketing us all in a sea of digital stars.

IKANOBARI MITSUKO
RESPONSE

TADASHIISSEI TOWER HAD, AT ONE TIME, BEEN THE TALLEST BUILDING in Irokai. It had loomed over the other buildings in Murasaki Prefecture, separated from them by the plaza that shared the company name but visible to all of them, like a monarch. Since the revolution, other structures had grown to dwarf it, and the very lay of the land had been rearranged – by popular vote, over the objections of the Geographic Society – to give it a more fitting location. Deposed, the twisting glass spire still stood at the edge of downtown as a reminder of Irokai's past. Having designed the district in to sit in concentric rings, however, most eyes turned naturally towards Wisteria Court – the new seat of government – and away from the former lords of the domain.

Hakushoku Station rose on the edge of the skyline as I crossed the plaza and stepped inside. The lobby was empty save for a single receptionist that looked up as I approached. "Ikanobari Mitsuko," I said unnecessarily to the wolf sitting behind the desk, bowing slightly and smiling. "I believe I am expected?"

The wolf motioned towards the bank of elevators behind him with one paw, holding out a slim crystal prism with the other. "Please go on up, Ms Ikanobari. He's waiting for you in the main boardroom. Will you need an escort?"

I bowed as I accepted the security token. "I know my way, *arigatō*." The Japanese was unnecessary, but the affectation was reflexive, and people had come to expect it. Jules would have said it was the way of expert systems to learn patterns. Adam would have said it was the nature of people to fall into habits. It was John, however, who would have asked about my accent. I smiled as I held the sliver of glass up to one of the doors, then stepped inside; the others knew enough to see those things, but it was John who chose not to look at them.

The ride to the top of Tadashiissei Tower was short, far shorter than any elevator outside would have been, and the hallway at this level had only one destination. The thick double doors swung open as I approached, revealing a panoramic view of Murasaki through the boardroom windows. Buildings of every description and style rose across the field of vision, dotted here and there by skyscrapers that blocked the view of what lay behind. Kajō Kūsō, former CEO of Tadashiissei and head of the newly formed Irokai Relations division, stood at the head of the table, gazing out at the world he had created.

"It's magnificent, isn't it?" he said as I approached.

"Oh, *hai,* it is," I agreed easily enough. "If you will forgive me, though, that is not why I came."

Kūsō turned as I approached, a broad smile settled easily on his narrow snout. His eyes shimmered. "No?" He gestured towards one of the chairs, then perched on the edge of the boardroom table. "Surely this isn't a social visit."

I remained where I was, my arms folded across my chest. "I had questions, about how it all came to pass." I paused a moment. "Are we secure?"

The *luong* laughed. "If you're asking if anyone is spying on the boardroom, the answer is not as far as I can tell. If you're asking if anyone is watching, probably Rei. He helps keep an eye on things for me, as his job duties permit."

Neither answer reassured me much, but nothing I asked would likely come as a surprise to my co-conspirator. "How much of what happened did you plan, really?"

"Enough," Kūsō admitted. "I'd assumed that the smaller attacks, the graffiti, the draconian – forgive the pun – service and license agreements, something would have sparked the outcry. Eventually, I had little choice but to escalate."

I sighed; it was the answer I had hoped not to hear. "Why John? Why me?"

The *luong* leaned back against his hands, tapping a talon against the tabletop. "Convenience and accident. Yours wasn't the only cell, just the first successful one. John's wasn't the only crisis, just the most obvious. Giri's would have served admirably, if he'd been uploaded instead of having been born here. If things had gone differently, Imogen might have ended up your leader instead. I actually expected her to be the one, but she was too busy enjoying not being sick to worry about Irokai's problems."

He shifted his position, tail thumping once against the dark glass. "That he was your lover was difficult, but at the time, his was still the best option. I took it." He sat up and spread his arms. "If you're looking for an apology, you won't find it here." A smile broke out on his snout. "Besides, you were a willing participant in it all. Weren't you, Fuki?"

"You are unrepentant," I agreed, nodding, ignoring the reference to my alias. "What would you have done had I chosen to quit rather than be part of your game?"

Kūsō chuckled. "I would have found ways to stop you from getting work and maneuvered you into exposing Tadashiissei's leader as a ruthless sociopath. If Johnathan hadn't quit, I might have had him fired."

"How do you continue to live with yourself, knowing the pain you have caused?" My tail lashed once, but I kept careful watch on my anger.

The *luong* shrugged again, then waved a taloned hand out at the windows. "Because all of this is now free. This is the world in which I wanted to live as long as I can remember, but I feared it for all the reasons that your friend Jules stated. I couldn't count on anyone to simply give me the freedom I sought, and I couldn't give it to anyone else without being told it wasn't mine to give. So, I had to force someone to stand up and demand it, someone that the outside world would recognize unequivocally as having a right to do so. That happened to be John. I thought it would have been Ms Franklin, as I said, but her interests lay elsewhere."

"So," I said turning away from the panorama. "The end justified the means."

I could hear the scowl that settled on Kūsō's snout. "In this case, I believe it did."

I sighed and lowered my head. "It pains me to admit it, but I agree with you, which is why I did not quit, why I accepted your terms, why I allowed myself to become part of your plan, and why I allowed all of the suffering that these events have caused. Understand, though,

Kūsō, that if the end justifies the means, then the punishment must fit the crime." I closed my eyes, quickly switching through administrative options. "You caused untold pain to those who did not deserve it, all to fulfill your vision. It is only fair that you understand the horror of their experience."

Kūsō shifted on the table. "I'm quite aware of how much horror I caused." His voice dropped to an angry hiss. "I reviewed the system logs. I've read every security report. I've heard the fear in people's voices, the looks of panic and terror. I even have the logs of the disaster on your lover's server. What more do you want of me?"

With my muzzle still lowered, I said, very softly, "I want you to fear, Kūsō." I spread my arms wide, and the hardwood door behind me shuddered to sudden life, roots sinking into the floor, vines curling from its top and snaking around the room. "I want you to understand that you will never leave this room."

"Mitsuko," the *luong* chided, "that's absurd. This is Irokai; I built this world. I can—" His voice died in his throat when I met his gaze again. The light in his eyes died as he stared at me. "Where's my menu?"

I forced a smile to my muzzle. "I have taken it from you. Hospitality must have the power to make real whatever their guests need or require. You need this." The vines spread as I waves my fingers, blotting the windows and slithering across the floor. "This is your last day, Kajō Kūsō. I hope that you made the most of it."

Kūsō jumped from the table, backing away from the approaching vines, but even as he shied back from his perch, they crept behind him and snapped towards him, ensnaring his legs. The *luong* let out a shout as he stumbled, his arms flailing as he landed on his back. "Mitsuko, this isn't necessary, really!" His voice quavered. "I've seen what I did; I understand!"

"Oh, *hai,* you understand," I agreed. As the advancing tendrils blocked the light from outside, luminescent flowers bloomed from the vines, casting an eerie glow around the room. Light seeped from my fur and eyes as I approached the thrashing *luong* on the floor. "But you do not yet *feel.* In the last moments I leave you, you will feel everything."

Kūsō's eyes went wide and his voice shook. "Mitsuko, please, you don't have to do this. I... I've seen eno— Aah!" His voice jerked as the tip of one vine forced itself through his scales, working its way inside of him. At the same time I had blocked access to his administrative interface, I also set his self to emulate flesh and bone as best as it could; blood seeped realistically from the growing wound, then burst from another as the vine left through the flesh of his thigh, forcing a scream out of his snout. "Please, no more!"

I nodded. "That is what the others said, as they begged for mercy. That is what Mielle and Isao shouted, as the Nanakōsei tower dissolved around them. That is what two thousand people cried as John's server almost crashed." Vines entangled his wrists, pulling back and stretching his body, while a second vine dug at his side, forcing itself into his stomach. Kūsō whimpered and sobbed as it squirmed into him, gagging as the flesh beneath spasmed. "You will receive the same amount of help they did."

"I— Please!" The *luong* tried to scream, but the word came out as a breathy wheeze. His eyes were wide and dull, exposing whites all around as he tried to thrash himself free, unable to stop the pain, helpless to escape. The reality of his situation was settling in, and the panic was following close behind. "I can't... why... you don't... please! Make it stop! Plea—" A thick vine forced itself into his snout, worming down his throat, muffling his mewling and reducing him to wordless sobs.

I knelt beside the once-proud head of Tadashiissei and put a paw to his forehead. "Oh, *hai,* it will stop, when there is nothing left of you to suffer." I stroked gently over the smooth blue scales as another vine pierced him, then another, filling him from the inside out, twisting its way through his system, branching and then forcing themselves back out again. The wooden tendrils lifted him off of the ground, stretching him out like a broken doll. He tried to scream, to beg, but the vines were indifferent to his pain. "Only then will you truly know what you have done."

I stood again as the creeping wisteria pulled him tight, broken joints splitting under the tension. "My suffering, Kūsō, is that I must live with what I have done. John and Jules know, and have forgiven me; in time, I may one day forgive myself." As I stepped to the door, the vines moved aside, opening a passage for me to leave. "They will not kill you, but you will learn many new meanings of pain as Irokai returns the harm you have caused." I tapped my ear, then set a small pulsing star by the exit. "When you are ready to apologize, they will recede, and this will be waiting for you. I hope, for both our sakes, it will not take too long." The boardroom then closed behind me, and I left Kūsō to his education, while I returned to the world that I hoped would justify my role in its birth.

KRISTINA TRACER
ABOUT THE AUTHOR

ANY BIOGRAPHY THAT KRISTINA COULD WRITE ABOUT HERSELF would either be too long to be useful or too short to be meaningful. However, let it at least be said that she wrote her first sixty-page novelette at age eight and hasn't figured out how to stop talking yet. A part-time author, full-time rabbit, and over-time dreamer, Kristy has three children – four, if you count the way her wife behaves. At present, she lives in the Pacific Northwest, where she hopes to convince most people that she really isn't out to take over the world, and to use the rest as an example to the remainder.

CPSIA information can be obtained
at www.ICGtesting.com
Printed in the USA
FSOW01n0915080115
4404FS